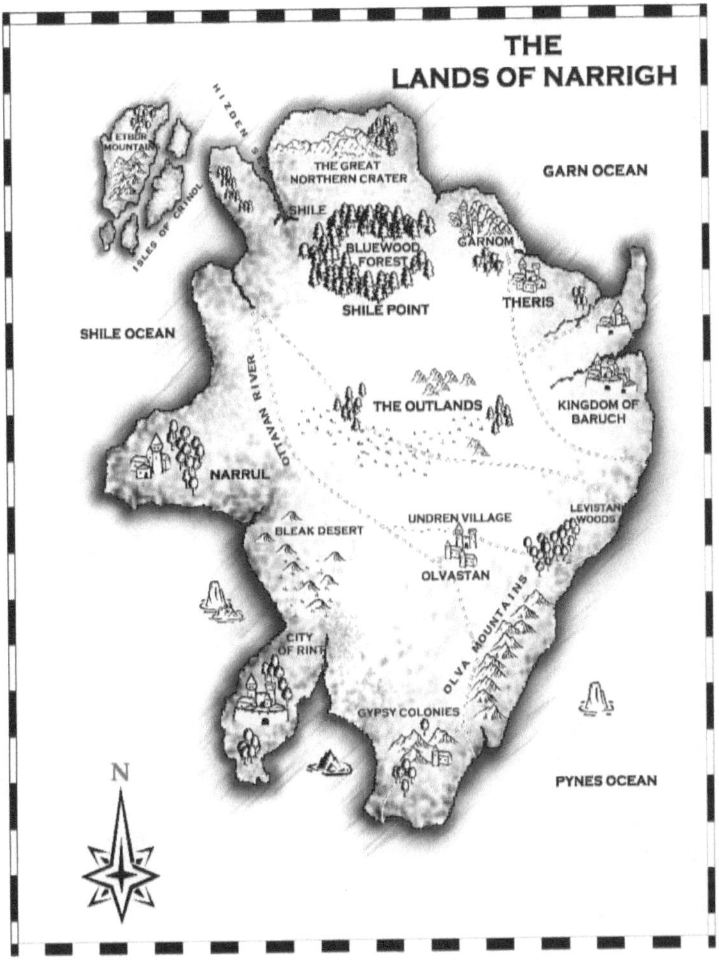
THE
LANDS OF NARRIGH
ETBOR
MOUNTAIN
HIZDEN
ISLES OF CRINOL
THE GREAT
NORTHERN CRATER
GARN OCEAN
SHILE
BLUEWOOD
FOREST
GARNOM
THERIS
SHILE POINT
SHILE OCEAN
OTTAVAN RIVER
THE OUTLANDS
KINGDOM OF
BARUCH
NARRUL
UNDREN VILLAGE
LEVISTAN
WOODS
BLEAK DESERT
OLVASTAN
OLVA MOUNTAINS
CITY
OF RINT
GYPSY COLONIES
N
PYNES OCEAN

RACES

Citizens

Darque Goblins

Drone Elves

Dwarves

Humans

Theria Elves

Traceless

THE QUEST OF NARRIGH

S. K. HOLDER

www.rogghornpress.com

FACTIONS

THE FURNACE consists of a Blade Army made up of Darque Goblins, Gamnod Humans, and Drone Elves.

THE STORM consists of a Score Army made up of Theria Elves, Olvastan Humans, and Dwarves of the West.

Chapter 1

It had happened on a Saturday.

Connor hadn't had much sleep the night before. He was all jittery with excitement. He had risen early to hang out the washing his mum had left in a basket on the kitchen table. He even completed his brother's chores: sweeping the kitchen floor and putting out the rubbish. After he was done, he sat in the living room, idly flicking through one of his old comic books. His best friend Riley was coming over.

Connor's mum was at work, which meant he could do whatever he wanted in the house as long as he didn't invade his brother's personal space. Connor planned to do that later when his brother had left for the cinema with his friends and before his mum returned. 'The Quest' would be his and Riley's to play.

The Quest of Narrigh was the biggest massively multi-player online role-playing game ever to be released by Tridan Entertainment. Its creators had deposited so many obstacles, that any player would be lucky to reach Level Twenty.

His fifteen-year-old brother, Luke, sauntered into the room. He was on the phone with his friend, Walter 'Bat' Bateman. 'Yeah Bat. Level Forty....told you I'd do it.'

Connor flung down his comic book, his eyes wide, his mouth gaping open. He had a name for the way he constantly regarded his brother; he called it the Look of

Awe. Luke seemed to appreciate Connor staring at him as if he were some sort of comic book hero. 'Wow! You got to Level Forty.'

Luke nodded, a smug grin on his face. 'Yeah, yeah I know,' he spoke into the phone. 'But it was me who put in the extra work. My fingers need a break though...laptop's playing up. I think it's overheated. What time will you get here?'

His brother had reached Level Forty in thirty-eight hours. Not bad.

Luke had allowed him enough game play to get some idea of the skill involved. Connor reckoned he could reach Level Forty in a lot less time than that, if he had more free time on his hands, if he could stay up late, if he had a computer in his bedroom. He had to share a laptop with his mum. It didn't help that she made full use of the parental controls, which prevented him from freely surfing the internet.

Luke ended the call and shoved the phone into his back pocket. 'You like that, huh? One day, I'll show you how it's done. What time's Riley coming over?'

'Twelve.'

Luke gave him a weary grin and then leaned over and ruffled his hair. His brother was such a sap. 'You stay here or in your room, understand?'

'I know. Why do you always have to tell me?'

Luke shrugged. 'Because.'

Because five years ago, Connor had packed a bag and gone in search of the dad he had never met, and whose name he couldn't remember. He knew he was never going to find him, but he didn't care. His mum had told him off for using her bottle of shampoo in his water-gun, and his brother had been ignoring him all day. He had left the house in a huff, having packed a change of clothes and some of his favourite toys and books. He was going to take the bus into town, but he didn't have any money. It was late and he had soon grown tired. His bag was heavy because of all the books he was carrying, and people were staring at him. When a woman in a trenchcoat asked him if he was okay, he ran into the park to get away from her. And that's where his brother found him, curled up on the grass, cradling his toy truck.

Luke had given him a clout round the ear for causing him and his mum to worry. Connor promised them that he would never run away again. He intended to honour that promise. Deep down, he didn't mind his mum and brother treating him like a baby. He wasn't ready to grow up.

He gave Luke the Look of Awe. 'Can Riley and I watch you game today?'

'Don't see why not.'

Connor grinned and reached for his comic book. Yes, the Look of Awe definitely came in handy.

As soon as Luke and his friends had tumbled out of the door, Connor didn't hesitate. He switched off the TV and skulked upstairs to his brother's bedroom with Riley following close behind.

Connor sunk into the swivel chair and wheeled himself up to the desk. He turned on the laptop.

Riley pulled up a chair next to him. 'Won't your mum

say something if she catches us in here?'

Connor pulled a tattered sheet of paper from his pocket. 'Yep.'

'What's that?' Riley rested his chin on Connor's shoulder. His chestnut locks tickled the side of Connor's face.

'Luke's password combos. He only uses five, so it should be easy.' Connor had watched his brother while away the hours at his computer enough times to memorise all five passwords, one of which was Connor's own name.

Riley took the sheet of paper from him. He turned it over. 'And what's this on the back?'

'Notes to get us started.' They weren't much. He had picked up a few smart moves from watching his brother play.

'They don't make any sense.'

Connor whipped the paper from his hand. 'They make sense to me.'

Riley placed two cans of soft drink on the desk. 'What's wrong with the screen?'

The screen was flashing a luminous purple. Connor dusted it off with the palm of his hand, and then tapped the ESCAPE key. The screen returned to normal. 'Seen too much action, I guess. And it's about to see some more.'

Connor logged into the game and pressed PLAY.

The Lands of Narrigh

"Eight hundred years ago, in the Age of Peace, Narrigh,

once collectively known as the Goldlands had eight regions: Narrul, Hizsen, Garnorm, Theris,   Baruch, Crinol, Shile and Olvastan.

To the North, lay Garnorm and Hizsen. Garnorm was inhabited by a race of humans known as the Gamnod, who were gifted in the crafts of counselling, sculpting, and tailoring.

The Darque Goblins dwelled in Hizsen and were renowned for their camouflage and enchanting skills.

The Isles of Crinol were surrounded by the blue waters of the Hizsen Sea. Here the Drone Elves dwelled. They were exceptional potion-makers and flame-wielders.

In the Etbur mountains of Crinol, dwelled the Traceless who had no name and no soul to speak of.

To the west, lay Narrul, home to the dwarves, who were famed for their mining and iron-forging skills.

To the South, lay Olvastan, where there dwelled humans, who believed in one God as opposed to the Gamnod who believed in many. The people of Olvastan were great farmers and tradesmen.

Further South, in the Shile region, there lived the gypsy clans, known for their herbal remedies and hunting skills.

To the East, lay the Kingdom of Baruch, bathed in gold and home to King Kalgar and Queen Irentha. The King and Queen ruled Narrigh with an iron-hand to maintain its prosperity and tranquillity. Their Score Army was both revered and feared.

Not far from the Kingdom of Baruch was Theris, home to the Theria Elves, who worked tirelessly to weave beautiful cloth and textiles for all Narrigh. They were also renowned for their enchantments.

One day, evil descended on the lands of Narrigh. It came in the form of a heatwave. It started with a flush of red in the sky, which rapidly simmered to a burnt orange and then a sun-soaked yellow. It descended on the land like some great floodlight, burning fire-bright and smothering the lands with a haze of shimmering heat.

A heat that was unbearable. It sent races and beasts alike scuttling to their homes, seeking shade where they could find it.

Some months later, a strong breeze swept across Narrigh. It cooled the land with its charm-less icy breath. Rain followed, marking an end to the drought, bringing the inhabitants of Narrigh out into the open.

A great rainbow formed in the sky. The people of Olvastan marvelled at its beauty, saying it was a gift from God to announce the beginnings of a bountiful harvest to come. The Theria Elves believed it was a gift from the Elfin Spirit, King Garlor, for their crafts. The Gamnod race thought the rainbow had been created by the Old One, whom they called Uom, to show them the way to a new world. The dwarves believed the rainbow was wondrous and that if they bathed in its arc, they would find mountains of gold and other riches. The Darque Goblins, however, feared the rainbow was an omen, marking the end of peace in their time.

And the Darque Goblins were right.

The rainbow stood in the sky for four days. On the fifth day, it faded as a smile fades on the lips, spitting fire and rock. It carved a great crater in the North. It poisoned the Garn Ocean and the Hizsen Sea. Many died. All lost their homes.

The surviving Gamnod people and the Darque Goblins appealed to the King and Queen of Baruch to give them aid, to let them seek sanctuary within the Kingdom.

King Kalgar and Queen Irentha believed that because the Poison Rainbow had wreaked so much damage over Garnorm and Hizsen, the Gamnod people, and the Darque Goblins must have done something terrible to anger their Gods. They also deemed that their customs and religions had no place in the other regions of Narrigh. Hence, the King and Queen granted them little aid and refused them entry to the southern, eastern, and western regions. They also had their Score Army erect a barrier named, Shile Point to prevent their passage. A gate to the North, it sat on the edge of the Dead Forest.

The Darque Goblins and the Gamnod were hurt and angry that the King and Queen had abandoned them. Evil rose in their minds and consumed them. They sought an alliance with the Traceless and the Drone Elves to help them gain vengeance over the Baruchians.

And so, the Age of War came.

From this war sprung two factions: the Furnace and the Storm.

The Furnace faction of the North formed the Blade Army. The Blade Army invaded the Kingdom of Baruch, and thus a great battle ensued between the Furnace faction and the Score Army. The Score Army were outnumbered. The kingdom was defeated, and the King and the Queen put to death. The Furnace held the Kingdom for three years until the Storm faction formed of Garnorm humans, Theria Elves and dwarves, drove the

Furnace's Blade Army back North and restored the Kingdom back to the Baruchians.

Hizsen became known as the Great Northern Crater and the races of the North became fewer and scattered.

After the Age of Wars comes the Age of Trepidation.

The Shardner government seeks to protect the races of four regions: Theris, Olvastan, Baruch, and Narrul, who remain forever wary of the North. They believe its lands are cursed. The threat of another northern invasion hangs over them. The fear of another Poison Rainbow weighs heavy on their minds."

"Far beyond the Poison Rainbow, lies the world of Odisiris, predominately occupied by a race known as Citizen. It is from here that the Poison Rainbow evolved. Unbeknown to the races of Narrigh, the rainbow created a rift between their world and the world of Odisiris.

The creator of these worlds knows of the rift and seeks to use it to his advantage. He hopes others do not seek to do the same. For he holds in his possession, a great artefact that if wielded, could disrupt the balance of the two worlds and ultimately lead to their destruction."

Connor hastily scrolled through the game's background story. 'I can't believe they try to hold up your game play with this crap.' He took a slurp of drink from the can. 'We don't need to know all this stuff.'

He set to work creating his own player character: a human warrior with his own suit of leather armour and a

Lightning Sword to help blast his enemies to smithereens. He knew warriors fought a lot and were brave. There was no time to read up on any other Professions. He would have to pick the rest up as he went along. He had not forgotten that his mum, who had returned home from work, was taking a nap and could wake up at any moment.

'Can't we just play your brother's character, Duffy?' Riley frowned at the screen. 'It'll save time.'

'Rookie mistake. If we don't want him to suspect anything, we need to create a new character, one we can delete when we're done.' Not that his brother would ever suspect him of foul play.

Riley guzzled from his can of soda. 'What good is that? We'll have to start all over again, every time he goes out. Just play Luke's character.'

Connor scowled at him. Riley was taking away all the excitement with his moaning. 'No. You don't mess with another player's character. You don't do that. Don't you know anything about the sacred code of gaming?'

Riley bowed his head. 'Only what you teach me, O Great One.'

Connor smirked. He didn't know anything about the sacred code of gaming either. He knew he didn't want to snatch Luke's personal victory away from him; he just wanted to beat it. And in time, he would. His brother need never know. 'Okay. I'll create a new character and I won't delete it. If he sees it, he'll think Bat put it there.'

Riley gave a nod and two short burps. 'Then I want my own character too.'

Chapter 2

Someone was talking to him, prising him out of the shell he called sleep. The voice was gruesomely loud. Pivotal.

'Northern beasts. Get up!'

Connor woke to find himself in the hollow stump of a tree. He was dressed in strange clothes: a leather tunic over a linen shirt, wool trousers, and soggy brown boots. There was a leather bag strapped across his shoulder and a thin metal chain around his neck. The beating of a thousand wings pounded in his ears.

'Riley?'

The stump moved. Someone or something was shaking it.

He tried to reassure himself. 'I'm still dreaming. I haven't really woken up.' That happened in dreams sometimes. You wake from one dream only to find yourself in another.

He attempted to steady the stump with his hands. The stump was slippery with moss and yellow fungus. He jerked his head from side to side, willing himself to wake. He gave his hand a hard, quick pinch. When his skin snapped back into place, a patch appeared that looked almost black beneath his brown skin. Regardless, the pinch had no impact on his current dilemma.

A grimy tusk flashed in front of his eyes. His dreams had never felt this real, or his nightmares. There was something out there.

Blood rushed through his veins, thawing out his stiff

limbs, sharpening his senses. Northern beasts?

The last he remembered, he had been playing *The Quest of Narrigh* on his brother's computer with his friend, Riley.

He must have dropped off to sleep.

He gave a loud gasp as a white-hot pain exploded in his ankle. A beast with a beak honed like a steel sword had taken hold of his right foot, clamping down on his flesh, crushing it. The size of the beast's head was three times the size of his own. On either side of its beak were two great tusks.

He breathed through clenched teeth, fighting to push back the pain. He had to dislodge himself from the tree trunk fast.

The beast casually lowered its head and peered in. Its yellow eyes fastened on its victim. Very slowly, it began to reel in its prey.

He fought to gather his wits. He braced himself against the trunk and desperately tried to draw himself up to the other end of the stump. The creature responded by forcibly pinching his ankle, determined to drag its squirming-meal out from its 'wooden container'.

His foot twisted and then cracked. He arched his back. His strangled cry echoed through the tree hollow. 'Come on,' he spat. 'Come on!' His eyes watered. Bracing himself again, he lashed out with his free leg. The beast moved to skewer it with its tusk.

He swung his leg away, snagging his trousers. He clawed at the bark, fighting the pain, vehemently trying to blot it out. He gave a deep-throated growl and, with one vicious kick, struck the beast's beak with his foot.

It opened its jaws, releasing his leg, which smacked the ground with a grisly thud.

He exerted all his energy into scrambling from the trunk. He wrenched himself up, only to find two of the great, seething beasts closing in on either side of him. Maggots dripped from the folds of their wings.

He staggered away, grimacing in pain. He was afraid his injured ankle would give out on him; afraid he wouldn't make it. Instead, he found his strides lengthening.

Very soon, he was running through a forest locked in shadow, his sodden boots squelching in the soil, the wind whistling past his ears.

Squawking noisily, the beasts rose into the air.

He spotted a boy just ahead of him, running low to the ground with his bloodied hands wrapped around his head. One of the beasts was on his tail, lunging at him with its talons.

He cast about the forest floor, looking for something to ward it off. He grabbed a sturdy, forked tree branch and charged at the wings of the swooping beast. If he could divert its attention, the boy could get away.

Wallop!

He found himself face down in the soil, floored by a blow from the beast's wing. He scrambled for his piece of tree branch to find it had fallen well out of reach.

Three of the rancid smelling beasts ensnared him. They cocked their heads and sunk their shiny pink claws into the forest floor.

A chill went through his spine. *They're going to eat me.* One night, he had hidden behind the sofa when his brother and his friends were watching a horror film about a man-eating bird. He had nightmares about it for months afterwards.

One of the beasts struck him on the side of the head with its beak. His punishment, he supposed, for trying to outrun them. He clenched his jaw. The pain penetrated his skull. Black and silver sparks flashed before his eyes.

The beasts set to work, scraping away soil from around him with their wiry claws, showering him with maggots. He felt himself sinking on a wet platform. Soil rained down on him in thick wet clumps, blocking his airways.

He would need to act quickly before they buried him alive.

Wheezing and coughing, he heaved himself onto his side and pulled the straps of his bag from around his shoulders.

Then without looking, without thinking, he tore the bag open and drew from it the first thing he could lay his hands on - an apple, soft and bruised. He flung the piece of fruit at the beasts. It missed them. He watched in horror as the lime green apple disappeared into the ground.

The beasts commenced using their beaks to break up the soil even faster.

Tears stung Connor's eyes. 'I can feel the cold shadow of death upon my face.' That was what the man had said in the film when the giant bird had started gnawing on his neck.

If this was a dream, wasn't it about time he woke up?

'You ran away again. Don't you remember?' said an Authoritative Voice inside his head. 'You wanted to come here.'

He fought to regain his reasoning. *What if I am in Narrigh?*

A Warrior had been his chosen Profession. He didn't have his armour, his Lightning Sword, or the enchanted shield he won in Level Fifteen. He raised his hands and thrust out his fingers. No light shot from them. No orbs of flame.

The thing around his neck! With determined fury, he grappled with his shirt collar. His fingers slid along the thin metal chain. Suspended from it was an egg-shaped pendant. There were bands set in the Egg's middle encrusted with gemstones. Instinctively, he took the band between his finger and thumb and rotated it in a frenzy. 'Help me, please!'

Just when he started to believe his instincts had failed him, a spectacular bolt of blue light shot from the pendant, pierced the air, and then vanished.

Screeching in fright, the beasts took to the sky, soaring above the treetops and out of sight.

Coughing up the last of the soil from his throat, he reached for his bag and hauled himself from the pit. He hobbled away without looking back.

The reality of the world around him grew starker and more perilous in his mind.

Chapter 3

Meanwhile, elsewhere on Narrigh...

The world of Narrigh is alien to Citizens. Technology is ubiquitous where they come from. They rely on it for their very existence. How well they can cope without it, in these extraordinary lands, only time will tell.

Skelos's moment of glory had almost slipped through his fingers like the intangible dreams of the wretched victims on which he conducted his experiments.

Almost.

He was in the Shardner's custody, exiled from Odisiris to a foreign land. They had put him to work on the Herming Moth Wings. Supposedly, his predecessor's invention was faulty. What did they expect when he had specimens no bigger than lizards on which to test them?

The Shardner will keep me here forever, out of sight, but unfortunately not out of mind.

He wiped the sweat and grime from his face and threw another metal Wing into the crate, sneaking a glance at the door where two guards were stationed. Half-crazed with weariness, they were still upright. Their shift would end in twenty minutes. He would get five minutes respite before a new set of guards came on duty, and he could get little done in five minutes, very little in this pitiful excuse for a lab. The laboratory was not designed with comfort in mind, nor was it designed to allow a scientist or his designated assistant to indulge in their scientific passions. The furniture was conventional, the utensils basic. There was a standard lab table, a double bowl sink, two stools and shelves stacked with beakers, test tubes, flasks, spoons, tongs and one microscope. In the corner stood a tall glass cabinet, which housed three groups of specimens: orange lizards, snout-nosed Ticket Shrews, and miniature red frogs.

Bored and agitated, Skelos lined-up the beakers on the nearest and lowest shelf to him. He had sent his assistant home an hour ago.

He had chosen to wear his favourite purple silk-lined robes rather than don the clinical black coat more suited to his Profession. The robes hid his widening girth, which was about all they were good for. He had tripped over and snagged the fabric more times than he could count.

Truth be told, he had no idea how to fix the Wings, and furthermore, he did not care. He was done with all this. He was superior to the races of Narrigh, a Citizen. First Status. Why should he work for them?

He strutted up to one of the guards and tapped him on the shoulder. The guard swatted away Skelos's fat finger with the steel baton he clutched in his hand, his face a rigid mask. He was a burly fellow with cauliflower ears and a crooked mammoth-sized nose. His ill-fitted black tunic bulged at the seams. Another Unmarked One[1], mused Skelos, who didn't see fit to bow.

'What?' said the guard.

'I wondered if you could fetch me something from the Stores.'

'Ain't no fetcher,' said the guard.

Skelos gazed at his companion who shrugged. 'You've been given everything you need, so get on with it.'

———

'Unmarked One(s) – non-Citizens.

The other guard was a Second Status Citizen, with all the arrogance of a First. He had dark brown skin, an athletic build, sinewy muscles and an angular jaw. *Now, he could prove to be a problem.*

'And how would you know what I need?' Skelos asked, inwardly seething.

The guards kept quiet. Skelos knew what was going through their minds. The store was ten minutes away at a jog; a Citizen might make it there in three minutes. However, once there, they would have to wait for him to find what he needed in the extensive storerooms, get security clearance and sign the logbook. All of which took time. Their shift would overrun, and they were not getting paid overtime to babysit.

'My assistant forgot to bring me a valuable ingredient,' said Skelos, 'and these Wings won't wait.'

The guards looked at each other. The Herming Moth Wings were a priority, every serving member of the Shardner knew it.

'We're not to leave our posts,' said the Burly One.

'Perhaps one of you can escort me to the Stores.' Skelos stared hopefully into the Burly One's eyes. *Please let it be you.*

'You go, Vastra,' said the Burly One to his fellow

guard. 'Make it quick. I want to be out of here on time.'

The other guard cocked his head at Skelos and pulled open the metal door. 'Let's go.'

The guard, named Vastra, hurried Skelos down the passage. 'What's the matter with you? Can't you go any faster?' he barked, waiting for Skelos to catch him up.

'No, I'm afraid I can't.' Skelos hunched a little and coughed, an act, which seemed to infuriate Vastra further.

'It's a good thing you've got brains or the Shardner would have been rid of you long ago. Now hurry the blazes up!'

Skelos refused to be rushed. The Avu'lore he had hidden in his robes was slowing him down, making him hobble, making him wish he had lifted a few more weights and eaten a lot less pies. He could not leave it behind. It was his most prized possession, his only possession of any worth.

As Vastra said, he had brains.

Chapter 4

Connor trudged deeper into the forest. Alone and exhausted, he clambered over mounds of soil and stumbled over gnarled roots. I'll find a safe place, and then I'll stop, he told himself. But nowhere seemed safe. The trees towered over him, casting eerie shadows, taunting him with their silence.

No ordinary forest, he reflected. The air was dead. Lifeless. If he was in a game, where were the Quest Givers? Where were the markers in the sky prompting him in the direction he needed to go?

He had called his player character, Connor the Brave. He didn't feel like Connor the Brave now, more like Connor the Coward. He could already feel himself welling up. He was surprised he hadn't wet his pants. He may have. It was hard to tell. His clothes were damp with soil. They clung to his skin, numbing him. There was no sunlight to dry them.

As he stumbled wearily on, he clung to the hope that Riley or his brother, Luke, would appear or even better that he would reach the edge of the forest and find himself back in his bedroom.

The pain in his leg had ebbed away, but his head had not stopped hurting since the beast had struck him with its beak. He rubbed a numb hand against his forehead, hoping some friction would ease the pain. It didn't. He tilted his head. Grains of soil fell out of his ears. He dug the rest out with his fingers. And that's when he noticed the black and inky blue scar on the palm of his right hand. He stared at it goggle-eyed. It didn't hurt. That didn't mean it wasn't poisoned, or worse, the beginnings of some hideous transformation. He noticed that his arms were bony, and his ribs poked from beneath his shirt. What was happening to him?

Whispers.

He snapped his head up. He could hear them clearly. He was not alone.

The whispers brought him to a clearing in the forest, where there stood a circle of trees knitted together to form an immense pen. Unnatural light streamed from the enclosure. The men, who had taken up residence inside it, had invaded the eerie silence of the forest.

Connor forgot about the scar on his hand. He found a small gap between two lofty trunks and peered through it.

Several stones littered the muddy bottom of the enclosure. They gave off a dim light. He blinked four times. He could not believe his eyes.

He counted forty or so riders mounted on sturdy grey horses. The riders were armoured, clad from head to foot in silver. Silver helmets covered all but their eyes, jaws and mouth. Their fine cloaks flowed about them like silk. Three of the riders dismounted. They spoke amongst themselves, heatedly, in some peculiar tongue.

His eyes swivelled up and down, left and right. The riders were human. It brought him little relief. Not all humans in Narrigh were allies. And as far as he knew, there were no Silver Riders in *The Quest of Narrigh* game. He glimpsed a small figure sitting hunched at the foot of a tree, draped in fur, their face concealed.

Most of the enclosure's branches arched inwards, shutting out the daylight, but some low-hanging boughs fell outside the cage.

He considered climbing along one of the boughs for a better look if he could find the strength. He was too tired and anxious to feel the familiar pangs of hunger in his belly. Nonetheless, he felt the cold in his veins.

He crouched on stiff legs, kneading his ankles with his balled fists. He felt pinpricks in his feet, nothing more. He blew on his hands and then rubbed them together until they were hot. He opened his bag. Inside, he found gold, silver and bronze coins, an apple, strips of dried meat, two leather flasks, a folded piece of parchment, a small grey stone and a slow-burner.[1]

So, I am in a game. He had twenty-two pieces of gold in all, sixteen silver coins, and twelve bronze. He had unloaded his more valuable items into the City of Rint vaults. The coins were loot he had gained from defeating his enemies. The food was all he had left over from an inn he had visited in one of the villages. He didn't know where the stone had come from. He didn't even remember winning it. It could be that it found its way into his bag by accident. If it was a magic stone, he had no idea how to use it. He shrugged. He was sure to figure it out in time.

You needed a special kind of flint to light slow-burners, not magic. He rooted through the bag and checked his pockets. He didn't have any flint, which was probably a good thing. He had never lit a match in his life. He didn't want to set fire to the whole forest.

He chewed a corner of the dried meat. It didn't taste too bad: sweet, salty, and as tough as rawhide. He opened one of the flasks with some difficulty. The lid seemed to have frozen to the rim. Once he had tussled off the lid, he put the flask to his lips. The liquid was clear and tasted of ginger beer and lemon. The beverage instantly warmed him up. He didn't stop drinking until the flask was empty.

He unfolded the piece of parchment and found it was a map of *The Lands of Narrigh.*

------

[1]Slow-burners - clay straws impregnated with strips of linen, dipped in animal fat and alcohol.

He could find his way out of the forest and return to the place in which he started out in the game: Undren village. He could probably make it home from there.

He rearranged the items in his bag, taking care to place the map at the top where he could easily reach it.

He wiped his mouth and set about selecting a low branch, one he could reach without difficulty before his sore muscles gave out. Fighting weariness, he grabbed a fistful of leaves for advantage. He secured one foot on a stump, the size of a large potato, at the base of the trunk and hoisted himself up. He moved slowly, hindered by the pounding in his head. He clutched the flat green leaves and scaly bark. The cold nipped at him, stabbing at his fingers.

He was making good progress when he suddenly heard an almighty crack. Something hot coiled itself around his neck and yanked him to the ground. It squeezed his throat. His eyes bulged and watered. His scream came out as a gurgle. The veins rose in his temples. He bucked and thrashed, digging his fingers into the thing wringing his neck: the hot choking-thing.

He heard a coarse laugh, and then he felt the choking-thing grow cold and slack. He clutched his throat, coughing and gasping for air.

Through his distorted vision, he saw the shape of a man standing over him, telling him pointedly, in English, to rise.

Connor did not rise. He lay on his side staring into the face of a Silver Rider, who glared at him malevolently through the eye-slits in his helmet. In his gloved hand, the rider held a small silver barrel. From it came squirming silver tentacles. The rider raised his hand and the tentacles fizzled and died.

'Alone, are we?' asked the rider.

Connor tried to open his mouth. His head swirled dizzily. He forced himself to sit up and take notice of the man who had spoken to him. 'Who are you? What do you want?' Except the words never left his lips.

'Now, what to do with you?' The rider ran one hand across his exposed stubbly black chin. His lips curled into a smile.

Another of the Silver Riders drifted towards Connor like a pale ghost. He towered in height, dwarfing his comrade. He met Connor's gaze. His eyes were the same colour as the deep green leaves of the forest and as cold as the ice that clung to them.

'What do ya reckon to this one, Osaphar? Shall we leave him here? Let the Dal-Carrion have him for breakfast?'

'Imbecile!' said the Tall Rider. 'Do not speak my name.'

The Tall Rider knelt over Connor. Connor flinched and shuffled back on his knees. His head smacked the bark of the enclosure. He saw the silvery outline of an eye stitched into the fabric of the rider's cloak, where it draped over his left breastplate.

Osaphar tilted Connor's chin with his hand. He stared at Connor's neck. A look of wonder shone in his pale eyes.

Panic seized Connor. He was sure the Silver Rider had seen his Egg pendant and meant to take it. What Connor didn't see was the dark rims on his neck, left by the hot tentacles, fade then disappear before the rider's eyes.

With his stiff-gloved hand, Osaphar proceeded to rake at the chain around Connor's neck. His fingers fastened around the pendant.

The Tall Rider twirled the pendant between his fingers. Connor wasn't about to let him take it. It was the only thing he knew how to use. He snatched the pendant clean out of Osaphar's grasp and hugged it to his own thumping chest.

Osaphar frowned and rose abruptly to his feet. 'He's to come with us.'

'Gods save us!' said his companion. 'Surely our undertaking doesn't include that of a half-starved boy.'

'You're reputable in your disregard for orders, Lomar, and if it were any other boy, I would allow you the privilege,' he paused. His gaze drifted to where Connor sat gaunt and bewildered. 'This boy, however, comes with us.'

With that, Osaphar seized Connor by his waist and soared to the top of the trees.

He landed, with a slight bump, inside the enclosure. He set Connor down, propping him up against a tree.

Snow began to fall. Connor's teeth chattered. He wasn't afraid anymore. The cold had dulled his mind.

Osaphar said no more to him. He wrapped him in fur and pressed a heated flask to his lips. The fur obliterated the cold sheet of air that swathed him. He downed the warm syrupy liquid, hardly tasting it. He cupped the flask in his hands and let the heat from it enter his body. He gazed expressionless at the others who sat astride their mounts like silver spectres. The snow melted the instant it touched their garments. Connor felt them watching him. A handful of the Silver Riders cast an idle glance in his direction, and then resumed their conversations.

He stole a glance at the hunched figure seated on the ground. In the soft flickering light, a little girl's hazel eyes gazed back at him.

One of the Silver Riders swept the girl roughly off her feet and placed her upon his horse.

Connor stared at the empty space where he thought he had seen her. His vision was hazy. He rubbed his eyes, determined not to fall asleep. Someone snatched the flask out of his hand and lifted him onto a steel grey horse. He gripped the horse's mane tight and sunk his legs into the animal's flanks to stop himself from falling. A Silver Rider clambered up behind him to take the reins.

Snowflakes settled on Connor's eyelids. He dipped his head, only to have it instantaneously lifted by a jolt from the horse as they galloped out of the enclosure.

The other riders followed. They rode hard as if spurred along by an urgency that could not be communicated in words.

Connor's eyes fixed on a vision of blue. Every tree and the very ground on which the horses trampled was as blue as the ocean was deep, a watery and fathomless blue. He felt giddy. His head lolled.

What did they give me to drink?

The blue forest vanished, replaced by perpetual darkness.

Luke didn't want to believe a computer had swallowed his brother. It sounded like a story straight out of a film and a bad one at that. The police had wanted his laptop. He didn't give it to them. His whole life was on there. If he let the police take it, they might wipe the computer's memory or mess with it. They might find things on there he did not want them to see. He had given them his old one, loaded with programs and files he no longer cared about. He didn't need the police to check the websites and accounts they assumed his brother had accessed; he could do that himself.

He had found a photo of himself and Conner and made it his screensaver. It was taken a year ago. They were at the beach, ankle-deep in ocean water with the sun on their backs. He glanced from his brother's beaming face to his own. They looked almost identical. He supposed Connor's jaw was less angular than his own, his stature a little shorter. And Connor had a lot more hair on his head. However, they had the same shaped noses, the same dipped eyes.

It had been almost three weeks since his brother had gone missing and just about the whole world knew about it. It was on the news, on the internet, the talk of the neighbourhood. Luke had not returned to school.

Connor's picture had been put up in the local area of south London. He and his friends had seen to that. When he wasn't putting up posters, or showing his brother's picture around, he was revisiting all the old places his brother used to go and the new ones, hoping to find a trail. He always came up empty. Connor had taken nothing with him. He hadn't run away. He knew that for a fact.

There came a knock on the door. He ignored it. He thought it might be his mum's friend, Ruth again, wanting to talk to him about his feelings. He wasn't good at those sorts of conversations. "Have you seen my brother?" He was good at saying that. He said it until his voice was hoarse.

The knock came again.

'It's open,' he snapped. Or perhaps it was his mum. She popped her head around the door occasionally to offer some support, although she was in no state to give it. She would always burst into tears and go back to waiting by the phone in the living room, afraid no one would think to call her on the mobile phone she carried with her everywhere.

Riley shuffled in, hair like a thatched roof on a windy day, a face full of freckles and regrets. Luke stiffened. He wanted to pound the truth out of his brother's friend with his bare hands. But Riley had not changed his story.

'He's in there,' he whispered. 'You must believe me. I care about him as well you know.'

'Tell me again.'

Riley took a deep breath and stared around the room.

He shivered as if he had a ghost on his tail. He sunk into a chair on the other side of the room. A good distance between Luke and the laptop. Luke didn't blame him. If Riley didn't start talking sense soon, he'd rip the chair out from under him.

'Connor got a list of your passwords. That's how he-we got into the game. He wanted to get to Level 40 same as you. We played for hours. I fell asleep in the chair and when I woke up the screen was flashing, and Connor vanished into it.

'You ever done drugs, Riley?' He stared at the screensaver. His chubby-faced brother grinned back at him. He was dressed in board shorts and held a football in the crook of his arm. He couldn't imagine Connor going behind his back, stealing his passwords, accessing his computer without his permission. Connor hero-worshipped him. He was a good kid. Riley must have put him up to it.

The legs of Riley's chair squeaked. 'You mean like aspirin?'

'You know what I mean.'

'No. Never.'

'What about Connor. He ever take anything?'

'No.'

Some of the tension in his shoulders eased. 'Alcohol?'

'Na-uh.'

He sensed Riley's cautious footsteps as he padded across the room.

He dropped a tattered piece of paper on the desk. On it were Luke's passwords, every last one of them in his brother's own hand.

'I forgot I had it,' said Riley. He hastily retreated to his chair. 'We just wanted to play the game.'

Luke felt sick to his stomach. *I shouldn't have let him watch. Shouldn't have let him play.*

He swivelled to face Riley. The kid looked gaunt and there were red rims around his eyes. Luke knew the police had asked all the obvious questions, but there was no harm in asking them again. He balled up the paper containing his passwords. 'Is there anything else you're not telling me?'

Riley ran his tongue around the inside of his mouth a few times, staring off into space.

'No. We were only playing,' he murmured.

Chapter 5

Behind a set of steel doors, fifteen inches thick lie the Stores. Forty-eight chambers of the Shardner's secrets concealed in boxes, vaults, and vats. Access is restricted to no more than fifty of the Shardner's special staff. Skelos Dorm is somewhere on that list, though he does not consider it a privilege...

At the height of his career, Skelos had had his own Stores, spacious enough and rich enough to rival any in Baruch, and he did not need a guard to accompany him there.

The doors opened. Skelos and Vastra stepped off the steel welcome mat onto the cave floor. The chambers flanking them were four stories high. Skelos's ears rang as the doors behind him clicked back into place. Locked. At the end of the passage was another set of steel doors, and a glass cubicle. Inside the glass cubicle sat two ardent Administrators. It was their job to inspect the items leaving The Stores and record them in the logbook. Once the Administrators were satisfied everything was in order, they released the second set of steel doors. The doors that led to freedom or so Skelos hoped, for there was no other way out.

He was pleased to see there were no Plowmen[1]. He had not received their touch in a while.

———

[1] <u>Plowmen</u> (Plowman – singular) are silent half-ogres who can temporarily disable a race's abilities, innate or otherwise. They are often found in prisons and vaults, anywhere that needs to be heavily guarded.

The guards believed that his age and weight prevented him from making any great escapes.

So far, he had proven them right. It was better for them to think him infirm, than armed and dangerous.

Skelos dawdled outside the first barrel-vaulted chamber. With Vastra looking on, he had almost forgotten what he had come for. It was apparent to him that the guard had never been inside The Stores. His eyes were flitting all over the place, awash with curiosity of what lay hidden behind each iron door, behind each dusty vault. Once Skelos found what he was really looking for, he would have to act quickly.

He kept on until he came to the chamber he was seeking. The chamber door was bolted, locked and chained. The sign on the door read, RAINBOWS ROCK. PLEASE SEE THE STORE ADMINISTRATOR FOR ACCESS. Skelos's jaw twitched then sagged. It was in there. He could sense it. Besides, he had overheard the guards talking about putting it in the most secure chamber in the Stores, the one that was always locked.

'I can get a Store Administrator for you,' said Vastra eager to speed things up. He shot off before Skelos could say whether he needed a Store Administrator or not. As it happened, it wasn't an Administrator he needed, it was a bloody miracle.

Skelos rattled the chains in frustration, sending a thunderous echo through the chambers.

'Shhh!' hissed a voice. He spun round to see Vastra striding towards him with one of the Stores Administrators. The Administrator's cheeks were hollow enough to spoon tea out of and he was as thin as a plank of wood turned on its side. He wore glasses and a matted grey coat that precisely matched the colour and the state of his hair. Gyan. Skelos had encountered the irritating rodent no less than five times. Gyan was a stickler for detail and liked to ask a lot of questions and Skelos only liked questions if he was the one asking them.

'What do you want with the Rock, Skelos?' asked the Store Administrator. 'Wings don't need Rainbows Rock.'

They called it Rainbows Rock in Narrigh. On his home planet, they called it Zichronite. He thought the word was too sophisticated for the races of Narrigh. No one fully comprehended the true nature of the Rock, though many had experienced its power and its wrath.

'That's what I'm going to find out,' quipped Skelos. 'I believe the Rock maybe of some use after all.'

Gyan prised a leather-bound book out of his pocket. How could Skelos forget: The Logbook.

'Tuesday the twelfth of November,' he read. 'Skelos informs me that Rainbows Rock does not work on Herming Moth Wings. "I believe it may cause them to malfunction", he said.'

Skelos blew out his cheeks. 'I think I may have made an experimental error in the quantity.'

Gyan flicked to another page in his logbook. 'Wednesday, October 2nd. Skelos informs me that he has never in his life made a quantitative error in his experimental works. He also informs me that he has an intense dislike for Store Administrators, who as he put so eloquently, are lacking in intellect and have the social etiquette of Goby pigs.'

Skelos shrugged, laughing inwardly. Yes. It would take a miracle all right.

Gyan closed his logbook and deposited it back into his pocket. 'You know I cannot allow you to take this Rock, Skelos, so why bother asking? Surely you don't want me to log that you're carrying out unauthorised experiments?' Gyan tapped at the pocket containing his logbook. 'The Shardner will not like it.'

'Fool!' Skelos hissed, unable to contain his anger any longer. 'If it wasn't for me, this place would be overrun with those foul beasts. What do you suppose I would do with the Rock? I'm under watch twenty-four hours a day. My progress is constantly checked by the hour. I've come here to procure urgent supplies for the good of the Kingdom. I drag this young man, who's nearing the end of his shift, into the bargain, and you have the nerve to tell me what the Shardner will and will not like. Go and fetch the highest serving member, if it pleases you because I'm not moving until you open that door!'

Gyan looked as if he'd had a narrow escape with a poisonous dart. His face was the colour of strawberries. He stood there blinking, his mouth hanging open. He then whipped out his logbook and slid a pen from its spine. He wagged his finger at Vastra. 'You will be a witness to this, young sir. This will all be documented, every word. The Shardner will not be pleased.' He leafed through the book, eagerly scouring for a blank page. 'You people think you're better than the rest of us, don't you? I think not. Indeed, I think not.' He found a blank page and scratched his head. 'Now let's see. What day is it?' He looked over his shoulder. 'Belstien! Where are you? Get over here. I need your—'

The logbook was thrown into the air and the pen along with it. Gyan watched them fly and watched them fall in horrified silence. Weak-kneed and trembling with fear, he turned to the culprit.

Vastra's eyes were slits. 'What do you mean, *you people?*'

Gyan cowered. Backing into the chamber door and cupping his hands together as if praying for mercy, he squealed, 'I was talking about scientists. I'm not referring to Citizens. I love Citizens. They're so-so... robust.'

'I agree,' said Skelos, a smile sprouting on his lips. He was beginning to think having a fellow Citizen tagging along with him, no matter how inconsequential, was not such a bad thing. He was willing to ignore the insult regarding scientists. It was true; they did think they were better than everyone else. 'Vastra, pick up the Store Administrator's logbook for him, will you. Let us prove to him we are not lacking in propriety.'

Vastra picked up Gyan's pen and logbook in a scowling, sulking manner that wasn't a jolt close to propriety or readiness. He dangled the logbook and pen in front of Gyan as if he were dangling a bone in front of a dog. Vastra snatched the pen and book from him as if he were a dog and stuffed the items in the deepest crevice he could find in his oversized pocket.

'Open it,' said Vastra, nodding at the unlocked door.

Gyan looked at the door then back at Skelos, his face a picture of bemusement. 'This door?'

'Yes, this door.'

Gyan swallowed. 'You must understand I cannot give Rainbows Rock out to just anyone. It is most valuable.'

Vastra cocked his head. 'More valuable than – say – your life?'

Gyan swallowed again, took a step back and bumped into Belstien's portly belly, the second Store Administrator on duty. Belstien yawned and rubbed his eyelid. 'What's going on?'

Gyan didn't bother to reply.

'My shift ended twenty minutes ago,' said Vastra. 'I've got places I need to be.'

'Right,' said Belstien, fumbling for the bunch of keys clipped to his belt. He made his way over to the door, his three chins wobbling.

'I'll have to log it,' said Gyan, breathing through his nose. 'Questions will be asked.'

'Never mind that, *Administrator*,' Vastra snarled. 'The scientist is watched night and day; I'll vouch for him.'

Skelos could hardly believe his good fortune. He selected two fistfuls of Rock while Vastra and Belstien watched over him. The instrument he was looking for was so small, lost in the sea of Rock fragments, he wondered if they would afford him the time to search for it.

Gyan stood in the antechamber, one arm folded across his chest. Gagging with rage, he still hadn't managed to close his mouth. Skelos was thankful he had ceased his whingeing. *Let me concentrate on what I'm looking for.*

Vastra was eyeing the Rock as if it were gold for the taking, which it might as well have been. Belstien was so blearily eyed with sleep he could scarcely keep his eyes open. At one point he rested his head on his neck and let out a hearty snore.

It would be on the uppermost shelf, Skelos demised, a prediction that proved to be correct. One single Shard with Rainbows Rock powder encased within it. He nudged some of the smaller Rocks off the shelf below him. They clunked to the floor.

Gyan bustled in. Vastra was already bent over, gathering the Rock in his big hands. The Store Administrator was about to push him to one side and then appeared to think better of it. 'Careful,' he gasped. He took the Rock from Vastra and positioned it back on the shelf. 'I shall have to log this. It's counted you know. Twice daily, each little fragment.'

Skelos doubted it and Vastra doubted it even more it seemed. Skelos slipped the Shard under his robe and spun round in time to see Vastra deposit a small fragment of the Rock up his own sleeve.

'You done?' he asked Skelos, almost respectfully.

Skelos felt for the metal case inside his robes. It contained a very potent Cloud Vapour. One whiff would knock a Citizen out cold and a few more men besides. He turned his back on Vastra to address Gyan. 'If you don't mind, Store Administrator, I'd like to have a word with you in private. Is there somewhere we might go to talk?'

A ripple went through Gyan's brows. 'Talk?' he

spluttered. 'In private? What could you possibly want to talk to me about? I hope you're not going to try to bribe me, make me turn a blind eye to your misdemeanor. If that is the case, then I should let you know, you're wasting your time.' He poised pen in hand, logbook at the ready.

'No.' He lowered his voice. 'I have information that I would like to share with you. Confidential information regarding the experiment bestowed on me by the Shardner. Your input will be invaluable.' Skelos flapped his hand in the second Store Administrator's direction. 'Or I could take Belstien if you prefer.'

'Belstien is my subordinate,' said Gyan, glaring at Belstien as if daring him to dispute otherwise. 'I have a meeting room in which we can converse. Follow me.' He stepped swiftly out of the door and began to walk up the gangway. 'Lock the door will you, Belstien and return to the cubicle when you're done,' he called over his shoulder to the stupefied Administrator.

Skelos followed Gyan and was irked to see Vastra tagging along beside them. He had rather hoped the guard would leave. Wishful thinking, on his part.

Chapter 6

Connor's mind appeared to have disengaged itself from his body. A strange tranquillity had come over him. Fluorescent lights and gleaming silver flitted before his eyes. He dreamt of flying horses and whispering trees. A torrent of sounds, smells and apparitions tore at his senses: muddled words and rushing water, the smell of dead wood, dead meat and stale beer.

The liquid from the flask had jumbled his thoughts. He knew he had spoken to the Silver Rider upon whose horse he rode. The man had responded to him heartily. His chatter seemed endless, yet through all of it, Connor only managed to catch his name, Hiera.

Stop drinking the tea!

He didn't want to stop drinking the tea. He felt no pain when he drank the tea. No fear. No sorrow.

'Stop drinking the tea!' The shrill voice drilled into his temples.

The flask fell, knocked out of his hands by the distorted shadow crouching over him.

'Mum?'

'Will you wake up!'

He felt a forceful grip on his arm. He couldn't ignore the gravity of the words, but he couldn't react to them either. He didn't know how. His head lolled from side to side. The corners of his mouth went up into a lop-sided smile.

'For goodness' sake, will you wake up!'

Something was passed under his nose. He caught a whiff of a strong acid smell. He pulled a face and jerked his head back. Whatever it was swept up his nostrils and made his eyes sting. He twisted his mouth and snorted into the back of his hand. A vial of clear liquid was pressed to his lips.

'Drink this.'

A mist rose from the vial, swirling thickly, floating in the murky light. His head started to swim. He seized the small wrist of the hand holding the vial. He wasn't about to drink it. No way.

The person crouching over him, wrenched his jaw open with one hand and thrust the contents of the vial down his throat. A small hand squashed his lips together, preventing him from bringing the liquid back up again.

He smacked the hand away, shuddering as the liquid, which tasted like hot metal, burned in the pit of his stomach.

A girl of about ten slipped into view. She sat back on her heels, her hazel eyes searching his face. She wore her thick hair in pigtails, tied with blue ribbons to match her blue silk dress. She had a piece of fur wrapped around her shoulders.

He looked around him. He was slumped in the hollow of a tree. Its sturdy roots bonded above the soil, forming a knotted shelter. He saw there was room for one more at a squeeze, but the roots did not go up high enough for him to stand or move about comfortably.

'I'm Amelia,' said the girl.

Connor shot her a wary glance. She didn't look as if she came from Narrigh or his world. 'Where am I?'

'In a Dacker tree.'

Wincing, he stretched out one leg. His toes grazed the inside of his boots as if they no longer fit. He checked the palm of his right hand again. The scar hadn't spread. Apart from his headache returning, he didn't feel much different from when he had woken up in the tree stump hollow, and that seemed like days ago. How long had he been cooped up like this? He rummaged around for his bag, sighing with relief when he discovered he was leaning on it.

Through an opening in the tree, he saw to his dismay, that he had not left the cold and forbidding forest behind, or the company of the Silver Riders. Some huddled in Dacker tree hollows of their own, others paced a small clearing outside, crunching ice under their feet, sniffing the air expectantly and glaring off into the distance. What were they waiting for?

'Where's your friend?' said Amelia. She continued to stare at him intently. 'The other boy.'

'You mean Riley? You saw him?'

'I saw another boy, out there, when the Dal-Carrions attacked.'

He hoped Riley wasn't the boy he saw the flying beasts carry off in the forest.

He drew himself up on his knees. 'Who are those men outside?'

Amelia took a sharp breath and removed the fur wrap from her shoulders. She spread it over her knees. 'Those men are the Shardner's Special Army. They gave you a Trance Potion. I used a Revival Potion to bring you round. We must get out of the forest. We're in danger.'

Connor's skin prickled with a sense of foreboding. There came that sound again, the sound of rushing water. Instinct told him, it was not the roar of the ocean.

Amelia's eyes flickered towards an opening in the frostbitten roots. Her face showed no fear or confusion.

A death-chill cloaked the forest. The snow had ceased falling. The trees were sparse in this part of the forest, their life eroded. No birds fluttered in the sky. No animals foraged on the ground.

'You can hear it, can't you?' he said. 'What is it?'

'Dal-Carrion. The winged-beasts. They're multiplying. That's what Hiera told me.'

'What's the Shardner?'

'The government.'

Connor had been so focused on trying to level-up in the game, he hadn't taken much time to learn about Narrigh society. He couldn't have afforded to, not if he didn't want his brother to catch him out. You had to be over fifteen years of age to play *The Quest of Narrigh*; He had only just turned thirteen. When you had completed your quest, which usually involved blasting something until it exploded or fell to the ground, you collected your loot. And once you had gained enough Experience Points you would then move up to the next Level. *They won't know to look for me here. They'll think I've run away again.*

He fumbled for the chain around his neck, feeling the weight of the egg-shaped pendant suspended from it. How was he ever going to get home, if he kept coming up against all these obstacles? He hadn't forgotten the pain he felt in his leg when the Dal-Carrion had bitten down on it. He wanted to run, not fight.

'Are you like...a Quest Giver?' he asked.

The little girl frowned. 'A what?'

'It doesn't matter.'

'Get it through your stupid head, this isn't a game,' said the Authoritative Voice.

Amelia played with one of the ribbons in her hair. 'The Dal-Carrion aren't easy to kill in their current numbers. The Shardner's Special Army want to capture them so they can study their habits and breeding patterns to help bring them under control – something like that.'

Connor didn't care what the Shardner's men wanted with the Dal-Carrion as long as they kept them away from him. *And what will the Shardner's Special Army do with me?* It was the most important question. The question he should have asked first. 'Where are they taking us?'

'To the Kingdom of Baruch, I think.'

A couple of nearby horses whinnied and reared on their hind legs.

Connor cast the strip of fur aside. The draught Amelia gave him burned through his bloodstream. He was breaking out in a sweat all over.

'What are they going to do with us in Baruch?' he asked, trying to ignore the increasing commotion outside.

Amelia scampered from the Dacker tree without answering.

Flexing his aching joints, Connor crawled out after her.

A low echo rumbled through the forest. The Dal-Carrion were approaching. Their beating wings could have been mistaken for a flowing stream, the waves of the ocean or simply the wind, but there was no mistaking the smell for anything other than the smell of death.

The Silver Riders flew from their Dacker tree shelters. Some mounted their horses and galloped out of sight, their voices drowning in the thunder of hooves.

'Be ready!' shouted one as he fled.

Connor found Amelia leaning against a withered tree, her hands folded behind her back. Thoughtful. Watching.

Less than thirty remained. Twelve on horseback formed an orderly line, a barricade across the clearing. The rest of the riders assembled themselves behind them, having tethered their horses to the trees.

Amelia seemed to know a lot about the Silver Riders. She had not asked Connor his name or where he came from. He fell in next to her, noting her curious detachment from the scene around her. He found her calmness disturbing. She reminded him of a doll, wooden and lacking in expression.

She stared straight ahead. 'This is the second catching!' she shouted above the din. 'They had another one two days ago, while you were sleeping.'

I can't have been here for days, thought Connor. Everyone will be wondering where I am.

He saw a vast shadow edging its way along the icy floor. Fear rose in his gut. 'Shouldn't we make a run for it?'

'No, not yet, not until the Herming Moth Wings have flown.' Amelia gestured to a Silver Rider running towards them, Hiera. He had a grimy orange beard and sunken auburn eyes. She flashed him a smile.

'You children get back in the shelter,' he growled.

'Yes, Hiera,' she said, without making any move to do

so.

Connor watched Hiera draw a bronze metallic object, shaped like a moth, from the pouch attached to his belt. Hiera thrust the object into the outstretched hand of a Silver Rider on horseback who sat near the end of the line. Each rider had two Wings, one clipped to their silver belts, the other clasped in their hands.

Amelia moved out, sprinting nimbly. She joined the Silver Riders on the east flank, all of whom were too preoccupied with the approaching Dal-Carrion to pay her any attention. She squatted at the root of a tree, dangerously close to a Silver Rider's horse.

She glanced back over her shoulder, beckoning Connor to join her.

His mouth flapped open. Did she have a death wish? One kick from the horse's iron shoe and she would be dead.

The Dal-Carrions squawks ignited the forest. Tree limbs creaked and snapped in their wake. The hairs on the back of Connor's neck rose. He steeled himself, fighting to find his inner strength, to latch on to it for good. He didn't want it to slip away again when he needed it so desperately.

He had started to edge his way out when he a caught a flicker of something in the peripheral of his vision. He whirled round to see a scintillating blue light hovering in the air, several feet away from him. It rippled like ocean waves bathed in sunlight. He stared at it in amazement.

'You can come closer,' said a voice.

There was no mistaking the light, but the voice? He didn't like the Authoritative Voice inside his head and now a new one had emerged. How many voices could he have in his head at once?

The light started toward him. He backed away from it. This had to be another hallucination, the last remnants of the Trance Potion trying to consume him.

He ran stooping, heaving at the smell fouling the air, determined to get to Amelia. He dodged Hiera, and narrowly missed a head-on collision with another Silver Rider who flew into his path. He finally reached her. He took her arm and dragged her clear of the horses.

Eight Dal-Carrion stalked into the enclosure, craning their long necks, their claws rising and falling with crude elegance.

Connor held his breath. What would happen when the winged-beasts made their deadly assault? How would the Silver Riders achieve a 'catching' as Amelia put it?

He gripped the strap of his bag, his fingers twitching, preparing to run.

Luke sat at the desk in his bedroom with his laptop open. He rapidly clicked the touch pad. The fingers of his other hand flew over the keys. His eyes flickered hazily from left to right and then back again. Every so often, he would stop to flap away the "bat" hovering at his shoulder.

The "bat" in question was his best friend, Walter "Bat", Bateman, and as usual he was flapping about nothing and shouting loud enough to punch a hole in his eardrum.

Bat wasn't convinced Connor was stuck in a virtual game world. He had offered his support all the same. His friend had helped him scour the local streets and post messages on practically every social media platform out there for any information about his brother's disappearance.

'Did you press enter? Press enter.' Bat rapped the computer screen with his knuckles. 'Go in there,' he urged. 'See what's in there!'

'I've already been in there, you twerp!' he slapped Bat's hairy finger away. Sit down before you run into a wall or something.'

He slammed his hand to his ear. Bat was giving him a headache. He needed to take a leaf out of Riley's book. Riley stood obediently at his side, waiting for his next set of instructions.

Bat rolled up beside Luke in a swivel chair. His dark hair swished over his shoulders. 'What's happening!' He sounded near hysterical. 'Why is it not moving?' He drummed his leg on the floor. Luke silenced it with a thump to his knee.

The only character Luke saw when he logged into *The Quest of Narrigh* game was the one he had created. He hadn't played since the night of his brother's disappearance. And why should he want to? Nothing held the same enthusiasm anymore, nor would it until Connor returned home. The situation was desperate.

He rose from the chair and offered his seat to Riley. 'Talk me through what you did from here?'

Riley licked the sweat off his top lip and shrunk into the seat.

Luke vowed not to get mad at him again. He crossed his arms to his chest. He held his breath.

'Connor created, we created some-some player

characters.' Riley stared at the keypad as if it were a nuclear bomb that he had been asked to detonate. He tapped the space bar.

'What was the name of his character? What race did he choose?' Luke stood directly behind the desk chair, clutching it on both sides. 'Bat write this down.'

Bat shot him a you've-lost-the-plot look as he fumbled around for pen and a scrap of paper. Luke didn't care if they thought he'd lost the plot. As incredulous as it sounded, it was the nearest thing he had to a lead.

'A human,' said Riley. 'Connor, The Brave. He was a warrior.'

'Was he alone?'

Riley hunched his shoulders. His head bowed, his back as stiff as a board. 'Alone?' He frowned. 'No, I was with him.'

'Besides *you.*' Luke let out an irritable sigh. 'Did he have a pet? Or any other characters with him?'

'There were lots of other characters and monsters, but I can't remember their names.'

'Where did you go from there? What did you do?'

Bat briefly rested his hand on Riley's shoulder. 'It's okay buddy. You're doing fine.'

It was not okay! He let go of the chair, his frustration shattered by guilt. This wasn't Riley's fault. He couldn't know any of this was going to happen. *I'll try to go easy on him.*

'We played the game,' said Riley, clasping his hands together. 'We reached Level 17.'

'You couldn't have levelled up that quick,' he snapped.

'We did. Connor did mostly. He got good very quickly.

He made it to Bluewood Forest. Then the screen flashed purple, like blinding purple and he disappeared.'

Luke stared at a spot on the wall. His computer had been playing up before that, but the screen hadn't turned purple, it had turned green.

'Hey,' said Bat. He gripped Luke's shoulder. 'Leave Riley to this. I'll get my dad to drive us to that new stadium by Clarkson.'

Luke spun around to face him. 'And what's my brother going to be doing there? Watching greyhounds' race? Don't you get it? Someone or something took him. He didn't run off.'

Five years ago, Connor had runaway. It was after their mum had told him off for spilling cola all over their new sofa. He had left a note detailing his futile expedition, it read: "Gone to look for dad". As far as Luke knew, Connor had no memory of his father. Their mum had once told him their dad's name was Joe Bloggs, and Connor being a child of five, had fallen for it.

When Connor had run away to look for their dad, he was gone for a whole night. He was a lot smaller then. His disappearance had ripped Luke apart. It was the first time he had cried in years. It was the last time he had cried. The police had found Connor hiding under a railway bridge alone, dirty and crying. Rather than comfort him, Luke had given him a clout around the ear and made him promise not to run off again. There was no reason for Connor to run away again. None whatsoever.

What if it was the other thing?

Bat backed away, raising both hands. 'I get it. I do.' Although, he had a look on his face that showed the only thing he was getting was stressed.

'He didn't leave this house,' said Luke.

Bat avoided eye contact with Luke as if he thought him beyond reasoning.

'You were half asleep,' Bat told Riley. 'Maybe you assumed it. If the light was blinding, he could have left the room without you noticing.'

'No!' said Riley. He jumped up from the chair, knocking it into the back of Luke. 'I didn't assume anything. I saw it with my own eyes.'

Bat responded with a compassionate nod. 'I'll go get us some drinks.' He disappeared out of the door.

Luke sat in the chair. 'We've got everyone out there looking. We stay here and play. We'll take my character back to Bluewood Forest and go from there.'

Chapter 7

Gyan escorted him to a small dingy room behind one of the chambers. This lightened Skelos's temperament; it was conveniently close to the exit.

The Store Administrator slipped a key into the lock, pressed his weight against the door, forcing it to swing open.

Slow-burners hung from sconces on the wall. Vastra took up some flint from the table and set about lighting them, coughing as he went.

Skelos licked his lips. He had one chance at this. Only one chance to get it right.

'Go,' he told the Citizen guard without so much as glancing at him. 'Wait for me by the exit.' Entrance or exit there was a strong chance that Vastra would overhear the conversation before he had the opportunity to execute his plan.

'Okay,' said Vastra. He held out his hand. 'Give me the case.'

'Case?' said Skelos, frowning at Vastra's empty hand, trying to decipher some hidden meaning behind the word. *A secret code between Citizens that I am not privy to, perhaps?*

'The case of Cloud Vapour you took from the first chamber,' said Vastra, smirking. 'I cannot allow you to take something of such potency in with you, if I am not present.'

Skelos rummaged around in his robes, found the case

and slapped it into Vastra's open palm. Turns out, Vastra wasn't as scientifically clueless as he had first thought.

Vastra's fingers closed around the case triumphantly. 'Don't think you can fool me, Citizen.'

Gyan leapt to the door like a startled cat. 'What's going on?' His eyes darted between them. 'What's he taken?'

Skelos leaned so close to Vastra, their faces almost touched. 'And don't think you can fool me,' he hissed at the guard through tight lips. 'You have something almost as potent up your own sleeve, shame if it were to fall out.'

The smirk slid from Vastra's face.

'A case you say?' said Gyan. 'If it's from The Stores, I shall have to take a look at it before we go in.' Although he did not look too eager to do so. No sooner had he taken two steps forward, he was edging back into the room as it occurred to him that Vastra sought to enter it. He gripped his logbook to his chest as if it were a protective shield. 'If I may,' he squeaked.

'My case,' said Vastra icily, half his body hanging over the door's threshold. 'It belongs to me.'

Gyan gave a ragged sigh of relief. 'I see, then please shut the door and leave us to it.'

Vastra did as he was told.

Skelos stood at the table. 'I want to show you something, and I'd prefer it if you do not speak until I tell you.' He glanced at the closed door. 'You never know who may be listening.'

Gyan pulled up a chair. 'If it's as important as you say it is, then I expect I shall be too stunned to say anything.' He laid his logbook on the table. 'Secrets are the best things to log I find.'

Skelos gave him a withered look. 'If you must.'

'I must,' said Gyan, grinning. 'This here is my own personal logbook. No one has ever read it, nor will they, unless I want them to, of course.'

Skelos tugged the Avu'lore from the folds in his robes and placed it on the table. It was a cumbersome thing for one to be carrying on the run, but he'd sooner destroy it than leave it behind.

Next, he brought out the single Shard he had taken from The Stores.

Gyan lurched to his feet, mouth hanging open, finger jabbing in mid-air preparing to make some accusation. Skelos guessed what he might say, 'Sorcerer. Wielder of dark magic!' or something along those lines. It was hard to say what he was a wielder of. The bold line between sorcery and science had begun to fade in his mind.

Skelos put his finger to his lips to hush the Store Administrator. Gyan hovered over the seat of the chair for a few seconds before sitting back down, his eyes as big as dinner plates. He seized his pen as if it were a glass of water and he was in desperate need of a drink. Unable to tear his eyes away from the Avu'lore, he wrote furiously in his logbook. Skelos saw that he had done a rough sketch of the Avu'lore globe and the Shard.

Two minutes. Two minutes, more or less. That was all he needed. 'I think I heard someone at the door. Can you check without opening it?'

Gyan stopped scribbling and stared at the door for ten seconds as if the challenge might be too great for him, given that it involved momentarily parting with his logbook. He picked up his logbook and crept to the door.

Skelos slotted the Shard into the globe. There were two more slots for the other Shards he had yet to retrieve. Slowly, slowly, he did not want to break it. The Shard transformed its shape. It became flat. It partially melted into the globe like sap dripping through furrowed bark. It sprouted ragged, sharp edges.

With the Shard in place, he laid his hands upon the Avu'lore. A mixture of colours began to swirl within it: indigo, violet, blue, red, yellow, green and orange. Every conceivable colour of the rainbow and many other shades in between were reflected on the walls in the ragged form of the Shard. He gave a snort of contempt. He had nurtured some reckless hope that he would not require the other Shards for the Avu'lore to work. He needed them, he realised, to unleash its full power. He stole a quick glance at Gyan who stood at the door, head cocked to one side, his arm raised. The Store Administrator turned unexpectedly gasping at the sight of the Avu'lore's blazing colours.

Hunched over the Avu'lore, Skelos watched Gyan groan and wilt to the floor, clutching the sides of his head.

Before he knew it, Vastra was thumping on the door. 'Open up!'

Skelos slid the Shard from the globe in haste. The colours within the Avu'lore died. He threw the Shard into one of his ample-sized pockets and deposited the globe separately within the inner folds of his garments. Feeling like his old self again, he went to help Gyan up. It was the least he could do.

'Thank you,' said Gyan.

Skelos handed him his logbook and escorted him to a

chair.

Gyan dug at his temples with his fingers. 'No, I mustn't sit. I have a bit of a headache that's all. You out there,' he bellowed. 'Stop that banging. We'll be out in a minute. Where was I?'

'Your logbook?' said Skelos, raising his eyebrows expectantly.

'Ah, yes,' said Gyan, handing him the logbook. 'Lots in there to read. It'll keep you occupied for months.'

Gyan unlocked the door and the two men stepped out together. Gyan was squinting. A small drop of blood dripped from his ear onto his collar.

Vastra and Belstien were waiting outside. Belstien was running his tongue over his teeth and fumbling with the bunch of keys in his hand.

Vastra scowled. 'I have to leave,' he said. 'What happened in there?'

'Nothing,' said Skelos, mopping sweat from his neck, *that's any of your business.* 'Can you give the case I gave you to Gyan? I no longer require it.'

Vastra's eyes narrowed. He handed Gyan the case containing the Cloud Vapour.

'What is this?' said Gyan, holding the case up to his squinted eyes.

'I took it from The Stores,' Skelos replied, honestly, 'and I don't think I'll be needing it,' he added, somewhat dishonestly.

'Right,' Gyan nodded, scratching the side of his head. 'I was urm—'

'Escorting me to the exit, seeing as I've nothing to check out.' He shoved past Belstien and Vastra, keen to be on his way. He could taste freedom on his tongue and found it to be both sweet and sour.

'Yes of course,' said Gyan, tottering after him.

Gyan slid back the heavy bolts and heaved the exit doors open. There were four guards posted outside the exit and another two further down the long passageway.

The four guards crowded in on them. 'Out of my way, out of my way!' Gyan flapped his hand, making the guards scatter. 'He has clearance. All is well.'

Gyan jerked his head around to speak to Vastra. 'You go on ahead,' he told him. 'I'll get one of the other guards to escort him back to his chambers. Unless you have some checking out of your own to do?'

Vastra coughed into his fist and sped out of the doors. Skelos resisted the urge to leap for joy. Taking Gyan's word that it would make for interesting reading, he tucked the logbook away. He then hung back for a minute, pretending to look for something in the pocket of his voluminous robes.

Once he was satisfied Vastra had passed the guards stationed at the end of the passageway, he prepared to leave, whispering to Gyan. 'Can you walk with me? I have a few more instructions I wish for you to carry out.'

Gyan nodded, red-faced and weary. His hand was stuck to the side of his head as if it had been glued there.

He won't last long, Skelos concluded, the Unmarked Ones never do.

He marched up the passage with Gyan, without breaking his pace. Without pausing for breath. There were two guards at the end of the passage, sharing a noisy joke, and a roaming Plowman with a rusty chain wrapped around its ankle. How many more of these nuisances would cross his path before he got to the surface?

Gyan swatted the air with his free hand as he passed. They continued on their way unnoticed by the guards.

The path he needed to take was looming before him. The slope to freedom, and it was a slippery one. He reassured himself. *They will hunt me down, but they won't kill me. They need me.*

And he needed more time. Time to stock up on provisions and to procure a disguise. He supposed he could grow a beard. *No one will recognise me with a wiry bush hanging from my face. I would hardly recognise myself.*

It was unwise to rely on Gyan entirely. Never put all your trust in one Citizen and all that. The same expression applied to Unmarked Ones, more so. What if the Store Administrator was reduced to a babbling wreck in the next five minutes instead of two hours? *If only there were a provisions room close by.*

'Oh there is,' said Gyan. 'A utility room. I will show it to you.'

Skelos cast Gyan a sideward glance, pleasantly surprised by his unexpected announcement. 'Marvellous. And don't forget your task on the way back.'

'Yes,' said Gyan, his eyes turning glassy. 'There's an emergency in the Stores containing Rainbows Rock. I must gather all the guards together. Once I have done this, I shall lock the chamber door. I have something I wish to show them; a case. I shall disperse its contents and show them all.'

Chapter 8

The scent of fresh blood rose from the Dal-Carrions wings. Connor noticed a string of worms hanging from the beak of one winged-beast, or entrails, if he shuddered to think about it long enough.

The Dal-Carrion seemed in no hurry to attack. They paused in front of the Silver Riders, cocking their heads to one side, regarding them with naïve curiosity.

The Silver Riders launched their Herming Moth Wings with a quick flick of the wrist. The Wings hung briefly in the air as if they were flies trapped in an invisible web. And then they sprung open, transformed into self-driven, whirring propellers, which expanded and flitted through the air.

The Wings accelerated rapidly over the heads of the unsuspecting Dal-Carrion and engulfed them. In a matter of seconds, the winged-beasts had disappeared, swallowed whole in the rotating swells of the Wings.

The Wings snapped shut and spiralled to the ground with a clatter. The Silver Riders on the ground hastily gathered them up.

Hiera collected his and charged up to one of the riders on horseback. His face burned with rage. He waved the Wings in the rider's face, spitting and shouting in a foreign tongue.

Osaphar exhibited a quiet reserve, but the two riders beside him began to cackle loudly.

'What's he saying?' Connor asked Amelia.

'I don't understand gypsy tongue,' she replied. 'But he's waving his arms about a lot so, I don't think it's friendly.'

One of the mocking Rider's sneered at Hiera. 'Shut up!'

Hiera removed his helmet and set it on the ground.

'*Tahark a sha dasamon!*' he cried, shaking his fist at the mounted rider. His auburn eyes were like flame.

'Put your helmet back on, gypsy nut!' bellowed a man, squatting at the opening of a tree. 'Nobody's interested in what you've got to say. We're following Shardner's orders here, not yours.'

'Maybe Hiera doesn't like what they're doing to the Dal-Carrion,' Amelia observed. 'Gypsies are funny like that. They care for all living creatures, even the ones that can rip you to shreds.'

Connor barely heard her. Another thunderous roar exploded through the shrouded forest. He couldn't tell where it came from.

Amelia dug her fingers into his arm, but not out of fear, he ascertained. She was warning him that the time had come to make their escape.

Connor cast about frantically looking for an opportunity, a breach between men, trees, winged-beasts and horses through which they could charge their way to freedom. Silver Riders barred the way ahead, and through the roar came the thundering of hooves from another company of Silver Riders galloping up behind them.

He glimpsed the blue light again skirting the edges of the enclosure.

'Your Seekers-light!' gasped Amelia, catching sight of

the light darting back and forth among the trees for the first time. 'Put it out! Put it out before someone sees.'

Connor called to mind the streak of light that had burst from the pendant when the Dal-Carrion were trying to bury him alive. The Blue Light. The Blue Forest. He seized the chain around his neck. The light had been there all this time.

Hiera's blood-curdling scream broke his moment of clarity. He shot around to see Hiera's Herming Moth Wings suspended in the air. The Wings had snapped apart and the head of the Dal-Carrion, minus its body, rose up from the mystifying depths of the open Wings, lunged at Hiera and impaled him on its ivory tusk by the neck.

A fountain of blood spurted from the gypsy's neck. The other riders looked on in morbid fascination. Only when they heard Hiera's neck crack, did one of the Silvers Riders draw his silver barrel from his belt, release the squirming tentacles, and in one fluid movement strike the Dal-Carrion, cutting its head clean off. The lifeless head of the Dal-Carrion and Hiera's limp body fell to the ground with a heavy thud. The Wings clamped shut and dropped lightly onto the tail of Hiera's cloak.

At that moment, hundreds of Dal-Carrion came charging from the sky, their enormous wings creating a canopy over the sombre forest.

In the mayhem that followed, Connor and Amelia took their chance, sliding under the bellies of the horses, dodging flying hooves, and scrambling over mounds of soil, until the cries of beast and men became an imperceptible noise in the distance.

Earth...

The dream wasn't particularly momentous in the scheme of things. That's why, Luke saw no point in blabbing about it to anyone else. He had a lot of crazy dreams. The Ring Dream was a simple one. He kept the titanium ring under the floorboards at the foot of his bed. He would crouch, lift the wobbly plank with the aid of his bank card, reach inside and grab a drawstring pouch. He would open the pouch and drop the ring into the palm of his hand, look over his shoulder and then he would wake up. That was it. Dream over. There was nothing under his bedroom floorboards but dust.

As he got older the Ring Dream had become less frequent. It had been two years since he had last dreamed of it, but it was hard to forget.

He had no idea why he was thinking about it now.

Bat had flaked out on the floor, his head leaning against a bookshelf that was showing signs of waning. He snored and every so often mumbled a few unintelligible words.

Riley was in the process of winking out. He kept yawning, his head flopping forward every now and then.

Luke's eyes hardly left the computer screen. He didn't want to stop playing the game. He couldn't. If he signed off, he might never see his flesh and bone brother again. And that would be the end of everything. His neck and fingers were stiff. His eyes ached. His head thumped. This is my fault, he reminded himself. He should have locked the laptop away. He should have covered up his passwords so Connor couldn't memorise them, couldn't get to them.

Once again, he had tried to put some of the blame on Riley.

'Why didn't you just shut the power off?' He had asked him. 'Instead of standing around screaming?'

As expected, Riley was at a loss for what to say and Bat had to step in. He had put his arm around Riley's shoulder and led him to a chair.

Luke slapped laptop's palm rest. He needed the glitch to come back. The one that turned things purple.

His player-character, Duffy, was trying to fight his way through Bluewood Forest. He had no idea why it was sometimes referred to as the Dead Forest when it was so full of life. He hadn't had to kill this many Dal-Carrion the first-time round. They were taking up the bloody screen; it was hard to see the forest floor.

'Do you want me to have a go?' asked Riley, lurching from his chair with one eye open.

'No!' He didn't want Riley to have a go. Riley would muck it up. He wasn't experienced in the game. He didn't get the game.

He managed to disperse the rest of the Dal-Carrion away with a Clanger Spell. The spell delivered a high-pitched noise, which sent the creatures fleeing into the treetops. He knew more were on the way. Duffy was in the heart of the forest. He had a clear picture of a group of men on horseback. He moved Duffy behind a tree trunk. He watched as a small figure, followed by another emerge from beneath a tumble of branches.

'There!' said Riley. He pointed at one of the figures, a round-faced boy with short black hair. 'Connor! Connor, can you hear us?'

Riley's shouts woke Bat.

Luke paused the game, freezing the characters in their tracks.

'Why can't he hear us?' said Riley, rubbing the sleep from his eyes.

Bat strode over.

'We found him,' said Riley. He pointed at the frozen figure on the screen.

'O-kay,' said Bat. He scratched his head. 'Let me try something.' He pulled the laptop towards him. He resumed the game and went into the player's communication box. There, he typed a message: Connor can you hear us? Are you okay?'

He gave Luke a nod.

Luke whipped the laptop from under his puppet-master-like-fingers before he could type another word. 'Get out.'

'What?'

'Leave.' He disconnected the charger and turned the laptop over in his hands a few times.

Bat raised his hands. 'Hey, I'm only trying to help.'

The plausible was fast becoming implausible. Not for one second, did Luke believe the figure on the screen was his brother. 'The both of you go home,' he said. 'It's late. There's nothing more you can do here.'

He wrapped his hands over his head. He needed to think beyond the game.

Chapter 9

There is a myriad of underground tunnels and caves in Narrigh. It is simple to lose your way in them. The lighting is poor, and the air is rarely pleasant. Take a wrong turn and you can stumble upon a bundle of riches, discover a secret door, or meet an untimely end...

Skelos found that the slope to freedom was more rocky than slippery. As he stumbled down a dark tunnel, he wondered if he would ever see the light again. Salt-water sludge and crystal formations hung low from the tunnel's roof, forcing him to continue his journey stooping and shuffling like an old man. The sludge water stench had burrowed its way into his pores, curdling in his throat. There was no end to this tunnel it seemed, and he found the trek dizzying.

He came to a bend, which brought him to a lofty stretch of tunnel where he could walk upright. He took the next bend at full pelt and skidded into a limestone chamber where he was startled by an old man, dressed in a stained grey shirt and a pair of ragged trousers. The Old Man pressed a cold dagger to Skelos's throat and clapped his hand over Skelos's mouth.

Skelos observed that the man was shorter than him. The top of his captor's head nudged his shoulder blade. He had a braided snow-white beard, which hung almost to his waist. His blotchy face was as dry and leathery as a lizard.

On the floor of the chamber was an oil lamp and a flask.

Skelos thought it best to negotiate first but found his attempts at conversation thwarted by the hand over his mouth. 'Release me.' He said the words inside his own head, hoping the old man had the ability to hear him. Was that how the Avu'lore worked? His mind was an open book, and he could control all those who read it? *It worked before, perhaps it will work again.*

His captor didn't respond. He simply tightened his grip on the dagger's hilt. 'Don't think I won't stick your throat if you try anything. I'm old, but I'm quick.'

Skelos pulled the dagger from his throat by the blade and shoved the man in the chest with his elbow.

The dagger clattered to the ground. The Old Man's jaw went slack.

Skelos tugged down the sleeve of his robe and wrapped it around his hand, sliced through to the bone. The wound was gurgling blue blood.

'You-you keep back!' said the Old Man. His steely-grey eyes bulged as he stared at the blood seeping through the fabric of Skelos's robes. He then began to scurry around in search of his dagger. Evidently, the shock had not left him paralysed with fear.

Skelos saw the dagger wedged in a crack in the rock. The Old Man had stared in the same spot twice but had not seen it. 'Who are you? What are you doing down here?'

The Old Man's eyes grew wide with indignation. 'I ask the questions. This is my territory you're on.'

'You own the tunnels, do you? I'm sure the Shardner

will beg to differ.'

'It's my patch, is what I meant to say,' replied the man, though his voice had lost some of its edge. 'Humph...well, my name's my own business, so it's sir to you. You shouldn't be down here. Danger waits around every corner of these caves, but you'd know that by now I suppose.'

Skelos flashed him a cautious smile. Until he learned the Old Man's Profession, it would do to be cautious. *And Sir may be of use.*

Skelos unwound his sleeve from his cut hand. His wound had healed quicker than he anticipated, save for a tiny patch of blue. He flexed his fingers.

The Old Man passed a disconcerting eye over Skelos's healed hand.

'I appear to have gotten a little lost, *sir*,' said Skelos. 'Do you think you can help me find my way out of here? The name's Gyan by the way, and I have coin.'

Chapter 10

Connor ignored Amelia's pleas to extinguish his Seekers-light. He was sure it would lead them out of the forest. *It might even take me home.* Home was a three-bedroom house in London, not a creepy forest with monsters, strange girls and no wheeled transportation.

He didn't want flesh-eating birds or the Shardner's Special Army to decide his fate. He tried to explain to Amelia that he did not come from Narrigh, and he had no idea how he arrived in the forest. She didn't seem interested.

'You're very stupid,' she said after a while. 'And you're sick.'

'I'm not sick and I'm not stupid.' He took hold of her wrist and stubbornly pressed on, forcing her to pursue the beacon of light without a thought to where it was taking them. He did not want to take his eyes off it, not even for a minute. His head was spinning. The blood gorged in his temples and his lungs burned. He swallowed hard, gulping the rising bile in his throat.

The sphere of blue light flitted amongst the growing foliage. After some time, it expanded into a floating pyramid, which glided along the forest floor.

The Seekers-light carried them to the Northern fringe of the forest where the ice had melted. A worm poked its head up from the cracked soil. The trees overflowed with dark fleshy leaves and the darkness unfurled around them. The catacomb of eeriness was broken.

Connor collapsed against a crooked tree and threw up. Amelia stooped down beside him, resting her hand on his shoulder. He crumpled to the ground. *The poison's taking hold now,* he thought. *I'm dying and there's no one here who can save me.* His mum wasn't around to take care of him, and he had no medicine to make him feel better.

He feebly pushed Amelia away and wiped his mouth on his sleeve. He snatched a few gulps of water from his flask. He offered the rest to Amelia.

She took a tiny sip and handed it back to him. 'We have to make it last.'

He returned the flask to his bag. 'How do you know about the Seekers-light?'

'Because I used to have one. It's called a Seekers Egg. It's supposed to keep you out of danger.'

The Seekers-light hovered close by, giving off a warm sensuous glow.

'Then it's working?'

'The Seekers Egg obviously doesn't belong to you, seeing as you know next to nothing about it,' she said, combing her fingers through her hair. 'It will take you to its owner. If it wanted to lead us away from danger, it would take us South where it's Dal-Carrion free, not further north.'

Connor knew the North was bad. The Dal-Carrion were not their only enemies. Gamnod people, Darque Goblins, Drone Elves, and Traceless Ones all lived in the North, not that he had seen any. It was possible they were hiding, lying in wait, and ready to attack. He glanced over his shoulder. He didn't know how far they had come, let alone from which direction. It was too late to turn back. He was too weak, too tired. 'Where do you come from?'

She showed him the palm of her right hand. Beneath her thumb was an inky blue tattoo of the letter 'I', or it might have been a '1', he wasn't sure. 'Same place as you.'

He felt a sudden tugging sensation in his temple. 'You're from Earth?'

'No stupid, Odisiris.'

He supported his weight against the tree. Fighting the tremors in his legs, he staggered to his feet. 'Don't call me stupid, and I'm not from Odisiris. Where's Odisiris?'

'A whole other world, a long way from here.'

'I'm from a whole other world too, but not that one.' To his mind, his world was small. It consisted of his house in London, the school at the bottom of his road, the local shopping centre and his friend Riley's house; five streets along from his own.

'Okay. Show me your right hand.'

'Why?'

'Just show me.'

Reluctantly, Connor showed her his hand.

'There,' she said pointing at the scar. 'You have the Mark.'

'That's not a mark,' said Connor snatching his hand away. 'That's a scar.' *Where the poison is seeping through and driving me mad.* And yet he couldn't help but notice the inky blue in his scar was the same colour as Amelia's tattoo.

She crossed her arms. 'How did you get it then?'

Connor hugged himself. Amelia was good at making him feel stupid. 'I don't remember. Who cares? How do you know my name anyway? I never told you.'

'It's written on your left ankle.'

'It is not!' Connor yanked off his left boot in a flash. He peeled off his damp dirty sock and lifted his foot up to his face. Below the knobbly bone of his foot was his name, tattooed in the same inky blue as his hand. He frowned at it. How did it get there?

Amelia handed him his sock. 'You're a Citizen. A Marked One. Your Status is determined by the colour of your blood.'

Marked One? He didn't like those words. They suggested you were a slave or you were earmarked for assassination. If anything, he was a warrior from Undren village. And his blood was red. He kept quiet. He didn't have the strength to argue with her. He put his sock and boot back on. He steadied himself against the tree trunk and tied a rough knot in his bootlace. He was feeling light-headed again. He watched the hovering blue sphere. Cracks had begun to appear in its rippling stream. 'What's wrong with it?'

'It's running out of energy. You must shut it off for a while or you'll lose the light forever. That's what happened to mine.'

'Isn't it magic?'

She rolled her eyes and smoothed down the hem of her skirt. 'Don't be silly. It's not magical. There's no such thing as magic in Odisiris. Seekers Eggs are the property of Sentinels. When we find the Sentinel who gave it to you, they'll tell you how you got here. They'll tell you everything.'

Connor didn't know if there were Sentinels in Narrigh.

He certainly didn't remember one giving him a Seekers Egg. He clutched the Egg in his trembling hand. He turned the stone band in an anti-clockwise direction. The Seekers-light vanished with a pop.

The trees were starting to cast shadows, making strange beast-like shapes Connor did not like. He saw teeth, claws, eyes and jaws.

It was getting dark, and they were on the wrong side of the forest. 'We'd better go.' He took a few faltered steps. 'We need to get out of the forest and find shelter before nightfall.'

Amelia gave him a surly glance that suggested he didn't have it in him. Connor grunted, pushed out his chest and marched past her just to prove he had.

Luke kneaded the back of his neck, which under normal circumstances, he would have found calming. But he couldn't relax. He still hadn't made any headway. He had so little to go on: the game, a purple flash and his brother gone.

Purple? Why purple and not green? And the laptop, he'd had it for what, eight months? There was no indication the machine was faulty. His mum told him she had purchased it brand new at an electrical store.

There was a knock at the door. 'Is it okay if I come in?'

He didn't answer. It was his mum wanting to know if he had churned up anything. He hadn't. She had no idea he was working on the premise that his brother's disappearance was somehow connected to the game, and he had made sure Riley didn't bring the story up to her again. The connection between the game and Connor's disappearance didn't make any sense either. But there was a connection that spilled from their virtual world into the real one. Even his mum knew it.

'Luke?'

'I'm in bed. I'll see you in the morning.' He didn't take his eyes off the screen.

'I can't sleep. If you need me, I'll be downstairs.'

He didn't need her. He needed to start from the beginning. Learn more about the world in which his brother had played: Narrigh.

He called Riley. He regretted sending him home. He couldn't do this without him. He was surprised when he answered. He had expected the call to go straight to voicemail. It had to be the early hours of the morning.

Riley answered with a croak and a whisper. 'Hello?'

'It's me. I know it's only been a little while. I don't know why I'm calling really.'

'To see if I've thought of something else. Well, I have.'

Luke shot to his feet. 'Seriously?'

'Yeah, I was gonna wait until the morning. It's small but—'

'Go on.'

'The backstory has changed.'

There was an initial backstory on Tridan Entertainment's website. It wasn't interactive and didn't warrant a thorough read as far as most gamers were concerned. But he wasn't most gamers. You got interactive stories throughout *The Quest of Narrigh* game when you levelled up or won something of significant value. Some read like novels.

He cast his mind back to the game installation. Bat had been there. He had elbowed him in the ribs and grinned at the screen like a hapless idiot when the dramatic music blared from the speakers and the film trailer of the game appeared followed by the history of the game world. They had both read it with eagerness. Every skilled gamer knew that if you really wanted to be part of the game, you had to immerse yourself in it completely.

'What do you mean changed?'

'I remember there were two parts to it, one long, the other short, but the part is missing from my cousin's installation and it's not in the gaming guide either.'

'You're right that is small. It was one long block when I checked it.' Anything could have accounted for two parts becoming one: screen size, a version update. 'Do you know what the second part was about? Did it mention a ring?'

'I don't know. I don't think so. I just remember it being split into two parts. Connor scrolled through it too fast for me to read, but it was the only thing that was different. Look, we know no one else went missing when they played the game, so there had to be something different when Connor played, and that's the only *different* I can think of, besides the purple flash.'

He was right. There were no reports of anyone going missing while playing the game. He had wanted to believe Riley when he said Connor was trapped in there, because it was better than thinking something worse, something more credible, like his brother was hurt, or lying dead somewhere. He took a swift glance at the backstory again. 'I'm still looking at one long block. If you think of anything else, call me in the morning.'

'Sure,' said Riley. He then ended the call.

'Someone took him straight out of this room.' The thought was there in the back of his mind but saying the words out loud made it seem more logical of all the scenarios he had entertained. The Ring Dream nudged into the forefront of his mind again: of how, he would crouch at the foot of his bed, lift the floor plank without any trouble, reach for the drawstring pouch—

His gaze shifted to the foot of his bed. He wasn't gifted like his brother; his dreams were meaningless. Yet, he couldn't shake the feeling that the Ring Dream was relevant to his reality. His bedroom wasn't visible in the dream, only the floorboards and the foot of a bed. Was he wrong to assume it was his? He and his mum shared the same model bed: his a double and hers a Queen.

He proceeded to her bedroom. He paused outside it, listening to the faint sound of the TV coming from the downstairs living room, before entering. He was careful to walk around the duvet which his mum had trailed across the floor. He padded over the used tissues she had discarded on the floor. She had left the curtains partially closed since Connor's disappearance. She didn't like to let in the light. It intruded with the enormity of the darkness she felt. She had hooked her mobile phone up to the charger, which she had left on the bedside table. She usually took it with her even if she went to the bathroom, in case she missed a call. He wondered if she was beginning to lose hope, if she anticipated that every call would bring bad news or nothing at all.

He moved to the foot of the bed and stared at the

floorboard. If a plank was loose, he had never noticed. Though, he hardly ever entered his mum's bedroom whether she was inside it or not. He felt a little ashamed with the act, considering she wasn't too far away, and they lacked a care-free relationship in which they could step into one another's personal space with ease. Attempting to resurrect the dream, he crouched down and pressed his hand on the section of the floorboard he recalled from his dream. His heart gave a jolt when it shifted. He took his bank card from his back pocket, sunk it partway into the groove and then flicked it up. He lifted the plank all the way up with one hand. Inside was a dusty pouch. He dropped the ring onto his hand. The dream hadn't been a simple one. This was no ordinary ring. He glanced over his shoulder. His mum was moving around downstairs, and he could no longer hear the TV. He closed his fist around the ring, shoved the drawstring pouch in his jeans pocket, and returned to his bedroom.

He slumped into his desk chair and took another look at the ring. It had sensors set in the inner rim. He tried slipping it onto his middle finger. A little too big, it came close to slipping right off again. He pushed it on to his thumb. It was a snug fit. At that moment his phone vibrated. He had a text message from a private number, which read:

STAY WHERE YOU ARE. WE'RE COMING TO GET YOU.

He made the connection at once. He had accessed a smart ring which was somehow hooked up to his phone.

He sunk his teeth into his bottom lip. He heard his mum's bedroom door creak shut. He seethed in silence. How long had she been hanging on to this ring and why the hell hadn't she mentioned it? He sent a text back:

Who are you?

Seconds later, he got his reply:

I think you know

Chapter 11

The undergrounds of the South consist of a heady mix of truncated tunnels and passages, connecting a web of sinister chambers.

The glowing jewels of the cave emit a light of their own from their craggy walls. However, there are chambers where the light has gone out, dug away by man or swallowed by the cave-dwelling beasts. These chambers sit dark and brooding, waiting to be occupied by whatever species the tunnels throw their way.

Some of the chambers are dank muddy ventricles, while others ascend into dry bone cavities, harbouring fierce draughts, their floors eroded by the natural forces of nature.

Skelos clambered after the Old Man in a tunnel that was becoming increasingly treacherous as it was narrow. The pools of water that had collected in the pitted ground embraced the nauseating reek of death.

His mind played tricks on him. He would see smouldering lights where there were none, and grotesque shadows that were not his own, appeared to jump from one rugged wall to the next.

The Old Man had climbed through a draughty orifice in the rock: the last winding passage, he advised, that would deliver them safely from the labyrinth of tunnels.

The section of the tunnel widened and Skelos and the Old Man walked abreast.

There was always the possibility he was walking into a trap? *But what is life without possibilities?* Yes, there was no end of possibilities and no end of trouble. And with this thought in mind...

'Where does this tunnel lead?' He had asked the Old Man this question before, and he had chosen to ignore him. It could have been because he had not added the word 'sir' or the word 'please', or it could have been because the Old Man was short of hearing. Needless, he tried again without the pleasantries.

'The route we are taking leads to Olvastan,' said the Old Man, holding his oil lamp aloft. 'Home to me and my kin.' The deep furrows in his forehead rose significantly. He increased his steps in a reckless attempt to boost the distance between himself and Skelos.

'Olvastan is days, if not weeks away, surely.' *At least for you.*

'The way is shorter through the tunnels.' The Old Man gave him a brief sidelong glance. 'You're dressed mighty strange, I must say. Are you from the North?' He cut through a dark, muddy passage, snatched up a sackcloth bag from a hollow in the wall and lowered it onto his shoulder.

Skelos had found no suitable attire to change into. He was still wearing his fine robes. 'No, the Bleak desert.'

No one in Narrigh was entirely sure if the nomads that dwelled in the desert were human. And he would rather say he came from the bottom of the Pynes Ocean than mention the North, not in the Age of Trepidation. Moreover, he would be a fool to mention he had travelled from Baruch. The Shardner had spies everywhere. He pressed a gold coin into the Old Man's hand to help ease both their anxieties.

'I don't know what you want from me,' said the Old Man. Stowing the coin away, he focused on the winding passage ahead. 'Cause I've nothing but the clothes on my back.' He picked up the pace, weaving between columns of rock and the slippery ground with ease, in a levelled off segment of the tunnel. 'We're not fond of foreigners here, you know. Never have been. Courtesy is as much as we can manage and we're a rare breed for doing that.'

'I need to get to Undren village.'

'We're not far from it.' The Old Man came to a halt inside a small dry chamber. He pulled a round metal instrument from his shirt pocket. 'We need to wait here for a bit,' he said returning the object to his pocket. 'There are guards about. They won't be off duty for another ten minutes.'

'You never mentioned guards before?'

'There are bound to be guards, aren't there? Like there's a sun and two moons. It's not getting past the guards that's the problem. It's getting past the Gate. There are high walls surrounding every village in Olvastan. The *Gates* are made from timber, craybine[1] and iron. Very sturdy. You can't get over them, for love nor barter, without a permit. You could access the village via the mines much easily of course if there were no danger.'

Skelos knew about the Gates and the permits required to go in and out of them. He had no such permit. His gaze fell on the bulging sack the Old Man had swung over his shoulder. 'The caves we've come through are mines?'

'Yes, some of them,' the Old Man declared, clutching

the bottom of the sack to his chest. 'Did you not see the shining rock?'

'Rainbows Rock.' Skelos gave a veritable sigh. For a short while there, he had truly been excited.

----

[1] Craybine – a clay-like substance, found several feet below ground, used to reinforce walls.

With the exception of a minority group, employed in the Shardner's service, the races of Narrigh knew only one use for Rainbows Rock and Skelos did not think it was a very good one.

'Every colour of the rainbow shines within its core. Some refer to it as Black Rock. Black, is the colour it turns when it reacts with sunlight. They're useless in sunlight. You need six of the best to get the same light you would out of an oil lamp. In the dark, the rock shines silver. Not a lot of people know that unless they've been in the mines and perhaps not even then.' He eyed him dubiously before changing the subject. 'What do you want in Undren?'

'Business. I need to find something. If you help me get there, I'll make it worth your while.'

The Old Man ran his hand over his flossy beard, his eyes saturated with greed. 'Best keep that *business* to yourself. Now situated at the end of this tunnel is a ramp built from fallen rocks. It is a short journey, but a might slippery because of the seeping water coming in from the sea. When we reach the top, we remove the grate covering and run. I have a retreat not far from here where you can change into something more fitting. You won't get into Undren dressed like that.'

Chapter 12

Connor and Amelia tramped the short journey out of the forest. The sound of rushing water at their backs spurred them on. Connor knew what the sound meant. It was the sound of the Dal-Carrion.

The young companions picked their way through the undergrowth, stumbling over the many mounds of soil, which carved up the forest floor.

They had crossed Bluewood Forest.

The sunlight was fading fast on the horizon. Connor's tired eyes met a sweeping grey desolate plain. It seemed to have no end. He had not expected to see such a dismal stretch of wasteland. 'Where are the villages?' To the south of Narrigh, there were lots of villages surrounded by high walls.

'There are no villages in the North,' said Amelia.

Connor stared at her in disbelief. 'There has to be.'

'No there doesn't have to be. You can't actually *live* in the North. The Dal-Carrion will eat you alive.'

He didn't know whether to believe her. When he had played the game, he had done battle with Drone Elves, Gamnod people, and a great many monsters, but he was never far from a city or village inhabited by allies. He was never far away from anywhere.

He dug a shaking hand into his bag and pulled out the crumpled map of Narrigh, his fingers nervously tracking the wavy blue lines of estuaries running south to North on the page. Jagged brown lines depicted the next landmark on the map: the Great Northern Crater. His heart sank. Why would he want to go there?

'Why indeed?' said the Authoritative Voice.

'We have to go back.'

'It's too dangerous. We need to hide below ground.'

They set off across the ashen plain in silence, encountering no one. A strong breeze blew in from the east. Connor felt his fever waning. There was no rest from the pounding in his head, but he could think clearly enough to dwell on the fact that he might never find his way home. *You've no one to protect you. You're all alone.*

He had a sickening recollection of sitting in his living room obsessing about *The Quest of Narrigh*. Now, he wished he'd never set eyes on the stupid game.

He felt a pang of fright. What if the Dal-Carrion had killed everyone in the North and they were the only ones left? He looked behind him to see the sullen forest trees fading from view, transforming to shadows as night crept in. A sheer face of rock opened in the distance, like a black abyss against the night sky.

At last, they found what they were looking for; a rectangular pit covered with logs wide enough for them both to slip inside. Dry leaves littered the bottom of the pit. Connor climbed in and Amelia after him, their movements laboured.

Once inside, they dragged the logs across the pit to cover it, hoping for protection against the cold and anything else that cared to venture their way.

Amelia fiddled with her hair, coiling it in and around her fingers.

Connor traced with one finger, the raised skin on the

bottom of his right palm. It held an abundance of questions, uneasiness, and dread. He broke the silence, recalling what she had said to him in the forest. 'What's Odisiris like?'

She cradled her knees and blinked at him in the semi-darkness. 'You really can't remember, can you? Odisiris is beautiful. There are no wars and no crime. It's not grimy like it is here. And you don't have to work. In Narrigh, children must work. I've seen them. And you don't have to do a lot of walking. You'd be happy there.'

A world with no wars and no crime. It sounded too good to be true. 'What does that mark mean?'

'I for Indigo. It's one of the colours in the spectrum.'

He tried to figure out in his head if Indigo was purple or blue. He quickly concluded it was neither and the scar on his hand definitely looked more black than inky blue. 'The spectrum?'

'A rainbow. Indigo is the mark of a First Status Citizen.'

Connor had seen more rainbows in the books his mum used to read to him when he was little than he had in real life. There was a substance called Rainbows Rock in Narrigh. You could trade it for items such as clothes, food, and drink. Connor won two pieces of the Rock once. They were next to worthless. They glowed in the dark at night, but not very brightly, so he had traded them for food in a village inn. But he'd only been playing then. 'Do all Citizens have a Mark?'

'*All* Citizens.' Amelia left her hair alone and went back to cradling her knees. 'To be a Citizen is to be marked.'

Connor chewed on a piece of dried meat. 'How did you get here?'

'I came with my uncle on a ship. He's a scientist.'

'What sort of ship?'

'An airship.'

An airship? *That can't be right*, thought Connor. He now wished he had read the game's back story. The world of Narrigh was supposed to be set in the olden days. They didn't have airships in the olden days. They didn't even have electricity. She was probably making it up. Anyway, what did Citizens have to do with Narrigh? Why was Amelia here? Why was he here? He stored these thoughts away with the many other unanswered questions he had whirring around in his head like flies.

He hadn't thanked Amelia for helping him escape the Silver Riders and the Dal-Carrion. He didn't know if he ought to be grateful just yet. The Silver Riders would have protected them from the Dal-Carrion and may have taken them to safety if they had been patient and stayed. Could he trust Amelia? She answered his questions bluntly, if at all and given the impending danger, she spent an awful lot of time daydreaming. He wondered what was going through her mind – very little – he imagined.

'I wish I could remember how I got here,' he said fiercely. 'Someone must know.'

Outside the wind howled threateningly and Connor felt the pain of loneliness for the first time. He got no companionship from Amelia. He rubbed his eyes, feeling the tears well up. He had been alone before, countless times, but loneliness had never tormented him as it did now. Overwhelming sadness gripped him. He was a whole other world away from home. He missed his mum, his brother, and his friends. What if he never saw them again?

'Don't cry,' said Amelia. 'We'll find the Sentinel. He'll know what to do. He'll help you.'

She then closed her eyes and did not speak another word.

Chapter 13

The Old Man's hut sits on the brink of a cliff. It is a misshapen thing, built from wood and a mesh of leaves. The sands of the Pynes Ocean are near enough visible amongst the thicket of trees that attempt to conceal it. There are no other dwellings situated along the stretch of coastline.

The windstorms have taken their toll on the cliff face and the bank is beginning to slide. In another decade, the Old Man's coastal side retreat will almost certainly crash off the cliff's edge into the murky depths of the ocean below.

The Old Man hurried Skelos in and then latched the door shut. He had been decidedly jittery since leaving the cave, and yet he had led them, competently enough, through the lowlands where sprawling Escarpard Root[1] devoured the footpaths from sight.

The Old Man rummaged inside a box under a blackened window. He retrieved from it, a worn black cloak. 'Here put this on,' he said, throwing the cloak on the floor.

Skelos's eyes wandered up and down the cracked and sunken walls of the Old Man's coastal retreat. The air of the place, or lack of it, had rendered him speechless.

———

¹Escarpard Root – a creeping plant, which locks on to any immobile object and literally chokes to death anything or anyone that threatens its domain.

The Old Man went to a wood-splintered table. It was stacked with books and keys of various shapes and sizes.

A Rogue. Skelos should have known. Rogues were good at sneaking about, getting in out of places they had no business getting in and out of.

The Old Man started to go through the books, picking up one and then dropping it onto the floor before homing in on another. His perusal of the books was overzealous and desperate.

Skelos had wanted to sit down, but soon realised there were no chairs, devoid of litter, on which he could make himself comfortable. Sacks, boxes, sheets of metal, and heaps of inexplicable junk lay strewn across the cabin, reaching the ceiling in some places.

The Old Man became exasperated. 'Put the cloak on, please.'

Skelos stared at the cloak on the soiled timber floor. 'It's too hot for these rags. Have you anything else?'

The Old Man dropped the book back onto the table. His movements' jerky, he turned to face him. 'I have water.' He took up a watering can from a shelf above a tiny-basin-of-a-sink. He then collected a chipped mug and filled it to the brim with water. The water slopped lazily from the mug as he cupped it in his unsteady hands.

Skelos took the mug from him and passed it directly under his nose. 'It's not seawater, is it?' *From the Hizsen Sea?*

'It's water from the well, equally refreshing warm or cold. I would drink it if I were you. The cloak is made from lambs' wool.'

Skelos didn't drink water if he could help it, but he couldn't pretend he was not thirsty. He had just completed the longest walk of his life. He sipped on the liquid, gingerly at first, and then in avid gulps until his mug was empty.

'Palatable enough,' he said with a shrug once he had finished.

'Please, you have to hurry.' The Old Man snatched the mug out of Skelos's hand.

Skelos gathered up the cloak. Dust and threads of fabric flew up his nostrils and into his eyes.

'You're not out to hurt anyone are you?' asked the Old Man.

Skelos answered him with a succession of sneezes. He pulled on the cloak.

The question struck him as bizarre. Everyone was out to hurt someone no matter what world they lived in. He secured the cloak clasp and noted it was embellished with a skull.

'No that is not my intention, though as I recall, it was yours not too long ago. Had you forgotten?'

Judging by his bewildered expression, it seemed as if the Old Man had forgotten. He regarded Skelos with new scrutiny. Donned in his black robe, Skelos must have looked like a giant bat.

The Old Man directed him to a large book he had left open on the table. 'See here,' he said, pointing a trembling finger at a faded map on the page. 'This is a map of Undren, a secret map of Undren I might add. It shows another way in.'

Skelos came to stand over the Old Man's shoulder studying the layout. The Old Man backed away.

He went on, lingering in the background. 'There's a tunnel north of the Gate. See? Go through, all the way through. You'll come to Levistan Woods. Once within the village walls, go to the Gate and present yourself to the Undren Guard. They'll recognise you as a priest and you'll be treated honourably. Tell them you're on a pilgrimage. Tell them that the guard, who was on duty when you arrived, gave you right of passage and granted you succour. Don't delay in saying them words, those exact words mind, or they'll likely be suspicious. They'll understand that to mean you paid the guard off with prayer, coin, or cloth. They'll not ask questions.'

Skelos raised an eyebrow. *A priest in black? That's a new one.* He gazed at the sack the Old Man had brought with him from the caves.

The Old Man talked faster now, eager to be done and be gone. 'Rip the maps out if you want. Don't matter to me. You can easily slip through at nightfall, without being seen.'

'How did you acquire such a book?' Skelos unrolled one of the parchments. He held it up to his face, turning it first clockwise, and then anti-clockwise in an effort to decipher the encryptions upon it.

'I brought it,' the Old Man replied boldly. 'There is plenty to buy on the black market, and to sell.'

'You've given me no reason to trust you. This tunnel you speak of, how do I know it will lead me to where you say it will?'

'I speak the truth,' said the Old Man, his voice rising in desperation. 'The tunnel's good and clear. No one will see you⎕'

'And the guards? Won't they talk? Realise I did not come through the Gate.'

The Old Man shook his head. Suddenly aware he was cowering, he stood tall. 'The guards change watch every six hours. If you're quick about your business, you'll be gone before anyone realises anything is, *nooo!*

Skelos snatched the frayed sack the Old Man had slung over the back of a chair.

'Give that back, it's mine,' he cried. He lunged to retrieve it and tripped. He toppled to the ground, spitting a tirade of abuse.

Skelos wrenched the sack open and spilled its contents onto the floor. Sizable fragments of luminous Rock shimmered on the grubby stack of books on which they had landed. The Old Man looked on aghast as Skelos reached for a fist-sized fragment. Skelos had no need for Rainbows Rock. What he needed was the Old Man's cooperation. He couldn't pull out the Avu'lore every time he needed to take control of someone's mind, not if he didn't want to leave a nasty bloody trail through Narrigh that would lead straight back to him.

In amongst the Rock was a small leather pouch. Skelos checked its contents and was pleased to see there was a little Binding Dust inside it. *Now here is something I can use.* He deposited the pouch and Rock fragment into his cloak pocket. 'You'll take me there.'

'I can't.' The Old Man hurriedly scooped the remaining rock back into the sack. 'I need to get back home. I'm expected.'

'You'll take me there,' Skelos repeated. He helped himself to a handful of keys from the table. 'You know full well what this cloak means. A sorcerer cannot get pass any Gate in any city or village without arousing some suspicion. And as we shall be in each other's company a little longer, I think we should at least be on first name terms.'

The Old Man watched his precious Rock fragment disappear inside Skelos's cloak. Skelos regarded the Old Man closely.

Like rogues, sorcerers usually worked alone. Occasionally, their conjuring skills were sought after by races stupid or desperate enough to procure their services. Sorcerers didn't swear allegiance to anyone but their own kind and were known to cast spells on the unwitting just for the fun of it. His path through the Gate would run more smoothly if the rogue were to accompany him, and they both knew it.

The Old Man nodded, realisation dawning on him. He levelled his gaze at Skelos and passed him the sack. 'I'll take you there and then you can give me back what's rightfully mine. The name's Barnabas, Barnabas Spinks.'

Chapter 14

'Don't move,' whispered Connor. He crouched at one end of the pit, his back pressed against the rutted wall, his chest heaving.

Amelia's eyes snapped open. She gave a low squeal, pulled the skirt of her dress over her bare legs and tucked in her feet.

There came a noise, both familiar and grotesque. Connor fixed his gaze on the bed of leaves. Something was moving beneath them.

Now here was a creature from the gaming world with which he was familiar. He had seen the dark scales of the poisonous Bakusa snake as it burrowed its way through the leafy heap. He had watched its quivering yellow forked tongue shoot up from the ground several times during the night. Bakusa snakes were easy to kill with a Lightning Sword. But he didn't have a Lightning Sword. He had a possible enchanted stone, which he had no idea how to use, and a Seekers Light drained of energy.

He had not slept. Gripped in the throes of fever, he wrestled Dal-Carrion whenever he closed his eyes.

This wasn't a pit, he realised. It was a trap, not made for humankind.

He stared wide-eyed at the ground. His body was drenched in sweat. He clenched his fists in readiness.

The snake smashed through the leaves, rearing its spoon-shaped head. It glared at Connor with red slit-eyes.

He felt a rush of new fear, cold and heavy in his

stomach. He shifted his body weight; afraid his legs would buckle.

The snake bared its three dagger-shaped fangs and swayed, weighing up its options. Its gaze never left his.

Any sudden movement and he was for it. He didn't have the strength, or the fight left in him to outwit any snake, and certainly not one as deadly as this. A small bite from a Bakusa injected a slow releasing poison into the victim's bloodstream. He knew that much, but little about the pain that went with it.

The clamouring of urgent voices above him interrupted his silent panic.

'I'm telling you there's someone in there. Hurry, lift the logs!'

Connor craned his neck, peering through a gap they had left between the timber. He glimpsed soiled skin, tattered sweaty cloth, and a curved blade.

No sooner had he lowered his head, the Bakusa dived, advancing towards him, tossing leaves into the closeted space. He drew his knees to his chest and cried for help.

Someone shouted, 'Stones! There're children in there.'

The logs were hurled aside. Light poured into the trap.

The snake lunged for Connor, its jaws wide open, preparing to sink its fangs into his ankle. Connor's heart galloped. The blood pumped hard in his veins. *I'm going to die!*

A man with a blotchy complexion and a tangled mane of blonde hair hoisted Amelia from the trap. Once he had set her down, he reacted swiftly. Drawing his curved blade from the belt around his waist, he rammed it into the snake's open mouth. Its head split in two and it hit the bottom of the pit with a sickening squelch.

Before Connor knew what was happening, a pair of meaty hands had seized him under the arms, lifted him into the air and onto the hard earth.

He squinted up into the face of a man with bronze skin. His face was streaked with dirt. His dark eyes exhibited bewilderment and disbelief.

Connor slumped against the man's broad chest. He had not one ounce of strength left in his body. The man briefly put his arm around him. He then took Connor by the shoulders and looked into his eyes as if he were trying to find some light in a dark fathomless tunnel. He then broke away from Connor to address the blonde-haired man. 'Get them on the cart Bel.'

The man Bel grunted. He wiped his blade clean on his grubby trousers and peered into the sky, one hand over his brow.

Connor staggered about like a newborn lamb. His heartbeat started to slow. He saw faces – the grimy, sweat-streaked faces of half a dozen men and women.

A tall pock-faced woman with bright red hair approached him. 'Dear oh dear,' she said. Putting an arm around his waist, she helped him onto a wooden cart, which looked as if it were being pulled by a long black shadow. His feet were sliding away from him.

Feeling as if he were about to suffocate, he wriggled free of the woman's truncheon-like arm, only to find himself clutching the empty air. His eyelids slammed shut and the ground rushed up to meet him.

Chapter 15

A weary traveller may choose from one of five inns in Undren village to lay their heads for the night, fill their bellies with a warm meal or revive themselves with a cool energy drink or beer. The inns have a large dining area, a fireplace and an adequate number of chairs and tables. The upstairs sleeping quarters are furnished with cosy feather beds, a chest of drawers and a small closet.

Hospitality varies from inn to inn and the clientèle can be less than gracious...

Barnabas had given Skelos the name of an inn that would welcome him without question. The innkeeper, Hans Runick was a man, who according to Barnabas Spinks knew how to keep other people's business to himself.

Skelos bundled up Barnabas's cloak and stuffed it into his bag. *Better to dazzle the man with colour, than to spook him with sorcery.*

He had wound a strip of linen around his right hand to hide his Status Mark. It was late and he wanted to lie down on a cosy bed for the night with no quibble. He took a short-cut down by the cobbler's yard, walking as quickly and as quietly as he could.

The Runick Inn was a two-storey building constructed of white stone and black timber frames. It had lattice windows and a hanging basket above the door. The inn was situated two doors away from the Gleary bakery. The smell of stale bread and sour milk turned Skelos's stomach when he pushed the inn swing-doors open.

He found the innkeeper on the cellar steps struggling with a beer barrel on the cold stone floor.

'Here let me give you a hand,' said Skelos, seizing one end of the barrel. Hans looked up half-startled, half-weary. He did not protest.

Together, they pushed the barrel up the steps. Once at the top, they rolled the barrel up to the bar.

'Thank you,' said Hans. 'Don't know how I would have managed.'

Hans Runick had acquired a bristle-tooth stubble from having not shaved for the past five days. The sides of his face were red raw from scratching it. He rubbed at his long, pinched nose and took a rag to mop the sweat from his brow. It was the third barrel he had rolled out that morning, and he was the worse for wear on account of it. His camel trousers and waistcoat were ashen from clearing the fireplace and washing down the floor and walls.

Hans regarded Skelos sternly from head to toe. His blue-green eyes were sunk too far in their sockets to have any imposing effect. 'You one of them performers from that festival in Pevistan?'

Skelos nodded. He gave a small bow and a slight swirl of his wrist. 'Indeed I am. The name's Gyan Sputsworth. Barnabas recommended me to you. He said you have some rooms. Best in the village.'

'I have rooms.' Hans busied himself with wiping down the tables that his wife had thoroughly cleaned the night before. 'You'll be wanting one I take it?'

Skelos perched himself on a stool. He threw a gold

coin on the bar and helped himself to a flagon of root beer from one of the barrels. He cupped the pale brown liquid in his hands. 'Hope you don't mind; I've come a long way.'

Hans stopped wiping. 'It's all right. I should have offered.'

'No problem. I can see you're very—' He was going to say busy, but the bar was empty and how many times did a table need cleaning? *Polish it anymore and the table will be aflame.*

Hans sneaked a glance at him. 'It's funny, Barnabas never mentioned you. What's the name of that festival?'

So much for not asking questions. 'The Chatville festival. Barnabas visited there once. He said that if I was ever in the area, he knew of a great inn.'

Perhaps, he had overdone it. The dull pink paper was peeling off the walls. The tables were so rickety, Skelos was surprised they were still upright, and the floor had more stains on it than a baby's bib. He took a large swig of root beer and swilled it around in his mouth before swallowing.

Hans brushed his rag over the same stretch of table for the twelfth time. 'I have to ask, what with the current threats.'

'What current threats are these?'

Hans regarded him as if he were a half-wit. 'Why the threat of a northern invasion of course.'

'There's always a threat of a northern invasion.'

Hans wrung out the cloth. 'And none of them should be taken likely. There's been talk of Northern spies in all the villages and a new resistance formed in the north. And there have been more sorcerers about than normal. Always a bad omen. I'll talk to sorcerers if I have to, but I don't want them anywhere near my Merriam or Fife.'

He went on exasperated. 'You know the Shardner's men are here. The last time they visited was the night of the windstorm. They wandered up and down for half an hour. Patted a few babes on the head. Their last stop had been the Rabbits Burrow where they stayed until closing.'

Skelos nearly choked on his root beer. 'Is that so?'

'They want to – how do you say it? Allay folks' fears.' He started wiping down the backs of the chairs. 'I've heard the Shardner's men are going to be at Braystay church this very night. You could go there if you want to find out more. Most of the villagers are going.'

'Will you be going?'

'No. I've no one to watch this place. But my wife and son are.'

Dear Meriam and Fife, I suppose.

Hans flopped into one of the chairs, smacking his cleaning rag across his lap.

'You originally from Pevistan are you?'

'No. I'm from Heverstock, but I have friends in Pevistan.' It was times like these that Skelos was glad there was no technology. He didn't have to worry about Hans undertaking a fast-paced identity check on some cutting-edge machinery. The innkeeper had no way of knowing whether he was from Heverstock or not without a lot of extensive digging about and a great deal of aggravation.

'Now, about that room, do you think you might take me up? I'm ever so tired. And if you can see your way to providing me with a change of clothes. I didn't think to bring any.'

'I have room in my barn and some old farmers clothes out there that may be big enough to fit you if you're not too fussed.'

Skelos brought back up the last of his root beer into his flagon. 'The barn? You said you had rooms.'

'All the rooms are full. I have space in the barn. Best I can do at this late hour, I'm afraid.'

'I'll pay whatever you ask for a room here.' He took out his drawstring purse and placed it on the bar top.

Hans didn't look at it. He was staring once more at Skelos's robes. 'I can't kick someone out of their bed. Not this late. I have a reputation. I'll leave the horses outside for the night if that will make you feel more comfortable.'

Since when did the offer of gold surpass reputation? Is the man so suspicious of my intentions, he would put me in a barn? Should I kill him? 'I don't sleep in barns.'

'Festival folk will sleep anywhere, even in pigsties, I hear. I may be able to offer you a room tomorrow, but not tonight.'

Skelos put down his flagon and surveyed his attire. There was a bloodstain on it from when he had cut his hand on Barnabas's dagger. A Citizen's violet blood did not look like blood to an Unmarked One. But it did look odd. Sloppy. He shrugged. He had been in worse predicaments than this. *I shall rise to the challenge and Hans shall pay for his insults later.*

He offered a grimace that almost passed for a smile. 'I'll take it.'

Chapter 16

Connor came around to find his head tilted. A tin cup was pressed to his mouth. He took a few tentative sips. Cool water trickled down his throat. His eyes hovered at half-mast. He saw the blurry outline of someone bending over him.

'Mum?' His voice sounded unlike his own, deep, and rasping.

'Your mother is not here.'

He felt a dull burning sensation in his right hand. He clenched his fist and forced his vision into focus. He blinked around at walls of splitting rock. A puddle of light poured, from some orifice, into the small cave. The bronze-skinned man he had seen by the snake pit, sat not far from where he lay, his coal-black eyes blazing like opals in the dimness.

Amelia sat in one corner with her legs bent under her, her face swathed in shadow, her expression blank, her eyes wide.

The bronze-skinned man placed the tin cup on the ground and helped Connor sit up. 'How are you feeling?' He took up a bowl and stirred its contents with a stick. Tendrils of steam rose from it along with the smell of decomposing fish.

The throbbing and tugging in Connor's temples had gone, but he still felt groggy. His throat was dry and scratchy, his limbs heavy. The smell rising from the bowl made him feel nauseous. 'I'm – okay.'

'Drink this,' said the man, setting the bowl in his lap. 'Rogghorn soup. It'll give you strength.'

Connor took up the bowl. His stomach instinctively growled. It had been a long time since he had had a proper meal. He closed his eyes and drank. The soup slid down his throat. It tasted of unsalted overcooked pasta: soft, tasteless and slimy.

He wiped his mouth and staggered to his feet, feeling the blood rush to his head. The walls leaned in on him. He swayed. His head was reeling.

'Careful,' said the bronze-skinned man, catching his elbow. 'You're not to go wandering about. You're still weak. Rest some more.'

'I can't rest.' He wobbled forward. 'I have to get home.'

'All the more reason for you to rest then.' The man let Connor regain his balance and then released him.

His eyes pierced the darkness. He stood motionless. The walls whispered to him. Voices rose from the dark labyrinth of winding tunnels.

He smelt tar, tasted salt on his tongue and heard the gentle lap of the ocean waves. He rested his hand on the rock. 'Where am I?'

The bronzed-skinned man sank back against the wall. 'The Great Northern Crater, home to the Sighraith Band. It's full of caves, tunnels, waste, and ruin. Now sit down before your legs fall out from under you.'

Voices rang out. Connor heard urgent, pounding footsteps. 'Did you hear that?'

'I hear them all right,' replied the bronzed-skinned man. 'Day and night I hear them. Now come away.'

Connor ignored the man. He teetered towards the

entrance of the cave and peered out. The wall across from him glistened with water. The ground was slick with mud. To his right lay a draughty passage, skinny and winding. There was no way of telling how far down it went. Slow-burners were clamped in brackets on the wider passage to his left where men, women, and children, scurried about like ants in their dirty clothes.

The Sighraith folk disappeared into walls beyond Connor's line of sight, all but one lone figure, who hobbled up the dim passage towards him on wooden crutches that thumped and squelched in the mud. One of the stranger's legs was heavily bandaged with a dry-bloodied cloth.

Connor slid back against the wall.

The stranger cried out, 'Hey wait up!'

Connor swung out from his hiding place. The stranger's head bobbed into the light of a slow-burner. The light sparked clean across the figure's face. He had a leather patch over one eye and a sprinkle of freckles on both cheeks. His hope mounted. Riley had freckles on his cheeks, too many for Connor to count.

As the figure drew nearer, he saw it wasn't Riley. It was a man, full grown. The man saw the dismayed look on Connor's face and grinned. 'It's not as bad as it looks lad. One of them Dal-Carrion almost had me for supper. I gave it a swift kicking. I hope it choked on my boot strings.'

The bronzed-skinned man sneaked up behind Connor, clutched his shoulder and wheeled him around. 'You shouldn't be out here,' he growled. 'Get inside!'

Connor found himself gawking at a bloodstain on the

top of the bronze-skinned man's thigh. He wore a knitted vest, a pair of patched trousers and ragged leather boots upon his feet. A knife with an ornate wooden handle hung from the broad belt he wore around his waist. He wore his long greasy hair in a ponytail. He looked to Connor like a warrior without armour.

'Aye,' said the man on crutches, hobbling past. 'Do as the Sentinel says.'

Chapter 17

Skelos sat on his bed of straw with his wrists perched on his bended knees. He tried to recall when he had had a pleasant life. It was a very long time ago before he had responsibilities, commitments, and regrets.

Darkness had fallen. Crickets chattered in the grass. Church bells pealed. And every half an hour or so, there came the vague echoing cries of some strange beast.

He hugged his cloak about him. He could have sworn he smelt some remnant of red dust when the rough fabric grazed his cheekbone. Specks of red dust floated before his eyes. He found it hard to get the red dust out of his mind once it had invaded it. His hands had stayed red for weeks after leaving the caves. He was convinced that it would turn him into one of those monstrosities that dwelt there. The nightmares had kept his mother, and occasionally his father, at his bedside for months. The red dust was the first thing he saw when he closed his eyes and when he opened them.

That was where the real horror lay, in the dust. The red dust was everywhere...

Reminisce Part 1
Stealth Quick

It was the summer of Skelos's thirteenth year. The sun scorched the grass. The soil cracked. Plants shrivelled up and died. Fires broke out in what little forests that were left on the continent of Pareus, in the south of Odisiris.

When the temperature dipped below seventy degrees Fahrenheit and the summer clouds had emitted a brief spattering of rain, Skelos's father had allowed him to go into the city with his two best friends, Eron and Osaphar.

They were not allowed to go far. Eron was the son of the vice-chancellor. His father had a hold on his son as tight as any manacle in those days and he would not let him go anywhere without two part-humanoid guards in tow.

It was not that Pareus was a dangerous city – far from it. It was simply the nature of First Status Citizens to go about their business unseen. They entertained the Second Status Citizens (of green and yellow blood lines) and humoured the Third Status (of orange and red), who they believed were beneath them. The Third Status Citizens were even known to bow to the First Status Citizens whenever their paths crossed.

No, they did not mingle freely with lower Citizens, which would have them travelling about the city proper, chatting to merchants, purchasing goods and procuring business face-to-face. They preferred to conduct their business, social and otherwise, utterly concealed. This heightened their regard; elevated their importance to that of their esteemed 'Maker'.

Skelos's father was extremely over-protective of his son. This had more to do with his abilities and less to do with his concern at having his child mix with Statuses so low they 'scraped at one's feet with begging bowls'. His protection of his son had augmented as he grew older and

Skelos soon grew to resent being cooped up day after lustreless day.

When Skelos suggested they give Eron's minders the slip and escape the city, in the base of a lightweight spacecraft, neither of his friends had protested. They were as eager as he was to make the most out of what was fast turning into the most boring summer of their lives. Naturally, they talked of the Red Caves, what Status boy and girl their age didn't? The one place they were forbidden to go, alone or accompanied, was the one place they dreamed of going.

The rumours surrounding the Outsiders who dwelled in the Red Caves were numerous and varied, from the plain to the outright astonishing. But the Pareusian children were no different from any others in the rumours they wished to divulge. They were the ones that made the hair stand up on their necks and sent a thrill-chasing ripple from their heads down to their toes.

And so, the stories went that the Unmarked Ones went about heavily disguised so that they might pass themselves off as human and venture out into the light. Their skin was covered in flaky scales and boils the size of small apples. They lived on snakes and locust, drank dust as if it were water and slept in their own excrement. Their brains were far too inept for *standard logic*. Their speech was impeded and their movements as slow as the red dust that lingered in their midst. There were talks of cannibalism and gross mutations among the diseased cattle.

Skelos had wanted to see it all with his bare eyes.

'I can't see anything,' said Osaphar. He went into the back of Eron, knocking the scrawny boy off his heels.

Eron steadied himself against the tomb-shaped rock behind which they hid. 'That's because there's nothing to see.'

'Yet,' added Skelos with a mischievous grin.

None of them had complained during the one hour that they lay cramped on the roasting floor of the sleek silver craft as it hovered out of the city and skimmed, almost like a bird on water, over the Imeruld Sea. Their selected mode of transport was auto-powered and had been pre-set for the Red Caves. Skelos hoped its intended passengers, two seven-foot-tall patrol guards, had now ceased scratching their heads at the Landing Port and simply taken out another vehicle, without reporting that their own had mysteriously vanished.

Nothing could shake Skelos's enthusiasm. This was the only adventure he was ever likely to have for what remained of his childhood. He was determined to enjoy every millisecond of it. 'Eron?' he said. 'How many guards do you think your father will assign to you after this jaunt?'

'*If* I survive the decontamination process, probably two hundred.'

They gazed at the red dust that had gathered on their bare hands. They eyed one another nervously.

Skelos shook his head. 'If it could turn us, we would have felt something by now.'

Eron gave a hesitate nod and ran the flats of his palms up and down his chest.

'Do you think it's got Citizens' blood in it?' asked Osaphar. The red dust shone like rubies in his raven-coloured hair.

Eyes widening, they puffed out their cheeks, blew on their hands, and wiped them on their trousers, creating enough friction to start a fire of their own.

'I think I swallowed some,' said Eron spraying the ground with his saliva. He pressed his wrist to his mouth.

'What does it taste like?' asked Osaphar, ever curious.

Eron chewed on his tongue. 'Like-like dust,' he said.

Skelos and Osaphar chuckled.

They surveyed the red dust plain for a while in companionable silence.

'Won't we have to go in to see something?' said Osaphar, after a time. He was as keen as Skelos to see an Outsider in the flesh. 'Osaphar the Bold' Skelos called him. He didn't scare easily.

Skelos considered this for a moment. He had been fully expecting to see Outsiders skulking around outside and had hoped to have spotted the odd mutant or two. He had taken the liberty of 'borrowing' his brother's electro-charged throwing net to snare one; the uglier the better. He had heard the caves were full of maze-like passages, and he didn't fancy running into a two-headed mutant that had the advantage of knowing where it was going.

Skelos shrugged. He took the net, contained within a slender silver box, and gave it a shake. 'We can draw one out I suppose.'

'One?' said Eron. 'How can you draw out just one? We must go in, either that or we sit here until we turn to dust ourselves.

'"Before the sun has risen, he believes he owns the day, that the day is his to command and that he will overcome every obstacle laid before him.'"

'Makers Will,' whispered Osaphar. His green eyes became glassy.

Citizens questioned the world around them and how it came to be. They adopted the term 'The Maker' to explain the unexplained, and events that they had no control over.

Skelos quoted the rest of the verse written by some anonymous poet many years ago. It had achieved cult-like status among young Citizens.

'"For he does not know that he lies in the palm of his Maker, and with each twist and turn of his Maker's hand he is moulded, and as he sleeps time rises up to steal another day."'

They looked at one another, hard.

Eron clenched and unclenched his fists.

'Stealth quick,' said Osaphar.

'Stealth quick,' agreed Skelos.

Chapter 18

Pain gnawed at Connor's temples. He gave them a rub and sullenly regarded the man who had forced him to sit down. To sit down would be to invite unwelcome sleep, and there was much Connor wanted to talk about with the Sentinel.

The Sentinel sat across from him, his knees raised to his chest. He nodded to where Amelia sat with her legs crossed. She looked as if she was in some kind of trance. The hem of her dress was torn, her knees were black, and she was wearing a pair of boots made from furry animal hide.

'That one's hardly said a thing since you got here, other than to tell me you were looking for a Sentinel. The name's Yate. Do you have the Seekers Egg?'

Connor removed the Seekers Egg from around his neck. As the Sentinel took the Seekers Egg from him, Connor saw that he had the letter 'V' tattooed on his hand. *'V' for Violet,* he thought, recalling what Amelia had told him about the colours of the spectrum.

Yate stared off into the passage, every muscle in his neck constricted.

Men and women thundered past, wielding swords, spikes, axes and knives. Their sackcloth garments were threadbare, and their skin was smeared with ash as black as the cave walls.

A dwarf with flat features and little hair on his head waddled in. He wore a pair of odd boots: one brown, one black. His trousers were patched with all manner of fabrics. In his hand, he held a rusty knife. Connor and Amelia were invisible to him. 'We're going back out,' he said breathlessly.

'How many parties have gone?' asked the Sentinel.

'Two,' replied the man, tugging at a scarf around his neck.

Yate's nostrils flared. He grasped the hilt of his knife. 'I said one.'

'Try telling them that,' said the little man before thrusting himself back into the scurrying mob.

The Sentinel watched him leave. He clicked his teeth in anger.

'Where are they going?' asked Connor.

'After the Dal-Carrion,' said Yate.

'The ones in the forest?'

'It used to be known as the Dead Forest. They call it Bluewood now. If you've seen the beasts, then you will have seen the mounds. The Dal-Carrion have a preference for burying their prey alive before feeding them to their young.'

Connor gave a hard swallow. Living graves! He had trampled over many mounds in the forest. He had narrowly escaped being buried himself.

The Sentinel briefly examined the Seekers Egg. 'It was mine.' He gave it back to Connor. 'Where did you get it?'

'I didn't steal it,' said Connor at once. Not that the Sentinel gave the impression that he mistook him for a thief. *His knife's sharp enough to cut out my throat,* Connor observed. 'I found it around my neck when I woke up in the forest. I don't know how it got there.' He didn't know what more he could say.

'Risky wearing it around your neck. The Shardner don't permit these sorts of gadgets in Narrigh. I traded the Seekers Egg on the black market and my good armour too, for these rags, can you believe it?'

'I don't understand. You're a First Status Citizen, aren't you?'

Yate nodded. 'You think Citizen Status means anything in Narrigh? Here you're just like everybody else. The Shardner strip you of your rights the moment you land. A Sentinel is meant to bring law and order, peace to the realm. You'll find no peace in Narrigh, only chaos.' He ground his teeth. His face darkened. 'I won't have them telling me what to do, curtailing my freedom.

'You wouldn't be the first one who's come here claiming to have lost their memory. The Shardner bash it out of you the moment you arrive. The Darque Goblins and most of the Gamnod have fled to the Isles of Crinol. The Sighraith Band are fugitives. Hunted and herded here, we are lost, but not for long.'

'Amelia said she came here on an airship. I think she meant a spaceship.' Connor looked across at Amelia to see if she was smiling. She wasn't.

'That's the only means of transport through the rift I know.'

'What rift?'

'Why the opening between our world and this one of course. You can't see it and you'll never find it without a navigator.' Yate spat on the ground. 'The existence of Odisiris is only known to the Shardner Council and those who serve under them. Believe me, you're being here is no accident.' He stabbed his finger at Amelia. 'And neither is hers.'

Amelia had been telling the truth; the spaceship was real. He just didn't remember getting on one. 'And you don't know how to get back home either?'

'You think I'd be sitting here chatting with you if I did?' He unsheathed his knife. 'Hold out your hand.'

Connor whipped his hands out of Yate's sight. The knife had dried blood on it!

Yate prised Connor's right arm from behind his back. He caught Connor's wrist before he could fend him off and pierced the tip of his thumb. Connor hissed through clenched teeth. The pain was no sharper than a needle. The blood oozing from the wound looked almost black. Filled with revulsion, he wiped the blood on his sleeve, grimacing.

Yate drew Connor's wrist into the light. 'Indigo blood, not red.' He wiped the knife on his trousers, and then put it away. 'You're a First Status Citizen. Highborn.'

Connor ran his finger over his thumb. It had quickly stopped bleeding. There was no wound where the Sentinel's blade had cut him. He must have been infected with Citizen's blood. It was the only explanation. 'I'm not a real a Citizen. I'm from Earth. That's a whole other world, in a whole other place.'

He was not dressed as a warrior, and he had lost all his weapons. If he learned how to be a warrior, then he could protect himself. He went inside his bag. He took out three gold coins and gave them to the Sentinel.

Amelia started to giggle. Connor shot her a look, and the smile froze on her face. He must not have given Yate enough gold. He gave the Sentinel two more coins. 'Can you train me?'

Yate gave him a puzzled look. 'Train you for what? The toilet?'

'I thought you could teach me how to use my abilities, how to fight or–or something.'

Yate gave him back his five pieces of gold. 'I'm not a trainer. I'm a Sentinel. There is no price for what I have to offer you. I can't teach a Citizen to do what should come naturally to them. And Citizens your age don't have true Professions. They are apprentices.'

'I think I'm a warrior.'

Yate gave a slow nod. 'That may well be, but I'm not a warrior and I don't have time to show you how to fight well enough to do you any good.'

Connor felt utterly helpless. He was alone again with the worrying, burning, stabbing pain in his head, alone wondering about Status Citizens, rifts, and home. Part of his memory had been chopped away and he didn't know if he would ever get it back. 'I need to get back to Earth, to my family. Amelia said you could help me.'

Yate took a waxy orange leaf from his pocket. He tore a strip from it. 'I can't give you back your memories Connor, nor can I take you home. Your mind is very fragile. Put too much pressure on it and it will break. Feeding it will only make it grow fat with confusion. The latter, I fear has already happened. Tell me what you do know.'

So, Connor told him about how he had been playing *The Quest of Narrigh* with his friend Riley before finding himself in Bluewood forest, of how he met Amelia and the host of Silver Riders. There was a lot to tell, and he was sure he had missed bits out. Important bits.

Yate chewed on the orange leaf while Connor spoke.

When he had finished telling his story as best as he could tell it, Yate spat the chewed leaf from his mouth onto the floor with such severity it made Connor flinch.

'And you recall nothing before that?' said Yate. 'No one's ever arrived in Narrigh in the stump of a tree.'

'No. I don't think that's when I got here,' Connor admitted. 'I think...' It was just a feeling. He couldn't be sure. It would explain his loss of weight, his change of clothes, the loss of his weapons and his newly acquired bag. 'I think I've been here a while. He was struck by a sudden thought. 'What if someone summoned me here or I came through a portal?'

'Summoning Spells only work between races, not between worlds. And there are no portals linking Odisiris with Narrigh. Besides Citizens shy away from the use of magic, we're not very good at it. Now, what do you have in that bag of yours?'

'A map,' said Connor, 'and some food, and...' What else was there? His fingers closed around something new: a cold pencil-thin object. He wrestled it out. It was a rod made of glass. 'How did this get in here?' He didn't remember seeing it before. It must have got caught in the bag's seams.

Yate took the glass rod from him. He frowned. 'Strange looking object.' He bashed it against the cave wall. It didn't shatter. 'Unbreakable,' he mused. 'It must be of some value. I'd hang on to it if I were you. What else?'

Connor fished out the map and the slow-burner. Yate looked at the map and flapped his hand. 'No good that one.' He slipped the slow-burner into his belt.

Connor was about to tell him to give it back and then changed his mind. He didn't want the Sentinel to bring back out his knife.

'Dried meat, an apple, two flasks, a map and what's this?' Yate came upon the small grey stone Connor had discovered in the bottom of his bag. He cupped it in his hand, his eyes wide. 'Where did you get this?'

'I found it in my bag with everything else. What is it?'

'I can't be sure without the proper equipment to hand, but it looks to me like a Worral Stone. The Gifted Ones carry them. You don't know this?'

Connor had never heard of the Gifted Ones. He shook his head. Anyone could have planted it there. 'It's not mine.' Connor looked at Amelia. She had been awfully quiet, and he knew she wasn't shy.

'I don't know why you're looking at me. It's not mine,' she said.

The stone couldn't belong to Amelia. He had found it in his bag before he met her. He tugged at the frayed thread on the cuff of his sleeve. If there were a gift for fear, then he would claim it as his own, but not this. The Seeker's Egg didn't belong to him. The chances were, the glass rod and the stone, didn't belong to him either.

Yate scratched the side of his neck. 'The Mark has been burnt from your hand, which may account for your weakness. But why would somebody burn it? And what did the Shardner's Special Army want with you?'

What had the man with the cold green eyes said? 'If it

were any other boy.'

Connor hadn't told Yate about the man with the cold eyes. He got chills in his spine just thinking about him. 'What are Gifted Ones?' he said at last.

'There are twenty-four Gifted Ones in Odisiris. Twelve Technopaths, who use this,' he tapped the side of his head, 'to bend technology to their will. Dangerous breed. And there are twelve Emissaries who can travel through the World of Dreams. I heard they can do all sorts, teleport in their sleep-dreams, see the future, read people's thoughts. For every one of the twenty-four who dies, a new one is born to take their place. The only way you can identify a Gifted One is with this stone. You good with technology, are you?'

Connor glowered at Yate. 'I'm not a dangerous breed if that's what you're thinking. The stone's not mine. I don't know how it got there. Maybe my bag got mixed up with someone else's.'

Yate regarded him through squinted eyes. 'I think I know someone who can help you.'

Chapter 19

Skelos ventured out into the streets of Undren. In the dark, he found he encountered less scrutiny. He manoeuvred the hood of his cloak so that it covered the uppermost part of his face. His head bowed, he walked at an ambling pace. The few residents who bustled past him were in too much of a hurry to wonder about the stranger in black.

He would have gone to the castle sooner if it were not for the guards. They patrolled in pairs, their heavy boots crunching on the cobbles. He sought to stay clear of them, hiding under arches and in doorways until they passed, and he could continue on his way.

He turned into a narrow unlit alley, rank with the smell of horse manure and coal. He chanced upon some discarded newspapers, strewn across the cobbled stones. He plucked one up. It smelt faintly of alcohol. He browsed through the headlines on the front page. The main story told of a meeting in the village church concerning a rumoured threat in the North. *No surprise there.* There were numerous other stories about goings-on in the village he had neither the time nor the patience to read.

He realised the streets had emptied, even the guards were gone, but he could hear the babbling voices gathered nearby, murmurs in the gentle wind and the groaning of doors as they opened and closed. A dog barked from its owner's backyard. From five streets away, there came the hollow clopping of horses' hooves on the cobblestones.

Skelos had to settle for hope. Hope he could recover the painting without getting caught; a painting that would bring him a step closer to reaching his objective. His sixth sense did not leave much room for hope. Hope suggested the pattern of events would change for the better. Part of him clung to the principle that Citizens control their own destiny.

Citizens were inept at tuning into all six senses. His sixth sense told him that events, whether good or bad, happened because they were meant to happen, that the actions you take, the places you go are mapped out ahead of time, at the will of The Maker.

Who knew where The Maker would take him next. Would his rise to glory be swift or would it be slow?

Reminisce Part 2
Blood, Flesh, and Bone

Skelos had spied the Outsider, hurrying into a cave entrance, clothed in a soiled robe. It was a small, thin-limbed looking thing. Skelos had hoped for something a bit more challenging. However, he was not in a position to stall. No other Outsiders had put in an appearance. Perhaps, it was not the season for them to be out of their burrows. Whatever, it would not do to be too particular.

Fleshy or withered, an Outsider was an Outsider. He could sense he was running out of time. By now, someone would have reported Eron missing, and it wouldn't take an intelligent Citizen more than a couple of hours to figure out where they had gone.

Drawing a breath, he fished out the Bolt-Shot whip he had taken, with ease, from his father's study and gave it a quick pat.

Osaphar swallowed. Eron sucked in his breath.

'Why the blazes did you bring that?' asked Osaphar.

'Why do you think?' said Skelos. 'This is supposed to be an adventure, remember?'

'You're going to kill a Mutie?' said Eron. He clenched his eyes. When he opened them, his irises were swamp-green.

'No,' said Skelos. They were missing the point entirely. He had three tasks he wished to accomplish. The first had been getting here. He hoped that his other accomplishments ran just as smoothly. 'I'm going to capture a Mutie and kill an Outsider. No one our age has ever done it. I say let us be the first. Leave our mark.'

'Right,' said Osaphar, nodding.

'I don't know,' said Eron, staring down at the Bolt-Shot whip. 'Can't we leave our mark in some other way?'

Osaphar and Skelos burst into fits of laughter.

'You mean like leaving a stick in the sand?' said Osaphar.

'Not unless it's got an Outsider's head stuck on the end of it,' said Skelos, wiping a tear from his eye. 'You can't get exiled for killing Outsiders and Muties, wet one. At least we can say we've spent our summer doing something worthwhile.'

'You know most of what they say about Outsiders is fantasy, don't you?' said Eron. 'Like the Map of the Other

Worlds.'

There were Other Worlds, but the map was make-believe. Skelos eyed Eron coolly. They were children. Make-believe was all they had. Why was Eron trying to snatch the dream away? This was supposed to be fun. 'I thought you wanted to be here?'

'Sure, I want to be here,' his friend replied. 'I don't see why we have to resort to killing – things. What do you know about killing anyway?'

'I think we've got ourselves a little Outsider lover here,' said Skelos, daring to move towards the cave. He looked over his shoulder. 'You coming Osaphar?'

'All the way,' said Osaphar jumping to his feet. 'You going to stay here and eat dust or what Eron?'

Eron jumped to his feet. 'Course not,' he mumbled. 'I'm right behind you.'

They shot towards the squat cave entrance where they saw the Outsider disappear.

Inside, Skelos saw the cave walls glow. It was as if they had a layer of gold painted beneath them, projecting an iridescent veil of light. Or was he becoming delusional in this deadly game? He could have sworn by the Palm-of-his-Maker, he saw a figure drenched in white robes scrambling out of the way as he whizzed past. And what was that noise? Wasn't it the guttural screams of some caged being?

The smell of excrement and stagnant water washed over Skelos, momentarily stunning him. He blew out of his nostrils and coughed into a closed fist. It would take more than a foul blast of air to make him turn back. The Outsider was not tortoise slow as the rumours would have it and there was still fun enough to be had in the chase.

Skelos deliberately slowed down to gorge on the thrill of it all. He let his victim slip out of sight every now and again. Let *It* think it was safe, that It had lost him. He had a vocation here for sure; he was a skillful Outsider Hunter if ever there was one.

He observed how the tunnels branched off, connecting lateral caves and recesses. He heard strange distant grunts, felt the ground-bugs bounce off the tips of his boots and saw no one. *How big was this place?*

'I say we go back,' said Osaphar. He appeared like a gust of wind beside him.

'I say you shut up,' said Skelos, 'and let me make my kill.'

Skelos had the whimpering creature in his sights again. He hesitated before activating the Bolt-Shot whip.

Five hot Lashes burst from the whip, hissing like a family of agitated snakes. The Lashes were so hot, they had turned from silver to a burnt orange colour. The temperature settings were broken. Two of the Lashes were slightly dimmer than the rest. His father had used the Bolt-Shot for sporting purposes: man to android. He had not used it for two years. Skelos, who had only ever seen his father and his father's friends master the Bolt-Shot, was amazed at its weightlessness. How could a weapon this dangerous be lighter than a molecule of gas?

Fear rose in his chest. He gasped. The Bolt-Shot whip could do that to you, even if you were the one wielding it. The Lashes travelled far and were said to slice cleanly through the flesh of any living thing unfortunate to receive its touch. It burnt flesh, but a *dimmed* Lash would lacerate flesh very much like a knife. So, he had two *blood-spillers* and three *burners.* Interesting.

Ravenous for victory, Skelos levelled the whip's handle with the Outsider's head. The Lashes were bright and limp. They trailed the ground, turning it black.

Skelos caught some red dust in his left eye. It felt gritty. He rubbed it and felt it turn sore and watery. He had reached the very pinnacle of boredom now. He wanted to finish with this one, and then go catch his Mutie.

He brought the Lashes down all wrong on the first try. Missing his target, he hit rock, blowing a miniature crater along the wall. It was the eye rubbing that had done it and the boredom. There was a technique to it, wasn't there? He should have brought the handle of the whip up, thrust it out and then brought it down upon his target. It wasn't as easy as it sounded. The secret was in the upper arm thrust.

The Outsider glanced over its shoulder. Long straggly hair partially hid the terrified eyes of a twelve-year-old girl. Hot tears ran down her cheeks. Her face was stained with dust, making it look as if she were crying blood.

'It's a girl!' cried Osaphar.

'It's an Outsider,' said Skelos, grinding his teeth, 'and it's going to get it!'

He drew back his forearm and let the Lashes fly. He brought the Bolt-Shot handle down fast. *Is this it? Am I close enough?*

Hiss!

Crack!

Black smoke rose from the hole he had blasted in the Outsider's shoulder. He stopped and waited to see if the flesh would start sloughing off the bone, to see if *It* spilled Its red blood; to see if It took on an even more grotesque form than It did now. It slumped to the ground like a doll made of silk and feathers, a small whimper of defeat escaping *Its* lips for the last time.

There was a shout from behind him. Skelos spun round to find Osaphar gone. Eron stood to one side of him, staring down at the body. He looked as if he had taken a whipping himself. His face was dark; his soul bruised. 'What have you done?' he asked.

What had he done? He shut off the killing weapon, and holding it tight to his chest, he made his way over to the Outsider.

The Outsider's eyes were shut tight, her eyelashes glistening with the forlorn tears *she* had squeezed out of them in her final moments. She had dropped her dinner when she fell; a little withered snake lay beside her. Her tiny mouth hung open in a silent scream.

Bone and flesh and blood. She was a girl, an Unmarked One, a child surviving – here – in the Red Caves and he had killed her.

'You shouldn't have,' said Eron. His sobs filled the cave. 'You shouldn't have.' He turned on his heel and ran.

'Wait!' Skelos shouted. He took one last look at the girl. Red blood streamed from her nose. He felt a sickness rising like waves inside him.

He sprinted after his friends. It would be two long hours before he finally caught up with them, and their friendship would never be the same again.

Chapter 20

Yate led Connor and Amelia down a long rocky passage and into the Hall: an oval chamber in which the Sighraith Band held their meetings. It had two entrances: The Near and The Far. The Near led to thirty or so ashen-coated dwelling chambers and stone rooms that bracketed the winding, cramped underground passages. The Far was a secret labyrinth of perilous tunnels that ran through the whole of Narrigh.

Slow-burners, set in brackets, dotted the jagged walls of the meeting chamber. Poorly crafted benches were scattered around its perimeter. Large woven mats lay in the middle of the floor. On one of these mats sat a man with long copper hair. His head was bowed. He wore a leather vest knotted with string and trousers made from animal hide. His skin was streaked with ash.

Yate commanded Connor and Amelia to sit. Connor did as he was told. Weary from the walk up the long passage, he was desperate for a rest.

Amelia shrugged her shoulders. She remained standing, assessing her surroundings with large round eyes.

The Hall smelt of burnt toast and sweat, but Connor preferred it to the cramped cave he had left. He sat cross-legged at a respectable distance from the copper-haired man. He hugged his bag to his chest. He was eager to learn anything that would help him find his way home.

Yate squatted beside the man. 'This is Wolth,' he said.

'One of the few Gamnod among us. This was the boy I was telling you about,' he told the Gamnod man.

'I thought you could help this one out,' said Yate. He seems to have lost his memory. Got it into his head that he's not a Citizen. Doesn't know how to use his natural instincts.'

The two men locked gaze.

'Sure it's not the Plowman's Touch?' said Wolth. 'The book of Uom says the Touch can hit you like a blow to the head.'

'Quite sure,' replied Yate. 'Connor, show Wolth the rod and the stone. He's a hunter. He's travelled all over Narrigh and seen many things.'

Connor placed the glass rod and the stone in front of Wolth.

Wolth looked from the stone to the glass rod.

Yate whispered to Connor. 'You'll need to pay him.'

'Right,' said Connor. He gave The Hunter three gold coins and immediately wished he had given him silver. He couldn't see himself making any more money. In the game, he had gained his wealth from striking down his enemies, but in the real Narrigh, he didn't have the strength or bravery to swat a fly.

He was relieved when Wolth gave one of the coins back to him.

'Two pieces of information. Two pieces of gold,' said Wolth. He plucked the stone and rolled it around in his fingers. 'This stone represents uniqueness and danger.' He placed the stone back on the mat. He then picked up the rod. He peered at it for some time before putting it to his ear and finally between his teeth.

'This glass stick has no use on its own. It is one part of a whole. Hold on to it.'

Yate gave Wolth a sharp nod of approval. Connor whispered in the Sentinel's ear, 'I paid two pieces of gold for *this*?'

'You don't like what I've told you?' said Wolth.

Connor didn't care that the man had overheard him. He was thinking of asking The Hunter to return another one of his coins. 'I thought you were a magi or something.'

'I can offer you counsel,' said Wolth, 'not spells. I have never seen the items you have presented to me before.'

That was painfully obvious to Connor. He had hoped for something more: a spell or potion that could spirit him home, or the location of a magic portal leading to his bedroom. 'Do you know a place called Earth?'

Wolth held out his hand. 'A coin,' he demanded. 'A coin or no answer at all.'

Connor scowled at Wolth. He was being cheated out of his money. It wasn't fair.

'Pay him,' said Yate. 'He will always have an answer.'

An answer full of riddles thought Connor but gave The Hunter a coin all the same. He made sure it was a silver one this time. He had learned his lesson.

Wolth placed the coin on the mat beside the gold ones.

'I met someone in Bluewood Forest some weeks back who claimed to have come from this Earth world you speak of. Yes, I am sure that's what he called it.'

'Was his name Riley?' Connor asked eagerly, 'or Luke?'

He reflected on this a while. 'A peculiar name he had,' replied Wolth. 'Ho-wood or Herwood. He had a wild look about him and jumped at the sight of his own shadow. Didn't seem to have a clue where he was.'

'Ho-wood' was not the name Connor had been hoping to hear. 'Do you know where I can find him?'

'Rotting in the soil,' The Hunter replied. 'Got caught in the mounds, didn't he?'

Connor sighed. He was no nearer to learning anything about how he came to Narrigh nor how to leave it. 'So, what now?' he asked Yate.

'You can talk to the Past Teller,' said Wolth, before Yate could form a reply.

Yate glared at The Hunter. 'No one has ever gone there and returned with their senses intact. How could you even think it?'

'What's a Past Teller?' asked Connor, looking at both men.

'A Traceless One,' growled Yate, 'who dwells in the Fortress of Shilemoor. One of the vanquished from the Age of War. They cannot be trusted. A Past Teller can return your past memories to you for a price that not even you can afford. It's out of the question.'

Connor knew then that the Sentinel had not gone through his bag. He didn't know he had plenty of gold and silver. He had more than enough to pay for his past memories. If he had his memory back, he'd know how he arrived in Narrigh, and hopefully, he'd be able to find his way back home.

He packed the rod and stone away.

Yate let his gaze drift to The Far and then back to Connor. His eyes revealed a quiet desperation. 'Never fear,' he said. 'We are rallying an army to march on the

Baruchian Kingdom. We will demand freedom and land. If the Shardner do not give us what we want, we will fight.'

'That's just great,' said Connor with an exasperated sigh. He had no plans to be around when the fighting started. He suspected he'd be the first one to die. And he was certain fighting would break out. The Sighraith Band lacked decent armour and weapons. They were no match for the Baruchian army.

Seven members of the Sighraith Band came charging through The Far led by a bare-chested man with shaggy hair and a bony face. 'They got Bel,' he gasped. His long neck and hands were splattered with crimson blood. 'We have to get to the forest before dark!'

Yate leapt up to join the thickening Sighraith Band, pouring in droves from The Near, then scurrying to The Far, brandishing oil lamps and slow-burners, knives and axes.

'Take the biggest Rogghorns we've got!' Yate hollered, his conversation with Connor forgotten.

There were children among them Connor saw, children not much older than himself. He watched an old man hobble by with a bloody rag wrapped around his head and a wooden pole in his hand. It looked as if every day for the Sighraith Band was a fight for survival.

Connor scrambled to his feet to avoid being trampled. The Sighraith people shoved him out of their way in earnest. Their only concern was to get to Bluewood Forest and rescue Bel. Connor considered offering his services out of courtesy; after all, Bel had saved him from the Bakusa snake. How could he not offer to fight?

'You're weak and you don't know how to fight,' said

the Authoritative Voice wisely. 'Best run while you still can. Time is of the essence.'

For once, Connor agreed with the Authoritative Voice.

A man brandishing a dented sword, and a woman wearing green scaly armour, were jostling Amelia between them. Connor grasped her hand, dragging her free. 'We'd better get out of here.'

He saw the Sentinel cutting a swift path towards them. He caught them by their elbows and steered them into a small alcove.

'You'll have to go on ahead,' he said. He thrust a small leather pouch into Connor's hand. 'Binding Dust, should you run into any trouble. In the hands of a child, it's safer than a dagger. We shall meet again.'

He nodded to The Near where two identical brothers in green tunics stood waiting. They had wispy white hair and startling emerald, green eyes.

Yate herded Conner and Amelia over to them. 'Take them through the tunnels.' He instructed the men. 'Head for the Kingdom.'

Then to Connor's amazement, the Sentinel morphed into a vicious-looking cat with a shimmering multi-coloured coat and bright orange eyes. The big cat sprung into the jostling crowd, growling and swishing its tail.

'You can close your mouth,' said Amelia. 'It's not that impressive.'

Connor gave her a scowl. He tucked the Binding Dust into his pocket, wishing he could morph into a big cat. He wouldn't have minded a dagger as well. In Narrigh, you could never have enough weapons, armour or potions. 'I don't want to go east,' he told the twins. 'Can you take me to the Fortress of Shilemoor?'

The twins looked at each other. 'That wasn't our instructions,' said one.

Amelia planted one hand on her hip. 'You heard Yate. You're not supposed to go off by yourself. We need to travel to the Kingdom of Baruch.'

'There's nothing for me in the Kingdom of Baruch,' said Connor. 'Nothing worth fighting for anyway. I need to get my memory back. You can stay.' He turned his back on her.

'Fine,' she snapped, stalking off.

'I can pay you,' Connor told the twins. 'I have silver.'

'Show us your coin and we'll show you the way,' said the other twin, grinning.

Chapter 21

Built from shabby rock and choking in rivers of moss, Callawly Castle stands on a steep hill overlooking Undren village – all the way down to the Gate – but scarcely over it. Clumps of evergreen grass sprout up from the shallow soil-filled moat. An old yet sturdy drawbridge leads to a broken twisted iron gate that once acted as a formidable shield against intruders. From here, a dull stone path continues to a set of wide oak doors, reinforced with more craybine to protect against the ferocious northern storms and the odd intruder...

A breach in the castle wall delivered Skelos into the arms of the cellar. Wood snapped and glass cracked under his feet. Vermin squeaked and scurried beneath the clutter of crates and old sheets.

Skelos stood perfectly still for several minutes allowing his eyes to become accustomed to the darkness and penetrate the shadows. The cellar door stood open.

He climbed the flight of stairs, pausing when he reached the top. Two lamps, secured in brackets, burned low on the sombre walls. A nail in the wall and a faded rectangular patch told him that a picture once hung there. He had overheard one of the guards commenting on how it would fit in nicely with 'the drab background.' The castle was drab by all accounts. All of its twenty-two rooms needed extensive repair work, too costly for its Ward, Jemrah Cullen, to contemplate.

The painting was among the list of 'luxury items' the Pareusian officials had permitted Skelos to bring with him from Odisiris. It had never hung in his own home. When he learned the Pareusian officials knew of his unlawful experiments and the whereabouts of his secret laboratory, within the Red Caves, he had been swift to conceal any evidence that might link him to a misdemeanour before they arrived to question him.

He had dropped his tablet of notes through a discreet opening in the floor and sent a bucket of water chasing after it. He rolled his subject's body in a sheet and stuffed it in the cupboard under his bench. It had not taken them long to discover the body. (He had left half the sheet trailing on the floor). But the body had not been his priority. He had found the painting in amongst a mountain of junk in a leaky chamber at the back of his laboratory cave. He had told the *Pareusian* officials it was a worthless family heirloom and they had let him hang on to it, mainly because they couldn't take the mouldy smell. To cover any suspicion, they might have about the painting, he went on to inform them that all the junk in the leaky chamber belonged to him. It didn't bode well for him when they discovered another body buried beneath all the junk, one that he had not known was there.

He came to a rectangular hallway. A strong aroma guided him through an open door to his left. He had entered a well-equipped, half-moon shaped kitchen. The stove was a black lump hewn from brick and metal. Brass pots, ladles, and knives hung from iron hooks jutting from the walls. Some indescribable carcass hung on a meat hook above the kitchen sink. A broad oak table was set with stale cheese and mouldy bread. There were sacks on the floor filled with potato and grain, and a large assortment of jars and bottles lined the rows of shelves fixed to the walls.

And then there was that familiar smell, mingled with the foulness of the others. It made him feel light-headed. He discovered its source in an alcove beyond the kitchen doors, where there sat two wooden barrels. He pulled the stopper from one and dipped his finger into the liquid. He tasted it sparingly. It had a subtle dry flavour that burnt the palate as it hit the back of his throat. Zaskian: a beverage from his native planet, produced on a small island off the west coast of Pareus.

So the Shardner has been here.

He took a silver-encased vial from his pocket. He plunged it into the barrel and brought it up again, full to the brim. He secured the lid tightly in place and stowed it away.

He heard a noise from the kitchen and made his way back inside. *Perhaps it's the infamous Ward. The poor lord of the castle.*

He found a man steadying himself against the table, one hand clutching a bloody wound in his leg. In his other hand, he held a Lightning Sword heavily coated with his own blood. He wore the leather armour of an Undren guard.

'You almost gave me a fright,' said Skelos. He watched the man crumple to the ground. 'Are we under attack?' He ripped the Lightning Sword from the man's hand, his heart thumping.

'There's been a raid.'

'And you are?'

'The name's Sledge Owen. Help me. Heal me.'

'I haven't the means to,' said Skelos, making no move to help the guard. 'Sadly, under all this camouflage, I'm nothing but a Citizen at best. What did they take exactly?'

Sledge shook his head and groaned. 'The picture in the hall and the last of the silverware.'

Skelos offered up a friendly smile. 'What was it a picture of?'

The man winced. His hand flopped to his side. There was blood on his teeth. 'Red flowers. I tried to stop them. I'm supposed to be guarding the place.'

'They took the frame as well?'

Sledge Owen gave a weak nod. The blood was now forming a pool beneath him.

'And what would the thieves do with such an item?'

His voice grew raspy. 'Me-melt the silver?'

'I meant with the painting.'

'Sell it on the ba-black market or-or take to auction?' The guard gave a loud moan.

Skelos didn't want to stand around helplessly and watch the man die. *The thieves may yet return.* He stepped over the dying guard and raced from the kitchen. He headed for the cellar.

He heard the clatter of steel. He snatched up the Lightning Sword and took a pinch of Binding Dust from his pocket. He aimed the Lightning Sword at the first person he saw: a member of the Shardner's Special Army, dressed in shining silver armour with a silver cloak billowing out behind him. The soldier's mouth dropped open. A bolt of blue light shot from Skelos's sword, striking the soldier in the middle of the chest, sending him flying backwards into the another soldier sprinting up the cellar stairs behind him with a bejewelled Bolt-Shot whip in his hand.

Skelos careered down the steps, flinging the Binding Dust into the obscured faces of two more soldiers, at the same time slashing the air with the sword. The Binding Dust produced a torrent of purple smoke. The next three soldiers bounding up the steps, collided with one another, pulled by the magical force of the Binding Dust. They fell in a gangly heap, trapped within the purple vapour, unable to break free.

The Binding Dust had missed an Undren guard, lying in wait at the bottom of the steps. Skelos drew his sword. The lightning bolt bounced off the guard's helm. It was enough to startle him. He spun around and Skelos caught him with an uppercut to the chin, sending him floundering into a stack of broken crates.

Skelos hurled himself through the breach in the wall and then sprang up. The bejewelled Bolt-Shot whip coursed through the air. He caught it with one hand as it passed over his shoulder. He dropped the Lightning Sword and dashed back to the barn.

Chapter 22

Connor stared slack-jawed at the black-scaled creature shackled to the front of the wobbly cart. It was as tall as the Silver Riders horses and the same length as a bus. 'What is it?'

'A Rogghorn. It don't bite,' said the one twin who had given Connor his name.

Thaul wore a smart pair of green gloves. It was the only way Connor could tell them apart.

The Rogghorn looked more than capable of eating or crushing him. It didn't appear to have any teeth, but that didn't mean they were not tucked inside its mouth, waiting to come out when it was hungry. The creature reminded him of a black centipede. It reared up, revealing a thousand white wavy antennae. Yellow pin-like feelers ran down the length of its fat round body. Reins had been attached to the bit in its mouth.

A large rock had been placed to one side of the Rogghorn to allow its rider to mount it.

Connor gingerly put out his hand and touched the Rogghorn's feelers. The creature gave forth a high-pitched hum. He thought he had seen its feelers somewhere before, and then he remembered they had been in the soup Yate had given him. He snatched his hand away, feeling sick.

'It's got no eyes,' he said, or none that he could see from where he stood.

'Don't need no eyes. Got them things, ain't it?' said the

Unnamed Twin, nodding at the creature's antennae. He untethered the Rogghorn from the cart. 'You want to pay us now.'

Connor was careful to give the twins three pieces of silver each. He kept his gold well hidden. The twins seemed more than satisfied with the payment. Thaul grinned and slapped his brother on the back.

'This Bray tunnel,' said Thaul, pointing to a gaping black hole in the wall, 'slopes down on the east side of the crater. It goes deep underground. The ground is rough. It's too dangerous on foot. You can take the Rogghorn. Ride clean on its back. It will take you straight to the fortress.'

'I thought you were coming with me,' said Connor. Waking to find himself alone in a forest full of giant flesh-eating birds was bad enough, but travelling through a dark, deep tunnel with no idea what was waiting at the other end, if indeed there was another end, terrified him.

'You want us to come with you. We'll want more coin,' said the Unnamed Twin.

Thaul gave his twin a nod. 'Thirty pieces of gold is our price.'

Thirty pieces of gold! That was more gold than he had on him. He began to delve into his bag, hoping there was uncounted gold hidden somewhere within the lining.

'Put your coin away, you stupid boy,' said the Authoritative Voice. 'You don't need them.'

'Can I owe you?' he asked in earnest. If they said yes, he had no idea when or how he would get the gold to them and if they said no, he had to make a choice: to stay with the Sighraith Band or to try to find his way home alone.

Thaul shook his head. 'We'll take the gold now. We'd be deserting our posts to come with you. Thirty pieces of gold will give us a fresh start South.'

Connor took a deep breath. 'I don't have it.' It was settled then; he would have to go alone. What was to become of him if he stayed? Yate thought he was a Citizen. He'd never help him get back to his real home. He swung his bag over his shoulder and tried to choke down his fear.

'That's the spirit,' said the Authoritative Voice. 'Now off you go.'

'You'll be there in no time,' Thaul assured him. He passed him the reins.

They felt heavy in Connor's hands and quite unnatural. He had sat astride a donkey before without reins. His brother had been holding him. It hadn't stopped him from crying and screaming that he wanted to get down. He had been seven at the time and almost as big as the donkey. *There were no reins, but at least there was a saddle and my brother.*

'You can have this for free,' said Thaul. He produced a wooden stake. 'It's knife-sharp.'

Connor went to take the stake from him. 'Allow me,' said Thaul. He stooped down and carefully slid the stake into the neck of Connor's boot, sharp end up.

'Thanks,' said Connor. He mounted the rock step, his bottom lip trembling, his hands sweating. He was afraid if he shed one tear the twins would tell him he had to stay behind, and they would probably take the rest of his coins just for wasting their time.

'Ground your heels into the Rogghorn's sides,' said the

Unnamed Twin.

Connor climbed on top of the Rogghorn's back. The creature's skin was a lot tougher than it looked – leathery and plump. He dug his heels into its sides. 'How will it know where to go?'

'Tell it,' replied Thaul.

Connor gave a hard tug on the reins. 'Moride Fortress. Shile-Shilemoor.'

The Rogghorn plunged into the gaping tunnel, gliding swift and daring over the pitted rocks and ridges that flowed in the network of gloomy tunnels.

Connor loosened his hold on the reins, hoping the Rogghorn would slow down, but the creature set its own pace, and he soon realised the reins were only in place to stop its rider from falling off. He found himself bouncing up and down on the creature's back and had to regain his footing several times.

The Rogghorn manoeuvred itself up and around boulders. It cut across slopes where yawning holes belched cold air, swathing the tunnels with a thick mist. It took a sharp and unexpected corner. Connor yanked the reigns up in haste, jerking them clear of a mass of jagged rocks. The Rogghorn gave a long sonorous hum, which sent tiny ripples down its body.

He winced. 'Sorry.'

The darkness ensued.

They hurtled on.

Connor thought of home. His mum would be out of her mind with worry. His brother would be in bits; that's if he wasn't fuming over Connor's deception with his laptop. Once again, he wondered if Riley was somewhere in Narrigh. *If I think about home long enough, I might just wake up there.*

'Optimistic, but pointless,' replied the Authoritative Voice.

'Why don't you ever say anything useful?' snapped Connor.

The Authoritative Voice went quiet, and Connor freed his mind of all thoughts.

Chapter 23

Built of irregular coarse blocks and cemented with craybine, Braystay church is not the most attractive landmark. It is, however, the most frequented premises in Undren village. The church's arched windows are small and featureless, save the stained-glass window above the altar, which depicts twelve stars. The building's tall eastern tower houses a large brass bell, which rings sporadically during the course of the day and night. A simple iron cross sits atop the tower.

Many meetings take place in the extensive hall at the rear of the church and the doors are always open for those wishing to seek spiritual guidance. It is said that the residing Parr himself sleeps on the pews to be close to the altar and thus the God he so faithfully serves...

Skelos entered the church via its high-arched door and slid into the back pew, unsurprised to witness half the congregation turn away from Parr[1] Lona's late-night sermon to scrutinise him.

Skelos was not well dressed for the occasion. He wore a brown frayed waistcoat over an ill-fitting linen shirt. (Half of the buttons had popped off when he had tried to do them up). His trousers had no buckles or fastenings, so he had used a leather cord to hold them up. Thankfully, the waistcoat was large enough to cover the damage. His right hand remained bandaged. He had found a straw hat and had pushed it as far over his forehead as it would go.

———

[1]<u>Parr</u> – a local cleric.

The woman standing next to him gawked at his hat. Skelos gave a thin smile. She had drowned her herself in a dove-grey shawl. A boy, no more than a toddler, clung to her skirt, sucking on his thumb. She stroked the back of his head and smiled back uneasily.

Skelos realised his error and whipped the hat off his head as a mark of respect. The congregation returned their gaze to the Parr.

The Councillors sat in the front pew in order of rank: First to Twelfth. The Shardner appointed twelve councillors to each village to keep law and order, collect money or goods for taxes, settle disputes, and decide the best way to spend the public purse. The public purse strings had drawn tighter ever since Gulliver Haydem had worked his way up from Twelfth Councillor to First, in the space of a year, through scrupulous associations and well-placed bribes.

'Will everyone please rise for grace,' said Parr Lona.

The sermon hasn't finished. Skelos's eyes lit up in horror. *It's only just beginning.*

He bowed his head along with the rest of them.

Parr Lona had adopted a solemn countenance. He swayed from side to side as if in a trance. He clutched at his chest with his skinny fingers. His stark brown cloth robes swished on the flagstones. As he became immersed in his own reverie, his clouded eyes rolled upwards. He mumbled a barely audible prayer. The whole congregation recited it in perfect unison with their heads bowed. They knew it well.

Skelos lifted his head ever so slightly. He could not fail to notice the four men in silver-grey cloaks who had remained seated. They were huddled together in the third row of pews with their heads held high, as if oblivious to the fact that everyone else's was bowed. Skelos was confident the Shardner's men would not see through his disguise. *Undren would be the last place they would look for me.*

Once the prayer had ended, the congregation dutifully took to their seats to allow Parr Lona the pleasure of reciting parables from a frayed leather-bound Bible on his pedestal. His voice was toneless, and his parables: his usual choice favourites. The congregation nodded along, content with what was familiar to them.

After some time, the congregation had half-risen from their seats in preparation for the closing hymn, when Parr Lona unexpectedly bade they remain seated. He invited the Shardner to address the congregation. The congregation were unaccustomed to such a break in their routine and a series of gasps and whispers rippled along the pews. They had not seen a disruption like this since the night of the windstorm.

Parr Lona stepped humbly aside to allow the Shardner members to take to the pedestal. They did not remove their hoods. But if there was any disapproval to be had, by this break in tradition, Parr Lona did not show it. It brought to light the gravity and importance of the matter to be addressed.

Some of the congregation could not bring themselves

to sit down. Others looked nervously towards the door as if they expected the entire parliament to descend on them at any moment.

The tallest of the cloaked figures stood behind the pedestal to speak. He had a prominent hooked nose and high forehead. His green eyes appeared colourless in the shadows of his hood. His sallow complexion merged with the silver-grey cloth of his robes, giving him an almost ghostly appearance.

Osaphar. Skelos shrunk in his seat. Their lives had taken very different directions. Unlike Skelos, Osaphar had chosen to come to Narrigh.

'People of Olvastan,' he began, 'Greetings. I am Osaphar. I hope our presence here does not cause you too much alarm. I can assure you that you are not in any immediate danger. However, I will not deceive you. It is a serious business that has brought us here today.

'Over the last few weeks, there have been some incidents which you may or may not be aware of.' Osaphar nodded at the twelve Councillors who set rigidly in the front pew.

Skelos tensed in his seat, wondering if he was one such *incident.*

'The first relates directly to this village, where we have three strangers in custody. I say strangers, not visitors, for they are not tradesman or explorers, and they are most definitely no ordinary men – so I beg you, do not approach them.

'About a month ago to the day, the bodies of four men were found floating in the Ottavan River. The river flows directly from the lake at Shile Point, as you well know.

The bodies were so badly mauled they were almost unrecognisable – yet the water did not turn red with their blood. Their bodies had been in the water for weeks preserved from decay, no doubt, in the chilly Northern flows.

'We know these men came from Shanistan, a village not far from here and that they had left by the Gate some six months earlier for no other reason than the thrill of adventure. We are still looking into how they were able to acquire their exit permits. I heard they were contemptible rogues, but nevertheless, they were killed by some man or beast not akin to our own.

'We sent our men to Shile Point where movement was reported in the forest. The mines here have been disturbed. As you are the nearest village to the North, it is assumed that any invasion, if there were to be one, would strike here first.'

The congregation reacted with harrowing cries and there came screams from the few children, in attendance, old enough to understand what Osaphar had said.

'We believe the three strangers are spies, sent from the North to assess the state of our land and peoples,' he continued. 'It is the Shardner's belief that they belong to a new faction calling themselves the Sighraith Band. We have heard they have formed a pseudo-alliance with the Traceless. They are intent on taking over lands, which are clearly more fruitful than their own. We cannot let this happen.'

Heated voices erupted in waves. Some of the one-hundred-and-twenty-strong congregation trembled in their seats, while others leapt up shouting and bombarding the Shardner with questions, which none could hear above the noise.

'Quiet!' shouted Parr Lona, disgusted that they could behave so badly in front of the Shardner's men, and in a place of worship.

Gradually, they settled down. This did not stem the flow of fear that continued to ripple through the pews like wind through a hornpipe. All of sudden, the sanctity of the church was of no consolation.

Skelos had never heard of the Sighraith Band. Did they even exist? Or was the Shardner trying to shield them from a truer, greater threat? Like the winged-beasts for instance? The Shardner liked to put fear into the people of Olvastan. It made it easier for them to conceal their mistakes and their secrets.

'I repeat you are not in any imminent danger,' said Osaphar. 'We have put a roof over their heads and for this they seem grateful. We shall be taking them in for questioning. For the time being, you will need to be vigilant. If you have heard or seen anything unusual in the last few days, be sure to report it to the Council or the church, however small it is, however irrelevant you think it may be. Please do not hesitate to come forward. And I beg you speak freely. We want to put an end to this Northern scourge. As I'm sure you all know, those who do venture North rarely return to⬚'

'Too bloody right they don't. And what has been done about it in the past? Nothing,' shouted a rugged-looking man in the seventh pew. 'It takes floating bodies for the Shardner to come a-calling.'

Collis Gray had lost forty-five sheep, two horses and

half his leg to the windstorm. As Gray struggled to get up, his mortified wife tugged at his shirtsleeve in an effort to keep him down. 'No doubt it's them that sends us bad weather an' all.'

Osaphar gave a stiff nod in Gray's direction. 'The Shardner do not neglect their obligations. We have been aware of the dangers for years. That is the purpose of the Gate, not to keep you prisoners within its walls, but to act as a protection against these insane Northern races and their relentless quest for superiority.'

Skelos knew the Northern races didn't have a relentless quest for superiority, just a relentless quest for survival.

'You may not know them by name, though you will know of them, and they are not to be trusted,' said one of Osaphar's comrades with brutal conviction. He stepped forward, pursing his wasp stung lips. His eyes roamed over the congregation, who responded by striking up further conversations amongst themselves for five minutes without interruption.

The word Skelos heard on everyone's lips was war. They did not want to believe it. There had been no battles in Olvastan for generations and there were no trained soldiers to speak of. Not even the guards were trained for full combat.

'Reckless,' the woman beside him muttered under her breath. 'Absolutely reckless.'

First Councillor Haydem stood up. He took residence at the pedestal, the muscles in his protruding jaw twitching. He was a short plump man with a crab-shaped face, excessively lined from too much scowling. His hair and beard were as wiry as a hedgehog's.

No doubt, he'll get plumper still, eating and drinking his way through the village coffers, thought Skelos.

'Osaphar,' said the First Councillor in a voice as brittle as dry wood. 'May I suggest that we hold a general meeting in the church hall tomorrow evening to allow the people to voice any concerns they have. I, in turn, will put their questions to you. Your prime responsibility is to detain these men and find out exactly what they know before starting talks of war and the like.'

Osaphar's bottom lip quivered with annoyance at having been interrupted twice: once by his colleague and the other by a First Councillor, who he did not intend to confer with on the matter at all.

'As you wish,' Osaphar muttered tightly. Noting an abrupt halt in the congregation's racing speculations, he raised his hand and the four of them swept from the church.

Iyah Baines the greengrocer stood up to speak. He peered from beneath his mane of foppish brown hair. His hooded eyes flared anxiously. 'First Councillor Haydem, I think I can speak for all us when I say we're none of us fools. We can't fight. We don't know how. How sure are we that the Gate will hold if we come under attack, if there's never been a reason for us to come under attack before?'

'You've just answered the question yourself, Iyah – for exactly that reason,' replied First Councillor Haydem. 'The Gates have stopped any pre-emptive attack in the South for many years. Even when we had the storm, the Gates still held did they not?' Gathering the skirt of his robes, he attempted to vacate the pedestal in haste.

There came vigorous nods of agreement.

Ephan Clarke sat on the adjoining pew to Skelos. The local butcher flung his fat behind from his seat as if he had been catapulted from it by an invisible spring. 'Yes, but Osaphar already told us that the old mine shafts have been disturbed. Now anyone can come and go as they please. How do you know that these men did not come through the mines?'

'What aren't they telling us?' boomed his daughter Clara, who had a habit of adding her opinion to everything her father said. She folded her thick arms under her buxom chest.

What indeed? Skelos asked himself. *Why Undren?* It was not the closest village to the North; it was one of the closest. There were settlements outside the village closer still. No, there was nothing to set Undren apart from any other village in Olvastan, aside from the mines. And Rainbows Rock was not a precious commodity here. He stroked his newly acquired beard. He had presumed the Shardner had secret headquarters in all the cities and villages. *What if I'm wrong? What if this is the only one?*

First Councillor Haydem stubbed his toe on the base of the pedestal. He grimaced. 'Erm... thank you, Clara. I'm afraid the Shardner have sensationalised things somewhat. They are not used to public address such as ours. Once we rid ourselves of these North Men, things will no doubt go back to normal. We are already in the process of checking the mines and resealing them where necessary. No one can enter the Shile flow from the North and come out in the South in one piece, so we're safe on that score. However, other security measures have been put in place. I will hold a meeting here at seven, the day after tomorrow, in the church hall. Your attendance will be appreciated. And may I implore you, where possible, to leave your little ones at *home*. That is all.' With these final words, First Councillor Haydem returned to his pew.

Parr Lona took his place back at his beloved pedestal to continue the church service, and although looks of uncertainty were in constant exchange, no one uttered another word on the subject until after the service, when tongues could wag more freely.

Skelos slid out from the pew, thinking about the three strangers and of how he would cope with another sleepless night in the barn.

Chapter 24

Just when Connor thought he couldn't go any deeper underground, the Bray tunnel peaked and the Rogghorn shot upwards, leaving a trail of green slime behind it.

The foul stink made Connor's eyes water. He scrunched up his nose and gave a loud sniff, stopping a trickle of snot running onto his lip.

The earth grew steadily warmer, and the darkness fell away. A fiery red earth glared up like the blood-red sun on a dawn horizon.

Connor held his breath. His muscles tensed with anxiety. His hands burned where the reins had cut into them. The Rogghorn skidded to a halt at the mouth of the tunnel. He was tossed off the creature's back and landed flat on his face. He eased himself up with his hands, spitting dry earth from his mouth.

'Stay here,' he told the Rogghorn. 'Wait for me here.'

He breathed an infusion of clay and wet grass. He could see the square fortress from where he stood. Hills faded off into the distance. The fortress was surrounded by a lush green landscape, dotted with clumps of trees and shrubs. Moss grew in the patches where the harsh weather had stripped the stone away. Escarpard Root enveloped the fortress-like a giant spider spinning its web. The arched windows buckled under the ravages of time. A dilapidated tower reached out at every quarter.

Connor stumbled up the rampart and onto a fractured courtyard, where there stood a lone figure, wearing a hooded cloak that concealed their face. Connor's heart beat faster. *The Traceless don't wear cloaks,* he thought, without being completely sure. He reached for his gift from the Sentinel, the pouch of Binding Dust.

The figure came towards him. It threw back its hood. Connor saw it was a female Drone Elf. Black antennae sprouted from behind her pointed ears. Her red hair was gathered in a bun upon her hand. Her skin looked like wax. Her glassy black eyes were as hard as a beetle's shell.

'I've come to see the Traceless One,' he shouted at her. He stopped where he was hoping she would do the same. 'My name's Connor. I've come for a past-telling. I won't harm you.' His fingers dug open the pouch. He took a pinch of dust between his finger and thumb, fervently wondering if a pinch was enough.

'I'll take payment for the Traceless One.' She continued towards him, making a buzzing noise as she went. Her feet had left the ground and her fragile wings poked out from beneath the bottom of her cloak. 'One payment for one past-telling, those are the rules.'

He started to back away. 'I'd rather p-pay them in person if you-you don't mind, but-but thank you all the same.'

'Manners can get you far,' his mum had often told him, and he was not likely to forget it.

'How will you do that?'

He tripped over a broken stone. He put out both hands to stop himself from falling, releasing his pinch of Binding Dust back into the pouch. 'I have gold,' he said.

He marched backwards, taking care to look over his shoulder this time. He didn't want to fall and break his neck.

He saw the Rogghorn was no longer sitting in the mouth of the tunnel, which brought him fresh terror.

'The Traceless have no need for gold,' she said.

'Silver then?' Though he didn't think that's what she meant. 'You-you can stop moving now. You're making me dizzy.'

The Drone Elf landed eight paces away from him. 'The Traceless will accept your soul for payment.'

Connor came to a halt. 'My soul?' He gulped. Yate had said the price asked for a past-telling was too high for him to afford. He hadn't been talking about money.

'Do you take anything else? I have items to trade.' He would hand over everything in his bag if he had to, little as it was. *Just please don't take my soul.*

'Do you have a Profession?'

Connor puffed out his chest. 'I'm a warrior.'

She laughed. 'You're the strangest looking warrior I've ever seen. Seldom does a warrior have items that the Traceless need.'

'I'm also a Gifted One.' He was certain Drone Elves wouldn't know about Citizens, but the word 'gifted' made him sound important.

'A Gifted One you say?' The Drone Elf dipped her head. 'A Citizen?'

'Erm...yes that's right,' said Connor. 'I have great power. If you get too close to me, I can cause you great harm.'

'What power do you have?'

His bravery disappeared as quickly as it had come. 'I-I don't know. I've sort of forgotten. That's why I came for a past-telling?'

'Your soul then.' The Drone Elf drifted back towards the fortress. 'Follow me.'

I'll go back, he thought. The Rogghorn will take me.

'If it's still around,' broached the Authoritative Voice.

The idea of travelling to Baruch with the Sighraith Band suddenly appealed to him. He could travel among them and wait for the opportunity to escape...*or use the Binding Dust now?*

'Use the Binding Dust,' said the Authoritative Voice, 'then run. You won't get another chance.'

'Shut up,' said Connor. The Voice was making it hard for him to think straight. What should he do?

The Drone Elf had reached the doorway to the fortress. She looked back at him. 'This way,' she said.

He knew the Authoritative Voice was right. He could still have his past-telling. He knew how to get his own way with his brother, his mum and his friends. So why not one of the Traceless? The Look of Awe may not work on them, but there had to be another way to talk the Traceless One out of not taking his soul. And if not, the Binding Dust would distract It long enough for him to escape.

The Drone Elf disappeared from view.

He broke into a jog, afraid he would miss the opportunity. He ran through the open doorway and stumbled upon a circular stairwell forged of stone. The Drone Elf had gone.

He heard her call down to him, 'Come.'

He climbed the spiral staircase, growing woozy as he went round and round, and up and up. When he reached the top, he found a small door of polished wood and no Drone Elf. He leaned on the wall for a moment, catching his breath.

The door stood ajar. He pushed it all the way open and slipped inside. The door clanged shut behind him.

A key snapped in the lock.

He hammered on the door. 'Let me out!'

There was no answer. His eyes were strong enough to make out the shapes of an assortment of objects that in the ordinary light of day would not have worried him in the slightest, however, in the looming darkness, they became like hideously deformed creatures lying in wait.

He cowered by the door, unable to pluck up the courage to tear himself away.

The monstrous winged-beasts sprung to his mind. They would find him here because it was dark and eerie. They would sense that he was more afraid than ever.

He expected to encounter, at any moment, some formidable horror.

His breathing became shallow, and his eyes widened in panic. He felt something brush against his leg, a rat or a mouse, no doubt. Whatever it was caused him to leap up and hurl himself among a stack of musty crates. He swivelled back to the door trying to regain his footing by standing on a pile of cloth sacks.

'Don't be stupid Connor,' he said, breathing fast. 'I'm here for a past-telling!' he called out.

He heard a light tapping sound on the stairwell outside. It grew louder and eventually stopped outside the door. There came one final tap, and the door slowly creaked open.

His throat tightened. A chill crept along his spine. Three bony pink claws appeared on the inside of the door. One...tap...two...tap...three...tap.

The smell of decay whooshed up his nose. He doubled up, retching, and then straightened up, scanning the room for a way out. An icy draught blew in from his left. He twisted madly, searching for a window or a hidden door.

He could sense his nightmare creeping up behind him. He spun around, petrified. Never had it been more terrifying. Never had it seemed more real.

The Dal-Carrion lumbered towards him, its beak honed like a steel sword, protruding from between its two great tusks. It fixed him with menacing eyes, which seemed to penetrate his very soul. Maggots oozed from under its half-raised glistening wings.

He took one deep shuddering breath and squeezed his eyes tight, willing the beast to go away. 'There's nothing there. It's not real.'

In the darkness, a ring of white light drifted towards him and he focused all his attention on it. He felt the bird's rotting breath on his neck. The maggots crawled on his boots and wriggled along his hands.

He watched the light grow bigger and bigger. Its glow intensified until it flooded his whole vision. He reached out fearfully and pushed the light away with his hands only to see a Dark Window lying behind it. His eyes flew open. He saw the door locked before him. The Dal-Carrion was gone.

He had been dreaming. It seemed his own fear had brought the winged-beast to life; the fear of not knowing what was to become of him, the fear of never finding his way home, the fear of the cold, dank room.

He went to the door and struck it with weak blows. His cries caught in his throat. There was something in the room with him. His hands shaking, he went for his pouch of Binding Dust. He poured some into his hand. Most of it went on the floor.

'You passed your first test, Connor,' said a hollow voice. 'The Traceless can expose your fears. I showed you one of yours and you made it go away.'

Connor gave a mad leap and ended up tripping over a wooden block, dropping his pouch, spilling the Binding Dust. He tried to scrape up what he could see of it with his fingers. 'Don't freak out,' he told himself. 'None of this is real.'

A halo of blue light fleeted across the wall. A small bulky creature, which looked like a cross between a bird and a platypus, glided towards him before fading from view.

The Hollow Voice sneaked up on him. 'You're not going anywhere. We made a deal.'

Connor pulled the wooden stake from the neck of his boot. He slashed the air in front of him. 'Show your-yourself or the deal's off.'

The stake was wrenched from his hand, the tip cutting into his palm.

He cried out, clenching his fist, dispensing droplets of blood onto the floor. He saw the stake lying between two crates. He reached for it again. It slowly began to move across the floor. He slammed his foot down on it. It wriggled under the weight of his boot as if trying to free itself.

He was now more annoyed than scared. He was in no mood for games. 'This isn't funny,' he shouted, his eyes roaming around the semi-dark room. 'This isn't fair.'

'You trying to kill a Traceless One is not fair,' said a voice at his feet.

Connor lifted his foot off the stake. The stake went still. He made no further effort to retrieve it. You couldn't kill a Traceless One with a wooden stake.

'I wasn't trying to kill a Traceless One. I was trying to defend myself. You said you showed me my fear and I made it go away, how?'

'You pushed it away, yes?' replied the Traceless One. 'You confronted it and you pushed it away with the light.'

The Traceless One sounded as if it had more than one voice that was neither male nor female.

A face without a body drifted into view. The face of the Traceless One was long. Its eyes were covered with a mesh-looking material. Its upper lip was turned down in a frown. It had a marking on its cheek: four vertical arrows pointing in different directions.

Connor's body gave way to involuntary spasms. He felt his throat close up.

'This room is as black as night,' said the face without a body, but you can see me, can't you?'

Connor gave a stiff nod. He really didn't want to see anything.

'You see with Citizens eyes.'

'Is that where the light comes from?' he asked. 'My eyes?'

'The light comes from inside your mind. Now if you require a past-telling, you must go to sleep.

'No,' said Connor. He thought it was over. How could he possibly sleep in this place? The Traceless would steal his soul. It would leave him for dead. 'I'm not tired.'

Something walloped him in the back sending him crashing to the floor. He groaned. His head was pounding again as it had done when he was in Bluewood Forest.

The voice of the Traceless became a faraway echo and his world went black.

Chapter 25

Those after something rare and special sit in the crowded benches of the stuffy Auction House. Its steps are crumbling under the weight of the many who take the steep climb, intent on doing their bidding. The most valuable items are the costliest, and the hardest to acquire – or so some would have you believe...

Skelos had risen early to make it to the Auction House in good time. He had had an uncomfortable night on his straw bed, sleeping behind a wall constructed of bales of hay, thinking about the strange men who had come to Undren and why they were here. What were they after? He had to know. The suspense was a haze of distraction in his complex endeavours. Undren was not the unassuming village he had supposed, and he was fast outstaying his welcome. *This village is like a magnet. Everyone is drawn here. The good, the bad and the insane.*

He halted in front of a large stone building with a black slate roof. He gazed at the sign hanging above the door: UNDREN AUCTION HOUSE.

He joined the fast-moving queue and quickly found himself inside the crowded hall. He inched his way along the lines of people, holding in his stomach, least one of the common village folk rebound off of it. He kept his right hand pressed to his chest and his head bowed, as he had done in the church the day before, with two aims in mind: to hide and look humble. The villagers liked humble. They trusted humble, even if it presented itself in the guise of a sorcerer. He was herded onto a bench by a man with a shock of yellow hair and a rather long walking stick. He tried to contain his rage when the man prodded him in the side with his walking aid; it was a further and painful reminder that in Narrigh, a Citizens' Status meant nothing.

He would have broken into the building the night before, if there were not so many guards on patrol and a body lying on the floor of Callawly castle. The Shardner's men would be drawn from the tavern, if only to ensure that no one left the village until they completed their inquiries. It was only a matter of time before he was discovered.

He had to crane his neck to see the Auction Master, a tiny man with a bowl-shaped haircut, who stood on a stage at the front of the House with the items for auction spread on a mammoth table. The House was packed to capacity. It opened at eight in the morning and Skelos had vowed to get there early. It was not to be. He was so sleep deprived; he had shuddered awake after ten o'clock. He had gone without breakfast, gone without washing. There were a lot of smelly people in Narrigh, and he was fast becoming one of them. His skin was itching. He mopped the sweat from his face with a soggy sleeve.

There was no sign of the Shardner and no talk of war or invasion. The occupants of the Auction House did not have time for gossip. They had to concentrate on the process of bidding and buying.

The Auction Master banged on the table with a

wooden hammer. 'Sold,' he shouted in a great booming voice, 'to number eleven in the grey jacket!'

Skelos sipped water from his flask. He stared wide-eyed at the list of items available on the parchment, given to him by one of the Auction Master's assistants. They had also given him an auction ticket number to present, if he wanted to place a bid.

The man with the walking stick had duly noted the colour of Skelos's cloak and quickly hobbled off. A woman in a green cloak, sitting on the other side of Skelos, did the same.

Before the Auction Master had called the next bid, the space around Skelos was quite empty, which suited him just fine. *The only smell I can cope with, in this stifling heat, is my own.*

A small boy, with messy hair and watery eyes, pelted up the steps leading to the stage. He added a long sword and belt to the table.

On the wall behind the Auction Master was a board. The Auction Master's assistant, a stocky fellow with a long grey beard, stood beside it with a piece of chalk in his hand. Most of the items listed on the parchment were also written on the board along with their starting prices.

Skelos recognised some magical items. There was plenty of armour, potions, and maps available. The potions were expensive: seven pieces of gold minimum.

The Auction Master called the starting bid, on a Lightning Sword, at one piece of gold. Several people held their auction tickets aloft.

The other items were tempting, but Skelos did not want to attract any more attention. There was only one item he needed. He found it way down on the list with no starting bid and a 'buy now' price of one bronze coin. The Auction Master had clearly seen no value in it. The last of the 'silverware', the Undren guard had told him about, was absent from the list. It seemed the Callawly Castle thieves had taken their more valuable plunder elsewhere.

'I hear five...six?' boomed the Auction Master. 'Do I hear seven? No?' He smashed his hammer upon the table. 'One Lightning Sword, sold to number fifty-four, in row nine, for fourteen pieces of gold!'

It was another forty minutes before the bidding closed. Skelos was already on his feet before the last bid was called. He weaved his way amongst the sea of people to the front of the house and asked the Auction Master about the painting.

'No-no, that's still here,' he replied. 'You-you want it?'

Skelos nodded. The Auction Master sent his youngest assistant off to retrieve the painting. He returned moments later, clutching the picture. The glass was broken, and a segment of the wooden frame hung loose. It was nothing more than a flaking oil painting, milling with poppies. It did not take your breath away or fill your head with pleasant thoughts.

Skelos tossed a bronze coin on the table and took the picture from the assistant. He slipped it into an old corn sack he had brought with him. He departed, scampering down the Auction House steps, his eyes fixed on the ground. He was content in the knowledge that his fortunes were about to change.

'Hey, Gyan!'

Skelos tucked his chin to his chest. His eyes swivelled

up, down left, right, scanning the people going about their daily business. *With half the Shardner, no doubt.*

A hand landed on his shoulder. His heart complained as loudly as a drum. *Gyan, here in Undren?* He swung around drawing the painting from under his arm to use as both shield and weapon.

'Gyan, it's me.'

Skelos let out a sigh of relief. *Oh yes, I'm Gyan.* He was almost pleased to see the old rogue. 'Barnabas, what are you doing here?'

'What am I doing here?' The old man shook his head. 'I should ask you what you're doing here.' He seized Skelos's sleeve, propelling him down the last of the steps. 'I told you to wear the cloak I gave you at all times.'

Yes, but why should I listen to you when you're no one and I'm□

'You've got Hans Runick put you in the barn because you didn't do what I told you.'

'This cloak draws more attention than a Plowman,' snapped Skelos. 'It creates suspicion wherever it goes.'

'I figured you for a smart man, Gyan.' Barnabas stabbed him in the arm with his finger. 'This cloak is your best protection. You choose to wear it now in a crowded Auction House, but not in a quiet inn. I didn't say Runick was stupid, did I? A black cloak doesn't invite questions, a flashy robe does. You'll have to move. You left anything up there?'

The Avu'lore globe, my Worral Stone, one Shard, Gyan's logbook, the Bolt-Shot whip, the device I stole from one of the Shardner's provision rooms, and the rest of my gold. All hidden in a bale of hay. He nodded, his face burning. He felt like a fool.

'Pick up 'em. I've got another place you can stay. A friend of mine's gone away. He left me the keys to his place. Wants me to watch it for him.'

Left him the keys? Skelos doubted that this was true. 'Does it have a bed?'

'It has three and a well, so you'll have plenty of water and there's some food in the pantry.' He gave him a piece of folded parchment. 'Summerwell cottage. I've drawn a map, so you know where to find it.'

'You're helping me,' said Skelos. 'Why?'

'First, I can do with some more of that gold of yours since my source of income's guarded and boarded.'

Skelos nodded. *Of course, the mines.*

'And second, Hans was asking me questions about you. Questions that left my tongue in knots, so I told him I never heard of you. That means he's about ready to squeal you up.'

'I thought you said he was discreet?'

'He won't be discreet if he thinks you're a Northern insurgent. The Shardner pay for information and the Shardner was here last night. Get back to the barn. Keep a watchful eye out and your hood up.'

Chapter 26

A dark window surged towards him. For an instant, Connor felt his breath sucked away by its extraordinary power. A brilliant light seeped through a tiny crack in the corner of the pane. Connor squinted. He desperately wanted to shield his face, but his arms remained locked at his sides. He felt as if someone had rammed a red-hot poker through the palm of his right hand. The tugging sensation in his head overwhelmed him. He tried to turn, to look away. He failed.

The window was opening.

The rift in the pane widened and more white light spilled out. What lay behind it? What was it, he didn't want to see?

A fierce pain shot through his body. Racked with spasms, his back arched. His jaw locked.

And all the while, the light poured in through the window, choking him with memories...

He sees a man lying on a slab of granite.

The Traceless One spoke to him. 'Here lies your father.'

His 'father's' hair is knotted with leather bands. His arms are folded across his chest. His eyes are closed. He is dressed in a fine silver tunic. His black cloak is draped over one shoulder. His brown face glistens in the fragile light that shines from eyelets in the ceiling above him.

'You're special,' said his father. 'You can do things other Status Citizens can't. It's a rare gift you have and a

dangerous one. There are those who would give all Odisiris to have your gift for themselves.'

Connor discovers he can fall asleep and wake up in any place he chooses, by searching for the keyhole-of-light and unlocking its door with his mind.

And he sees things. Things that happened in the past, long before he was born, and things that will happen in the future. He cannot make sense of all the jumbled images. He becomes frustrated trying to unravel them.

'This gift is not to be wielded as a toy,' says his father. 'Use it wisely or not at all.'

He tries not to think about his sleep-dreams. It is not easy. He does not want anything bad to happen to anyone. He wants to put everything right in the world, but sadly, he cannot change time. There is no order to his dreams, no dates for him to go by, no way of knowing when something is going to happen – just that it is.

'You created a Dark Window in your mind,' said the Traceless One, 'to conceal the visions that plague you.'

In a labyrinth of red stone tunnels, Connor spies on a spy. Lurking unseen behind a stone pillar, he observes the back of the spy. He has a thick neck and a head of straggly brown hair. The spy peers through a snake-shaped crack in the wall. Connor peers with him. Through it, he sees a cave alive with colour. The colours dance, weaving patterns on the wall. There are two people present: a figure in a white hooded robe and a bare-chested man with slicked-back oily hair. Connor cannot see the face of the hooded figure, who stares upon what looks like a crystal ball, positioned on a high stone table. The ball spirals with colours, the same bright colours that ignite the cave, the colours of the rainbow. Three partially dissolved objects extend from the crystal ball. They resemble serrated knives, fashioned from deformed icicles.

The bare-chested man stands just behind the figure in the hooded robe, his arms folded behind his back, his muscular torso rigid. His sea-green eyes are fixed on the crystal ball. Blood trickles from his nose onto his lip. He licks it off with his tongue.

'May I go?' the man asks the hooded figure.

'Not before you have taken your own life.'

The bare-chested man's brows dip. 'With what?'

'With the blade you hold behind your back, the one you were going to plunge into my neck as you watched me observe the Avu'lore; the artefact, I am using to control you.'

The bare-chested man grins. 'My apologies.' He brings the knife from behind his back and slits his own throat. The blood bubbles from the yawning wound. He collapses. The knife clatters to the ground with him.

Connor chokes down a scream and flees. He runs down one dark passage, followed by another...and another, passing figures and shadows. He cannot tell if they are human, animal or something else...

Connor enters the World of Dreams.

He lets the wind carry him westwards across the rolling desert plains. The sand is lapped up in the prevailing wind. The rain lashes against his face. His head feels as if it is encased in ice. As he struggles to control his breathing, he realises two things: the first, that he is not alone, and the second, that he is flying. He spreads his arms out like a bird in flight, exemplified with all the grace of an eagle.

And when he sees the black and silver-winged birds, he swerves with inept precision to avoid them. Unlike a bird, staying airborne does not come naturally to him. It takes all his concentration. He cannot allow himself to relax or become distracted, least he plummet into the ocean depths.

The barren land is out of his reach. He tells himself, he must not panic. It's an optical illusion after all.

He hears a man's voice. He tries to ignore it, to concentrate on his aviation. Soon the whisper becomes a wail.

He flies. His concentration is waning, preparing to drag him into the abyss. His father's words come back to him. 'There are those who would give all of Odisiris to have your gift for themselves.'

He looks down. The ocean is blood red. A boat bobs on the water. It looks like an eye, staring up at him. He shuts his eyes, willing it away. Too Late. The ocean rushes up to meet him. He lets out a small cry.

His feet hit the water. He skims the surface, leaving a trail of white foam on the ocean floor as he is dragged upwards. He lets forth a raw gasp.

The cold air subsides, and a warm breeze ensues. He feels as if he is floating.

'Boy, are you, all right?' The voice is resonant.

'Who's there?' he asks in his mind. He opens his eyes to a blue sky, shrouded by the face of the man who has gathered him in his arms. He stares into the man's bright blue eyes and asks, 'Where am I?'

'Running away indeed. You didn't get very far, did you?'

Connor pounced into consciousness. His eyes popped open. He scrambled to his feet, spinning, searching for the Authoritative Voice. He was still in the fortress. He had never left. There was no sign of the Traceless One.

'Those aren't my memories,' he yelled. 'I'm not from Odisiris. I'm not a Citizen!'

'Ah,' said the Authoritative Voice inside his head, 'but you are.'

Chapter 27

The sun has baked the craybine in South Narrigh, transforming its colour to a pasty grey. The sun rises in the west and sinks in the east. In the evening, the sky darkens, the clouds drift across the sky and two pearly moons appear...

Skelos trudged up the sloping hill looking over his shoulder, convinced someone was following him. He took a detour, clambering over the birch fences in the neatly divided fields. He listened to the insects buzzing and the birds singing in the treetops and jumped at the sudden whooshing sound of gushing water from some faraway stream. The sun shone down on Undren like a plate of molten gold, shimmering over the folding hills and vales. He checked behind him, above him and beneath him. He saw nothing untoward. Where were the guards? In the trees and hedges, or in the nettle-filled paddocks?

It was late afternoon when he arrived at the small, thatched cottage with his belongings. It was not hard to find. The further out you went; the less habitable homes were to be found.

Skelos found Barnabas sitting in a rocking chair outside the cottage. He had not expected him to be there. The Old Man's eyes were closed, and his cotton-wool beard lay plaited in a heap on his chest. He had pulled a frayed cap over his face to prevent his nose from turning a deeper shade of red.

The old rogue must have heard him. He lifted his flat cap. He opened his twinkling grey eyes, which were tainted with mischief and misspent youth.

Skelos saw that he was not the same man who had accosted him in the mines. This Barnabas was calm, confident. He preferred it when the rogue had been snivelling at his knees. *He no longer fears me, and he should.*

'Were you followed?' asked Barnabas.

Skelos couldn't be sure that magic hadn't followed him. You couldn't always see magic, couldn't always sense it. 'Do you think I'd come here if I was?'

'Yours is the second room on the right.' Barnabas jerked his thumb in the direction of the cottage door. 'If you want to clean up, you can get to the well through the back door. There's Dasenberry juice and corn cakes in the kitchen. You can bring them out.'

Skelos went inside the cottage. The room Barnabas had allotted him was sparsely furnished, but there was a bed with a towel and a small bar of soap laid out for him. The bed was dressed in a flowery quilt. A plump feather pillow sat at its head. He prodded the pillow with his finger. He gave a satisfied nod. The room was also furnished with a green armchair, a writing desk, and a small wooden closet. He rapped on the floor with his feet. There were loose floorboards. *Good.*

He went down on his knees. He pulled the painting from the corn sack. He carefully extracted the broken glass and dropped it into a gap in the floorboards. He then dragged out the canvas, rolled it up and returned it to the sack. He found what he was looking for, preserved within the frame's shell, just as he had left it. He placed the Shards in the case along with the other one he had obtained from the Stores. He sighed. 'Thank-the-maker. Only one more left.' He had given the last Shard to his niece. It had been a mistake. As her guardian, he had insisted she come to Narrigh with him. He didn't know the Shardner was going to separate them. He heard that she'd run off. To his knowledge, the Shardner had not found her. *But by the-Will-of-the-Maker, hopefully, she will find me.*

He removed his cloak and then his own robes. Underneath, he wore a white vest and a pair of black trousers. He found the panel in the closet was loose. He lifted it. It was a convenient hiding place, which meant it wasn't a safe one. He would look for another one later. He deposited his robes in the space beneath it, along with the Avu'lore globe, the two Sharda, his Worral Stone, Gyan's Logbook, the bejewelled Bolt-Shot whip (which he had not found the time to fully admire, but felt it was warranted) a large leather pouch filled with coins and the Compulog: the electronic equivalent of a picture diary. He had procured the black, faceless wrist device from one of the Shardner's provision rooms, with the help of Gyan, the Store Administrator.

Once he had washed and taken the care to bandage his right hand, he inspected the other rooms. There was a child's room with a cot. Suspended above it was a mobile of rotating wooden horses. On to the next...

Barnabas had clearly claimed the larger bedroom as his own. His clothes swamped the double bed. A map lay open on the floor. It was a map of a portion of the South. The curved rivers and streams that flowed into the Pynes Ocean were depicted on the map in blue ink; the towering Olva Mountains in mud brown, and the countless acres of land were shaded green. The high walls surrounding all sixteen villages were marked in red. The rogue was bound to have more insightful maps than the one he had left out so conveniently. Skelos had to refrain from rifling through Barnabas's things. It wasn't the right time.

He entered the kitchen. It had an adjoining family room set with a low table and three well-cushioned chairs. Most of the kitchen was taken up with an arched fireplace. The fireplace was stacked with logs. A pot hung over them, suspended from a metal rod. A jug of purple-coloured juice, a plate of corn cakes and two tin cups sat on a tray on the kitchen table. Skelos's left eye began to twitch. Barnabas expected him to bring out the refreshments like a common servant. First Status Citizens did not carry trays.

He sighed. 'Could my life become any lowlier?' He gathered the jug and tin cups in one hand and the plate of corn cakes in the other and took them outside.

He set the refreshments upon a crate embedded in the front garden. He made himself comfortable, as best he could, on a weathered log.

Barnabas gently eased himself to the edge of his chair to get a better look at him. 'You look smaller without your robes,' he observed. He poured some of the purple juice into a tin cup and discreetly added a drop of white liquid from a small silver flask he carried in his waist belt.

Skelos poured himself some juice. He stared into the

cup unnecessarily as he drank. The juice was warm and syrupy sweet. He thought he could do with some water from the well to wash it down.

'You don't have to hide your mark from me,' said the Old Man nodding at Skelos's hand. 'I've already seen it.'

Skelos shot Barnabas a glance. He had forgotten to hide the mark from the Old Man. Tattoos were not uncommon in Narrigh. But Barnabas was sharp.

He took a bite of a corn cake, savouring the light sponge right up until it melted on his tongue, caring not for the crumbs that spilled onto his chest. *Funny? I can't taste any corn.* He took a generous gulp of Dasenberry juice. 'I hurt my hand.'

The Old Man raised his white-feathered brows. 'You don't have to hide your ability to self-heal from me either, I've already seen it. What I don't understand is why you're hiding the mark now. Has it got something to do with the Shardner and the dead guard in Callawly castle?'

So, word has spread. Skelos pressed his lips to the tin cup. Barnabas was bold and no doubt full of secrets. He gave him a cold stare. 'The Shardner are not here for me, and I've never heard of Callawly Castle. If you want to know the Shardner's business, why weren't you in church last night? More than half the village was there. It's fortunate they didn't board up the mines with you in them.' *Or should I say unfortunate?* Barnabas took a swig straight from his flask. 'The Shardner had no business closing those mines. Those Rocks help put food on the table. It brought a lot of trade from the gypsies.'

Skelos noted that Barnabas had not answered the question, so he took the opportunity to ask one of his own. 'The Shardner said they have three men in custody they believe to be northern spies.'

Barnabas's twinkling eyes became like steel. 'They have no one in custody, I can tell you that. But three travellers came to Undren, not two nights ago.'

'And how do you know?'

'Cause I was the one who found them.'

'I suppose you brought them up from the mines.'

'They made me bring them up, same as you. Scared the hell out of me they did, but they're not northern spies. I know that much. One of them had a mark like yours.'

Skelos felt a twinge of panic. 'A mark exactly like mine?'

Barnabas nodded. 'They said they were looking for something. Never told me what it was. They would have got into Undren with or without my help. I didn't expect them to outstay their welcome. Their business had not been as straightforward as they would have me believe. They haven't found what they were looking for.'

Skelos's panic whittled away as he greedily ventured to what that something might be. Something of inexplicable value? Or someone? These strangers were not with the Shardner, or else they would have boldly entered through the Gate.

'Where are they now?'

Barnabas washed down the last of his Dasenberry juice and then gave a burp and a sigh. 'If the Shardner's men haven't gotten to them, they'll be in the old barn on Enoch Gleary's unused land – not five fields from here. Odd-looking bunch. One of them was riddled with thorns. And then there was another with black belts strapped to his chest and about a thousand pockets on his breeches. His eyes were the colour of Dasenberry juice one minute and the colour of deep oak bark the next. And the third, well he seemed plain looking enough, if not a little miserable. Had a good stock of hair he did. They weren't very engaging. Don't worry, I didn't tell them I'd already met one of your lot. I'm a keeper of secrets me.' He gave Skelos a quizzical look. 'What does the mark mean?'

Skelos smiled. 'It means we're untouchable.' *I shall have to find another hiding place for my valuables before I leave for Enoch Gleary's barn.*

The Old Man shrugged, indifferent. 'No one's untouchable in Narrigh, not even a sorcerer.' And with that said, he closed his eyes and gently rocked himself back to sleep.

Chapter 28

Connor had cried himself hoarse. His head was throbbing, and he had bruised his knuckles hammering on the ironclad door. He forgot all about his plans to outwit the Traceless One, to charm and distract It into letting him go. The door was his only way out. He had no other means of escape. There was no window to jump out of, no gap in the floor for him to slip through.

'But what about our payment?' said the Traceless One. 'Our agreement?'

'That wasn't a proper telling.' He had told the Traceless One this repeatedly. A past-telling is what he came for, and so far, the past-telling had proved to be false. And It had refused to give him another. He had *not* run away. He could not enter the World of Dreams and teleport from one place to the next. He tried not to give the past-telling any more thought. *Thinking about it might make it true.*

'It was a proper telling,' the Traceless One argued. 'It was what you asked.'

Connor hopped from one end of the door to the other. 'I don't have a keyhole-of-light in my mind.' If he could fall asleep to teleport himself out of this nightmare, he would have done it by now. And if he fell asleep in the fortress, he might never wake up!

'You're a Gifted One, a Citizen.'

'How many times must I tell you, I'm not a Cit—'

He stopped himself before he dug himself into a hole

bigger than the one the Dal-Carrions had almost buried him in. The payment was his soul and if he gave that up the past-telling would count for nothing. They hadn't taken his soul yet. If he refused to pay them, he'd never leave.

He stopped hopping and announced to the room, 'You're right. I am a Citizen.'

'Then why did you deny it?' asked the Traceless One.

'I was scared.' And he was still scared.

'We understand fear. We would also like to see the future. So, we will gladly take you as payment.'

'I don't see the future with my mind.' He pulled the chain from around his neck and held up the Seekers Egg. 'I see it through this. This is-is the Dark Window. All my visions are stored in here. Visions of war, big floating ships made of iron, dragons...' He trailed off. He couldn't think of anything else that might enthral them.

'Dragons?' hissed the Traceless One.

'Huge flying lizards that breathe fire,' said Connor. 'If you take my soul, you won't be able to see the future. If you let me go, I'll give you the Dark Window.' He removed the chain from around his neck and held it in his fist. His heart galloping.

'We will take both yourself and this Dark Window of yours,' replied the Traceless One.

'No!' said Connor. Why hadn't he thought of that? Of course, they would want both. 'The Drone Elf told me you take one payment for one past-telling. The Dark Window is more valuable than my soul, and if you think about it, you don't need a keyhole-of-light to get about, you can make yourself invisible.'

A long silence followed. Connor heard what sounded like a thousand voices whispering. He realised the Traceless One was consulting with the other Traceless. Connor was determined to do all he could to convince them not to take his soul.

He clumsily turned the stone bands. A blue light shot from it and then disappeared in a flash. He had forgotten the Egg's power was fading. 'Please,' he hissed into it, turning the band anti-clockwise. 'Do something, I'm running out of time.'

A translucent clock appeared with two silver hands. It floated in the darkness.

'Time is of the essence,' said the voice of the Seekers Egg.

The Traceless started whispering again. Connor wished he knew what they were saying. He wished he could see a look of awe on their faces, and then he would know he had won them over.

Finally, the bodiless head of the Traceless One drifted into view again. 'We have agreed. This is an exceptional item. It is worth more than your soul.'

Worth more? thought Connor. 'Does that mean I can go?'

'Yes, once you have given us the Dark Window.'

Connor threw the Seekers Egg, aiming it at one of the walls. He watched it freeze for a second in mid-air before vanishing.

'I need to get to Undren village. Do you know the way?'

'You should use your keyhole-of-light.'

'I can't. I'm not tired. And I don't want to be knocked

out either,' he added quickly. 'My head still hurts from the last time.'

'We do have one exceptional item that can take you South. A Storm Shifter.'

A small, corked glass bottle drifted across the room. Connor reached out and grabbed it. He shook it. It felt empty. He tugged at the cork stopper. How was a storm going to take him to Undren? Wouldn't he need a boat?

'Use it when you are out of the courtyard,' said the Traceless One. 'Set it on the ground, open it and then state your destination. It will only work once.'

The door creaked open, and Connor raced out before they changed their minds. He hurtled down the narrow stairwell and back across the courtyard to the tunnel where he had asked the Rogghorn to wait for him. He stumbled a little way into the tunnel. He didn't want to use the Storm Shifter, not unless he absolutely had to. For a start, he didn't know how it worked or if it would work. He knew how the Rogghorn worked, even if it wasn't the most comfortable of rides.

But there was no sign of the Rogghorn.

He returned to the mouth of the tunnel and unplugged the cork from the bottle. A watery mist rose from it. 'Undren village,' he said.

Shouldn't he have put it on the ground before he opened it? Did it matter? Concluding that it probably did matter, he went to push the cork back into the bottle. The bottle slipped from his hand and rolled along the grass. A grey mist billowed from it, like smoke from a burning chimney, only there was no fire.

Connor's senses were reeling. He had a bitter taste in

his mouth and his skin tingled. He could smell the sweet fragrance of flowers: daffodils, pansies, honeysuckles, and poppies. He smelt oak, birch, and grass.

There came a sudden gust of wind, which ended too abruptly.

He peered at the sky. The clouds drew in to obliterate the sun. There came another gust, stronger than the first, which caught him off guard, forcing him to his knees. He struggled back to his feet.

Windstorm!

He opened his mouth in terror. He heard a clap of thunder. The sky darkened to a reckless grey. Trailing clouds shifted and merged to form one giant snowball. The wind howled and whined like a pack of hungry wolves. Lightning ripped white across the sky. An almighty roar erupted from the orb of cloud and with it a profusion of sounds: glass shattering and the resonant creaking of timber trying to hold out against the wind's force.

The wind howled fiercely in Connor's ears. He took the violence of the storm head on. The wind thrust him forward. He gritted his teeth, struggling against it.

It sniped back.

A vast rotating column came weaving its way across the land. A high-pitched whistle and a boom of thunder accompanied it.

Connor had seen a film about tornadoes: great cones shrouded in wind, mist, and rain, but he had never witnessed one with his own eyes. He watched in horror as the tornado lapped up two huge oak trees that looked as if they had stood sentry outside the fortress walls for decades.

Then the wailing tornado twisted sharply to the left and advanced towards him like a lightning-charged spinning wheel. He started to run. The wind walloped him from behind, slashing at his spine like a belt of ice. Tears stung his eyes. His head felt numb. His lips turned indigo. He lost track of where he was going. He rambled around in circles until the tornado ripped him from the ground and smothered him in its cold embrace.

Chapter 29

Enoch Gleary is a fifth-generation farmer of significant standing in the Undren community. Approximately, ten acres of his land is unused, on account of the poor soil. On one of these acres, sits a weathered barn, nestled in long rank grass and nettles. Unattended paddocks border it. The unassuming traveller may find this abode cosy, if they do not mind the view...

As Skelos drew near the barn, he was struck with a compelling desire to turn back. He did not want to know and yet he needed to be sure. If Citizens had come through the mines, they would not be under the Shardner's service. They could be outlaws. Fugitives. *We could forge an alliance. They may have items I can make use of and vital news from home.* He quickly shrugged off the idea. He didn't need allies. He was on the brink of obtaining one of the most powerful artefacts in the universe and he had no intention of returning to his home planet, so what did he care for news.

He found himself knocking on the barn door, his trepidation mounting. He did not know what he expected to see when he entered the barn's stuffy interior, some marvellous spectacle he did not doubt, an ordinary barn full of extraordinary men. He had changed into his farmer's clothes and bandaged both his hands. If there were Citizens in the barn, they would be suspicious if he only concealed his right hand.

It wasn't a man who opened the door, but a young woman with dark eyes, shaped like teardrops. Her skin was deathly pallid. Her black hair was wound up in a bun on top her head. She had a metal stud impaled in her chin. She looked him up and down. 'Yes?'

She was at least five foot ten, by Skelos's estimate. She was dressed in spiked black and red armour. Skelos didn't quite know what to make of it. *If I fell on top of her, I would bleed like a waterfall.*

Had it not been for his mouth hanging open, Skelos would have commended himself for concealing his surprise. She had opened the door quite boldly for someone who was supposed to be in hiding. Had she seen him coming?

'I'm a friend of Barnabas. I have some news from him.'

'Barnabas? You mean The Rogue?'

Skelos swallowed, nodding.

The girl stepped aside to let him through.

The air was bloated with the scent of sweat, straw, and oil. Shafts of sunlight broke through the cracks in the shuttered windows.

Her companions, both male, sat on dank bales of hay. They had taken a plank of wood and spread it across several other bales to form a makeshift table, laden with a single oil lamp, and bowls of partially eaten soup and bread.

The strangers were far younger than he imagined. He guessed they were certainly not older than twenty if that, yet there existed an air of maturity about them that he had only ever seen in the gifted scholars of Pareus. *One long-haired, one short, and not a Dasenberry-coloured eye in sight.* The long-haired one stared at him with such piercing annoyance that Skelos averted his gaze to a spot on the wall.

He stopped five paces short of their table before realising the young men had made no attempt to rise to greet him. He removed his farmer's cap and stuffed it into the pocket of his waistcoat. He cast his eyes over the remnants of food and drink at their table, hoping that if he looked at them long enough, he would find himself back in Summerwell cottage.

He was caught off guard by a sudden movement, a scurrying flash so fast, it made his head swim. The girl who had opened the door for him was now seated with the others. Skelos dropped his cap. As he stooped to pick it up, all three rose from their bales of hay.

He was confounded. *They think I'm bowing to them? The impertinence. None of us are that important.* Except for the old King of Baruch and he had long since passed away. In Odisiris, the only Citizens you bowed to were members of the Parliamentary Elite. Parliamentary Elite! Skelos eyes widened briefly. *No, they would never come here.*

The man Skelos had taken the least note of stepped graciously forward to shake his hand. 'I'm Duffy.'

Skelos caught a flash of the letter 'I' engraved on his outstretched palm. He felt his hand crushed beneath its grip before he could decline the courtesy offered him. They locked gaze. *He's a child masquerading as a man.* Skelos took in the sharp slants of his eyes and his radiant brown skin. He noticed the contours of precision on his short-cropped hair. He studied his finely chiselled face, the prominence of his cheekbones, the definition of his nose, the fullness of his lips and the intensity at which he presented himself at that moment. There was an animated quality to him that Skelos had seen before; he couldn't quite place where.

He realised he had been staring for too long.

'Something wrong?' The other male glared at him menacingly. His dark hair swept over his shoulders. His eyes were small, blue and less intriguing than Duffy's. He had a smooth olive complexion. However, it was his expression that was most marked. It represented a silent rage that Skelos was certain had nothing to do with his presence there at all.

Duffy drew a bale of hay up to the table. 'Please join us.'

They do not recognise me. They do not know me. They do not suspect.

He sat on the hay bale, cupping his hands together in a priest-like manner.

'I'm Lin,' said the girl who had opened the door for him. She leaned forward and gripped his hand less firmly than her comrade. The Mark she bore was identical to his own.

Skelos couldn't care less about names. Chances were they had given him fake ones. Where had these three come from? What were they doing here? He had an uncanny feeling, he already knew.

'Thorn,' said the other male. He didn't extend his skinny hand to Skelos. The insult left him unperturbed. He had not come to exchange pleasantries.

The three waited for him to speak. *It would not do to*

show fear – that was paramount to guilt.

'Why did Barnabas send you?' asked Duffy.

Skelos answered frankly. 'My name is Parr Reighnam. I'm from the church and I've come to warn you that you must leave.' The words came to him easily enough, rolling off his tongue without as much as a waiver. *How can they not believe me?*

He helped himself to a jug of warm water from the table, poured it into a bowl and slurped it down with casual indifference, all the while thinking of what to say next. He had to be extremely careful with his words and actions from now on. 'The Shardner arrived last night to find out what brings you to a place where you are not welcome. Did Barnabas not tell you?'

His hosts exchanged anxious glances.

'We haven't seen Barnabas since we arrived here,' said the girl. 'How does the Shardner know we're here?'

'You were seen,' said Skelos, 'by a couple of local farmers who believe you to be Northern spies?'

'We're not spies,' said Duffy. He watched Skelos polish off the warm liquid. 'We're not looking for any trouble nor do we intend to stay long.'

The words were like a sweet melody to Skelos's ears. How quickly all their minds could be put to rest. Questions asked, answers delivered, and then no more. Their presence in Undren would only upset his plans. If he could persuade the young Citizens to leave, the Shardner's men would follow, and he could go about his business in peace.

He noticed a faint quiver in Duffy's hand. As for Thorn, he was practically chewing the skin off his lips.

They're scared, unsure of themselves. All the good for me. He started on the bread, breaking off small pieces and popping them into his mouth.

His three hosts watched him like hawks.

'Why didn't Barnabas come himself, *pa?*' asked Thorn. 'Why did he send you?'

Skelos chewed sluggishly on the stale bread, holding his hand up momentarily to signal that he could not talk with his mouth full. He swallowed the last few crumbs of bread with exaggerated effort. 'He had to leave on some family emergency. I am a trusted friend. Can I ask how you travelled here?'

'We came through a portal,' said Thorn.

A portal in the mines, leading back to Odisiris. Impossible!

'A portal? Leading from where?'

'Forgive us. We've had a long journey,' said Duffy, shooting Thorn a reproachful look. 'Weariness is causing some confusion and making us a little tense. What my friend meant to say is we are Gamnod from the North. We're looking for someone.'

Not for me, I hope. 'I see.'

'A boy,' added Thorn.

Skelos briefly glanced towards the door. 'Have you mentioned this to anyone else?'

Thorn met his enquiry with a haughty laugh.

'Why don't you go and check outside?' Duffy spoke to Thorn through his teeth.

Thorn replied with a smirk. He remained where he was.

'I'll go,' said Lin. She jerked to her feet and stalked off.

Thorn slid into Lin's seat, opposite Skelos. Duffy also rose. He came to a stand behind Thorn.

'We asked your friend. He said he didn't know, and now we're asking you,' said Duffy in an undertone. 'The boy we're looking for goes by the name of Connor.'

So, Barnabas knew what had brought the young Citizens to Narrigh, after all.

Skelos disliked having their penetrable gaze fixed upon him, imploring him to tell the truth. He nodded absently. 'Is he blood-kin?' The answer to this was all too plain now.

He felt the sweat rise on his brow. Duffy drank in everything about him, every movement, from the gestures of his hand to the momentary flicker of his eyelids. And as much as Skelos tried to put a wall between himself and Duffy's cold stare, he found he could not. 'He's my brother.'

'He's thirteen,' Thorn said in a dreary whisper. 'His name is written on his right ankle. He may be confused. Scared.' He stood up. He walked purposefully from one end of the barn to the other. Skelos could tell that his mind had left the room and abandoned itself elsewhere.

Duffy churned his lips. He sunk onto the bale of hay.

'And what makes you think he's in Undren?' asked Skelos.

'Because we've looked everywhere else.'

Even if they had been in Narrigh twenty years, they couldn't have looked everywhere. If they had looked everywhere, they'd be dead by now. They're not just guessing. They know the child is here. 'Certainly, if anyone here answered to the boy's description, then I for

191

one would know. Every person in this village attends my church. We have a register of names, and I can assure you unequivocally, that there are no children wandering around with their name written on their ankle. Handy though, should they forget it.'

Duffy's stare grew icier still. 'I saw him enter a portal to Undren.'

'You saw nothing,' Skelos wanted to say. Portals were notoriously difficult to locate. He had never come across one. They were not sign-posted. He wondered how much more informative they would be if he revealed himself to be one of them. He expected they would bombard him with questions or worse panic and kill him.

They were desperate for a lead. He decided to give them one.

'Did you consult the book of Uom? I hear you have the answer to everything in there.'

Duffy frowned. 'The book of Uom?'

'The Gamnod Book of Knowledge. You should have carried your copy with you. I hear most Gamnod people do.'

'There is only one copy,' snapped Thorn, from the other end of the barn.

'Well, perhaps you would like to show me the portal where you came in, so I may—'

'No,' said Thorn, his tone more cutting than ever. 'You've either seen the boy or you haven't. We travel alone.'

Skelos gave a light cough to clear his throat. 'I know of gypsy colonies in the far South. You could reach them in four days on horseback. You may find him there. I can offer you a map, if you don't already have one.' He swivelled around to face Duffy. He dare not tear his eyes away from him now.

'We're fine,' said Duffy. He lurched to his feet to indicate their meeting had come to an end. 'We have all the geographical equipment we need.'

With Duffy following close behind him, Skelos made his way to the door. He opened it. There was no sign of Lin.

'I'm sorry, I couldn't have been of more help to you,' said Skelos. 'But please heed my warning and leave as soon as you are able. The Shardner's means of extracting you from the village will not be the most – how should I put it? Conventional.'

'Thank you,' said Duffy. 'We shall depart within the hour.'

'Is there anything else I should know about the boy? Something that will help you in your search?'

Immediately, Skelos wished he had not asked it. He noted that Duffy's composure was a powerful testimony to a wealth of information that he shared with no one. His brown eyes probed Skelos's own.

'Wherever he is, we will find him, and we will destroy those who mean him harm,' came his reply.

Skelos broke his gaze. He stumbled out of the barn and into the green expanse beyond without looking back. The sweat from his brow trickled freely onto his eyelashes. *These Citizens will be my undoing.*

Chapter 30

Connor stirred. His clothes felt damp where the dewy grass had kissed them. He scratched his nose, inhaled the sweet scent of honeysuckles, and reached blindly for an invisible blanket. There was a chill in the air and his hands and feet were cold. It was a while before he mustered the courage to open his eyes. A bright light had crept under his eyelids, and they quivered in its wake.

He stumbled groggily to his feet. His eyes creaked open. He felt as if an iron fist had clouted him about the ears.

The sky above him was beginning to clear, as was his mind.

He had been swept up in a tornado. All signs of it were gone and he was still alive. Still in one piece, but where?

Dawn was breaking. He was surrounded by folds of green and a head of purple-tinged clouds. To his left, the sun crested over the horizon. He looked South. He saw the formidable Gate and a dark ribbon, winding beneath the hill crests towards it. To the east, he saw the Olva Mountains: small black crystals on a green band.

The Storm-Shifter had dropped him near Undren village. If he wanted to get through the Gate, he would have to barter his way in. He didn't really have anything with which to barter. He could say he was lost, that his mother lived in the village. They wouldn't turn away a child, would they?

He found his bag lying on the edge of a grassy knoll. It

had broken open. The glass rod was still there, the Seekers Egg, the Worral Stone, two strips of dried meat, three silver coins, and seven gold ones. The tornado had swallowed up everything else.

He put the glass rod inside the sock of his boot and scanned the sloping low road that would take him into the village: a dry mud path where grass failed to grow because it had been trampled on a thousand times by man and beast alike. He slung his bag over his shoulder, drew a long slow breath and began marching in the direction of the Gate.

The weight of his bag grew less as he journeyed on; the burden of responsibly grew heavier on his shoulders.

Much to Connor's good fortune, the Undren Gate was open. A man driving a cartload of Goby pigs (so-called because of their swollen cheeks and fins) was on his way out. The man was riding fast, leaving the guards on the Gate flustered and scattered. Connor slipped through the gate with ease. He was silently patting himself on the back when a hand thumped his shoulder. He froze, afraid to turn around.

'And where do you think you're going?' The Undren Guard had thought he was trying to sneak out of the Gate. He shoved him hard in the back, sending him into the horde of villagers.

Connor ran, eager to get away from the guards at the Gate. However, the further he journeyed into Undren, the more restless he became. He hadn't thought this all the way through. On a computer screen, the village of

Undren was clean, orderly, and small. In reality, all the buildings looked giant and unfamiliar. It was a busy place, dusty and packed full of people, carts, horses, and other animals. Connor was afraid that something was going to trample on him. And he was afraid to ask for help. If he stood still for too long, someone or something would shove him out of the way.

He was in Undren, the place where he started out in the game. He hoped something would trigger his memory. There had to be someone in the village who remembered him, but all the villagers he made eye contact with, returned nasty and suspicious looks.

He shrank into an empty doorway and pulled out his map of Narrigh. It named only a handful of Undren's major landmarks: The Gate, the Olva Mountains, the woodlands, the church (marked with a cross), the Auction House and the Village Hall. You couldn't zoom in and out of the map as you could on a computer screen, and you couldn't tap on a question mark symbol to receive useful tips on how to reach your destination. Worse, he had to get about on foot. If he wanted to retrace his steps, he would need a more detailed map of Undren. He had enough silver to buy a map of the village showing all the roads and landmarks. He made his way back toward the Gate, turning left onto a road he knew. Adle Road. He had frequented it – in the virtual world – on two occasions. Adle Road was teeming with shops. From what Connor remembered, there was also a bank and an Alchemist, which sold healing potions.

Villagers, walking in packs, repeatedly drove Connor into the road. Laden with boxes, bags, and other goods, they hardly seemed to look where they were going.

He came to a draper's shop. There was a reedy woman in the shop front, dressed in a high-collared white blouse and a long black skirt. She was holding a tape measure up to a roll of rose-patterned fabric. There were no other costumers inside the shop. Feeling confident that she could help him, he went in.

A bell rang above the door when he entered. The door groaned shut. He slowly padded across the shop floor. 'Excuse me,' he squeaked.

The Draper set down her tape measure and started to unroll the fabric.

'Excuse me.' He parked himself between two giant boulders of grey silk.

'We're closed.' She took a pair of scissors from the neck of her skirt and proceeded to cut the fabric.

'Sorry, I didn't know. I just wanted directions.'

The Draper returned her scissors to the neck of her skirt and shot him a glance. 'And what are you doing back here?' she said frostily.

'Erm...have I been here before?'

'Well, that's gratitude for you. I sowed the trousers you're wearing. They didn't look like that when they left my shop. I warned him, I said, "Get the cheap fabric, nothing pricey. You know what these children are like. They'll be shredded by the morrow, and you'll spend the rest of your years sowing and patching the things up."'

He looked down at his threadbare trousers, frowning. 'When was I in here?'

'You've some gall, I'll say. I'll have to ask that Warden to teach you some manners.' Her neck constricted. 'No "please", no "thank you", no "Madam"!'

'Who's the Warden? Please. Ma'am. Madam.'

The Draper slotted the roll of rose-patterned fabric between two others propped against the wall. 'I don't why he bothers with you strays. You don't want to go to school. You cost more to feed than a Goby Pig and you leave trouble and dirt wherever you go. He said that he had been charged with your care. Who charged him with your care is anybody's guess. But anyone would know to look at you that you didn't come off the streets of Undren. So, where did you come from? That's what I'd like to know.' She moved closer to him, her skirt rustling as she walked. She peered at him as if she were looking at a tiny and unusual insect. 'Did you arrive on a 'cursed' wind? Or are you a sorcerer's apprentice?'

'I didn't come in the wind and sorcerers don't have apprentices, thank *you*.' He made a hasty exit, slamming the shop door behind him.

What a nightmare! If all the shopkeepers in Undren were as batty as The Draper, it was going to be a long day.

He continued to weave his way along Adle Road, considering where he should go next. He slowed down when he came to a packed sweet shop. The shopkeeper had displayed the sweets in the window in tall glass jars. Connor's mouth filled with saliva at the sight of all the multi-coloured treats. The shopkeeper didn't look as if he had time to catch his breath. Connor watched him snatch a jar of boiled sweets from the window and fight his way back to the counter, purple-faced and wheezing.

'Psst!'

Connor looked up and down the bustling road.

'Psst!' There it was again. It came from a narrow alley next to the sweet shop. Connor went to the neck of the alleyway. It was stacked with broken crates and tall wire bins, overflowing with empty glass bottles and jars. He saw a pair of boots protruding from the bottom of a mountain of crates.

'Are you talking to me?' he asked the boots. They were brown and badly scuffed. He hoped there was a human body attached to them and not something repugnant and beast-like. A head appeared.

'It's me, boy.'

Connor recognised the man's bright blue eyes. He had seen them in his Past-Telling. More curious than afraid, he walked down the alley to meet him.

The man's hands shot out, and before Connor knew what was happening, the man had squeezed him to his chest. 'Why did you take off like that? I've been worried out of my wits.' He released Connor from his clutches.

Connor gawked at the staunch middle-aged man standing between the two crate towers. He had a broad face and a cloud of chestnut brown hair. He wore a pair of weathered trousers and a faded white shirt.

'I'm sorry, sir. Who are you?'

'Your guardian, Jemrah Cullen, as if you didn't know.'

'I don't know. I've lost my memory.'

Jemrah pushed up his shirtsleeves. 'What again? I'm not officially your guardian, of course, but someone had to take care of you. Seeing as how you landed on my property, I thought it might as well be me. Come in a bit,' he beckoned, 'so you're not visible from the road.'

Connor stood between the crate towers. 'When you

say landed, do you mean on a spaceship?'

'Spaceship? Is that a fancy word for a boat where you come from?'

He tucked in his bottom lip. He had no idea how to explain outer space. 'No...not really.'

Jemrah hoisted up the thick belt around his waist. 'Part of your memory was gone when I found you on the castle grounds, hovering in the air, fast asleep, dressed in your warrior's garb.'

'You're the castle Warden.'

'That's me. You said you were playing a game with your friend and that's all you remember. So, I took you in.'

'You arrived the day after the windstorm. I thought it might have swept you up from a distant land and carried you here. I knew you were no ordinary boy. Your cuts and grazes healed quicker than it took me to drink a mug of ale. You were having terrible nightmares. I knew it was the Mark.' He gripped Connor's wrist and gawked at the scar, his eyes big and gleaming. 'The sorcerers' pestilence. You don't know how many times I burned this thing off.' He released Connor's wrist. 'It gave me nightmares of my own, I can tell you.'

Connor hissed through his teeth and massaged the dark bruise Jemrah had left on his wrist.

Ignorant of the pain he had inflicted, Jemrah went on with his tale. 'I was planning to get your name on the village register to enrol you in school. Next I hear, some of the Shardner's men are riding in and they want to use Callawly Castle as their headquarters. So, I took you with me to the City of Rint, out of the way. Then you ran off.

You didn't want to hear about going to school.

'Things have taken a worrisome turn while I've been gone. The villagers are itchy with restlessness. There's war talk and a dead guard up at the castle. First Councillor Haydem wants to see me. I don't want to see him, or any of the others. I'm going to pick up my horse and cart from the stables across the way.'

'You were going to send me to school in Undren village?' Connor clutched the side of his face. The Warden's admission had made him woozy.

'Is that all you got from what I just told you? I was trying to protect you.'

'By burning my hand?' No wonder he'd been having nightmares while in Jemrah's charge.

The Warden let out a frustrated sigh. 'It was half a minute of pain. You can't be wandering around the village with those sorts of marks. You'll get yourself killed. Stones! You'll get me killed.'

'Did you give me an egg-shaped pendant? It was on a chain, I wore around my neck.'

'You had better keep that thing out of sight. That's Shardner's plunder. I got it on the Black Market. I was going to sell it on, but you were so taken with it, I let you have it.'

'I don't have it anymore. I lost it.' His eyes welled up with tears. He fought the urge to blink. He wasn't alone. There were people in Narrigh willing to help him, but not in the way he would have liked. 'Thank you for taking me in, but I don't want to live in Undren or anywhere else in Narrigh.'

Running from the City of Rint so Jemrah wouldn't

send him to school; it did sound like something he would do. But how did he end up in Bluewood Forest? If he was a Dream Emissary, he could have travelled in his sleep-dreams, or did he get there on foot, goaded by the voice of the Seekers Egg? He had no way of knowing.

'One day, who knows, whatever delivered you to Narrigh, will snatch you right back up again, but it won't likely be today or tomorrow.' He pulled a wrinkled handkerchief from his shirt pocket and gave it to Connor. 'Don't go getting yourself all upset now. I'm leaving Undren tonight for the City of Rint. You can come with me.'

'How long did I stay with you?'

'A month, more or less.'

Connor bunched up the handkerchief in his hand. He was determined not to give up. 'I've got a vault in Rint. There might be something in there from home.'

'You emptied it on your last visit.'

He dropped the handkerchief. 'What about my armour and my Lightning Sword?'

'I exchanged them for food and the clothes you're wearing.'

'But I need those things!'

Jemrah plucked up his handkerchief. 'If you still had those things, you're more likely to be dead than alive. You had better stick with me. Wait for me in the Verity Tavern in Gisil Lane. It's an odd-bod place. Quiet. You know the one?'

There were five taverns in the village. Connor knew them all by name. The Rabbits Burrow and Undren Tavern were the most popular drinking-holes. The

Murkin Mere was situated near the outskirts of the village, and the creepy Crocksford Arms was located in some dubious alley where nobody ever went.

Trying to control his emotions, Connor nodded and sucked in his breath. Getting home was going to take time and he had nowhere else left to run.

Chapter 31

The Verity Tavern had been left to rack and ruin by its careless owner. Few walked through the doors of the dilapidated drinking hole with its shabby walls and creaking floorboards.

Third Councillor Victrow refused to have it knocked down, for he had bought it as a present for his idle son, Brockta, who had run off to Shanistan and returned, a corpse, in the Ottavan River.

Connor sat at a balcony table. He had a clear view of the door and of the clock on the wall beside him. He ordered a mug of a Dasenberry juice, a bowl of pea-green soup and a chunk of bread from a hawk-nosed woman with puffy eyes.

Time dragged its heels.

As he waited for the Warden, he had plenty of time to think. Jemrah was right. He wasn't going home today, and he wasn't going home tomorrow, but some day.

A short while later, the hawk-nosed woman brought out his order. She did not say a word when she placed it on the table. A hooded stranger, toying with an empty glass by the window, drew her curiosity and Connor's too.

The stranger glanced up at Connor more than once, making him forget his thirst and his rumbling belly.

The stranger slammed his glass down on the table. It echoed like a dull stone in a bottomless pool. The figure then rose and made its way up the balcony stairs towards him. The stranger's movements were slow and hesitant. A gold and purple hem peeked out from under his black cloak where his boots met.

His heart hammered in his chest. Whoever was under the cloak might not even be human? He had learned that Parrs' wore hooded cloaks and Drone Elves, but sorcerers wore them too. Sorcerers preferred black or grey cloaks. All sorcerers in Narrigh were inherently evil. Worse than Plowmen, you could not trade or barter with them. They couldn't take away your powers, but they could cast a spell on you, and you wouldn't even know it, not at first – not until something went wrong; like you became as still as stone because they had cast an Immobility Spell, or you woke up in a cemetery because they hit you with a Death Star curse.

Parrs' didn't go to taverns, he told himself and no Drone Elves came this way. A sorcerer then? A raw fear raged in his belly. The stranger came over to his able. He was a rather large man with a nose shaped like a funnel and a thick dark beard.

'Hello,' he said, smiling. 'Do you mind if I join you?'

Connor did mind. He didn't want a Sorcerer at his table. He opened his mouth to speak. Fear had struck such terror in him that the Sorcerer had hauled up a rickety chair and sat down before he could form a reply.

He now understood why the others had left: the elderly couple who had sat just inside the doorway hobbled out when the Sorcerer arrived, and a thin man who knocked back one flagon of ale, staggered out shortly afterwards, ignoring the barmaid's pleas for him to stay and the offer of free drinks.

'Can I get you a drink?' asked the Sorcerer.

Connor stared into his bowl of soup. He didn't like the way the Sorcerer looked at him with his blazing speckled brown eyes. He thought about getting up and leaving, but that would cause suspicion and he didn't want to draw any more attention to himself than he had done already.

The Sorcerer ordered a flagon of cider from the barmaid. Connor watched him cautiously sip the frothy liquid and wince before placing it back onto the table. 'Are you sure I can't get you anything?'

'No!' He glanced at the window by the door. He must have been in the village for hours. It was already growing dark. He could wait for Jemrah outside. He willed himself to get to his feet. The only problem was he couldn't feel his legs.

'Are you waiting for someone?'

'It's none of your business.' He thought he saw a flame burst from the Sorcerer's gleaming eyes. Was he casting a spell on him at that very moment?

And what was that! A crude mark had 'appeared' on the palm of the Sorcerer's hand. He shrunk back horrified. 'What's that?' he breathed.

'What?' A look of confusion erupted on the Sorcerer's face.

'Your hand.' Connor began to shake uncontrollably. He felt as if something was crawling under the skin of his own hand, consuming him. The Sorcerers Pestilence!

Baffled, the Sorcerer looked down at his own hands, turning them over, repeatedly. Then he nodded slowly as if in understanding. He showed Connor the palm of his right hand.

'You mean the Status Mark? You have seen it before,

perhaps on your own hand.'

'No,' said Connor at once, baring the ugly blue-black scar on his right hand. 'I don't have a Status Mark and I'm not a sorcerer.'

'You think I'm a sorcerer.' He gave a good-humoured grunt. 'Don't be fooled by this cloak. I'm no sorcerer.' He took a sharp breath and drew back, taking his arms from the table. 'My name's Gyan. I can help you get back to Odisiris.'

'I don't know you and I'm not from Odisiris.' He wedged his hands between his knees and rocked back and forth ever so gently. His own voice scared him. His ankle was all covered up and yet the man knew his name.

'You remember something of your homeland, a sense of not belonging. I can see it in your eyes.'

Connor smothered his face with his hands. 'Don't look at them then.'

'I'm not going to hurt you, I promise. You don't have to be afraid.' The man's voice came in a low urgent whisper.

'I won't go with you.' How many times had he been told he was a Citizen?

'Enough for it to be true,' said the Authoritative Voice.

'What about your family and your friends? Don't you want to see them again?'

Gradually, Connor withdrew his hands from his face. The hammering in his chest had slowed and the man's face seemed less harsh, his eyes softer.

'I live with my mum and brother in London.'

The man nodded eagerly. He smiled. 'Your brother said you might be confused. He's here in Undren, looking for you.'

He was lost for words. His brother couldn't be here in Undren…unless he was trapped in the game too. 'You-you spoke to him?'

'Yes, and I assured him, I'd keep a look out for you.'

'What's his name?' Connor held his breath, waiting.

'Duffy, or so he told me. You look very much alike.'

Duffy was the name of his brother's player character. If Luke wasn't in Narrigh, then how would Gyan know the name, Duffy? He didn't remember telling anyone in Narrigh that his brother had used that name.

The Citizen propped his elbows up on the table. 'I'm curious to learn how you came to Narrigh. Your brother seems to think it was through a portal.'

'I used a Storm-Shifter to come to Undren, but I don't remember how I came to Narrigh. The Shardner's Special Army found me in Bluewood Forest, and then I met this girl. She told me she was a Citizen▯'

Gyan's jaw began to twitch. 'Girl? What girl?'

'Amelia. She helped me escape. We went to the Great Northern Crater.' He stopped there. He knew better than to talk about the Sighraith Band and their plans of invasion.

The Citizen put his fist to his mouth. 'Did you come to Undren together?'

Connor didn't answer. So, what if Gyan knew Luke's player character's name? It didn't mean he could trust him. What if he wanted to hurt Amelia? What if he was working with the Shardner?

'I can take you to your brother. We can all leave Narrigh together. First, there is something I wish to show you.'

Gyan caught the barmaid hovering in the background. He saw her off with a chilling glance. He placed his flagon of cider on the next table. He glanced around and then brought a black case from beneath his cloak. He opened the case and took from it a slender glass rod. He eyed Connor cautiously. 'Have you ever seen one of these?

Connor pushed his bowl and mug of Dasenberry juice to one end of the table. He stared at the glass rod for a long time. Amelia must have put one of the rods in his bag when they were in Bluewood Forest. Hazy images of his past-telling swept through his mind: the Avu'lore, the spy in the gold and purple robes and the white-hooded figure that used the Avu'lore to make his would-be killer slit his own throat. Wolth said the glass rod was part of a whole. What if that 'whole' was the Avu'lore and Gyan had stolen it?

The tavern door creaked open. A woman dressed in a green and gold embroidered cloak floated in. She took residence at Gyan's former table. The barmaid came scuttling from the kitchen, grateful for a less disconcerting customer.

Connor chewed his bottom lip. He swayed his head indecisively.

'It's all right, you can tell me. You're not in any trouble, I swear. It's very important.'

'Amelia has one. She's staying in a cottage in Burlington farm.' He knew of a Burlington Inn and was pretty sure there was a Burlington farm around it somewhere. 'I know the owner. I can fetch her for you. It's not far. I'll have to go on my own though. Mr

Burlington doesn't like strange men – I mean strangers.'
There was no Mr Burlington.

Gyan reached his hand across the table and squeezed Connor's arm. 'If you can't fetch her, don't worry. The important thing is that you bring me the Shard.' He held up the glass rod. 'This, this is a Shard.'

Gyan placed two silver coins on the table to cover the cost of the food and drinks. He returned the Shard to its case and slid it under his cloak. 'There are many eyes upon us, Connor. You get the Shard, and then we'll find your brother. Tell me, do you know of a secret place we can meet?'

Connor didn't hesitate, 'The Crocksford Arms. No one ever goes in there.'

Chapter 32

Connor tore through the village streets. He had to keep moving before Gyan caught up with him. He didn't believe Gyan would help him find his brother. He had seen the keen look in the Citizen's eye when he asked him about the Shard; it was all he cared about. If Luke was somewhere in the village, he had to find him and fast.

He had been told by more than one person that he was a Citizen. He was starting to believe it. He certainly hadn't been himself since arriving in Narrigh. What if he had turned into a whole other person when he had entered the game? What if there was a keyhole-of-light in his mind? It would mean he had powerful abilities: he could teleport. Teleport between worlds. Teleport home!

A mixture of fear and excitement welled up inside him, causing him to break his stride. He stumbled into some undergrowth and grunted in pain. This was not the time to lose his concentration or his bearings. Not that he had any bearings. Luke could be anywhere.

He shot through the shadows. The night breeze brushed against his face. His keen eyes did not fail him.

He took a shortcut down by the cobbler's yard, hurrying past the honeysuckle-coloured and cream painted shops. He raced to the brick houses circling Whitley Park. The flock of geese, gliding across the large pond hissed and flailed their wings.

He knocked on arched doors and frosted glass windows, calling his brother's name. Curtains twitched and doors creaked open. Those who answered claimed they had not heard of him, those who didn't, put out their lights or shouted into the night, 'Stop that bloomin' racket!'

He flew on, taking plunging strides across paving stones. A child running unaware, and he did not care if anyone saw him. But no one saw him. He ran at lightning speed back to the village proper, down the Gallion Road, where the market traders came once a month to sell their wares. The bare, rickety stalls were ripe with the smell of sour fruit and rotting vegetables.

The sight of a stray guard, ambling along the road towards him, stopped Connor in his tracks. The guard wore a crimson leather tunic under his breastplate. He also wore metal-capped boots and the sloppy grin of a man who had downed too much cider. An empty sheath hung from his braided belt. The drunk guard wheeled his sword in his hand. He sliced the air, chortling gaily.

Connor felt the ghostly stab of the sword in his chest. He rushed into the nearest alley. His head was pounding. If Luke were in Undren, where would he go?

'Hurry,' said the Authoritative Voice, 'time is of the essence.'

His empty stomach gave a noisy grumble. When wasn't time of the essence?

Once the guard had passed, he came out of the alley and walked swiftly along the streets, keeping close to the shop and house doorways. He checked over his shoulder every now and again to make sure he was not being followed. He felt considerably cooler after all that running, and the chilly night air was beginning to bite him.

A thin mist clung to the air and two slivers of moon lay in wait behind the trailing clouds. Connor walked until he came to a row of fields. The fields were unkempt and swollen with weeds. He took up a long twig and used it to thrash his way through the host of thorny plants that overran the dense field where an old mill stood dismal in the distance, its one dilapidated sail churning sorrowfully in the night breeze. He had seen the Old Getty mill in the game. The mill's hexagonal tower was built on a base of brick and craybine. He had no idea what lay inside it. It might be full of critters and booby-traps. Then again, it could contain a secret portal. All he had to do was throw a stone through one of the broken windows, that would give him a good indication as to whether or not it was safe.

The tangle of weeds and nettles determined his pace. He could not run. His first twig snapped in half. He had held it too tight. He had to stop and forage around for another. He found one, not much thicker than the last, gathered three more and bound them together with crisp blades of grass.

When he drew close to the mill, he crouched low in the grass. He swallowed the lump of fear lodged in his throat and stared into the undergrowth. Listening. Watching. He felt a tugging in his forehead and rubbed it fiercely with the heel of his hand. He thought he glimpsed a dim light in one of the windows, but it was only the light of the moons.

He charged toward the mill. When he reached it, he snapped his twigs in half and pushed them through a jagged hole in one of the blackened windowpanes. Once he was satisfied, there was nothing sinister inside, he pushed the mill doors open.

A draught swept in from the roof. The mice and Ticket Shrews that had made their home in the nooks and crannies began to stir. Outside an owl hooted.

A broken narrow stairwell led all the way up to the top of the tower, where a rusty brake wheel was a few windstorms off from becoming detached from its wooden shaft. An old sack-hoist rope hung down through an open trap. An assortment of cogs, hubs, timber and corn sacks, littered the floor.

Someone had been here. They had left a single oil lamp burning on the floor. He squatted near the lamp and warmed his hands on what little heat it generated. The timber walls creaked and sighed around him.

If he couldn't find Luke in Undren, then he would go to the next village and look for him there. He would search for him in the Bleak desert if he had to.

'Folly,' said the Authoritative Voice. 'Stay here for a while, where it's safe and warm.'

The Authoritative Voice was talking nonsense. The Old Getty was neither safe nor warm.

Connor threw down his bag and yawned. He was going to fall asleep if he wasn't careful. He stood up, grabbing hold of a frayed rope dangling above his head. He thought about the world he had left behind and the life that went with it. He had a simple life in a modest home and his mum and brother took good care of him. Now he had messed it all up.

He gave the rope a tug. It spiralled to the ground. He leapt out of its way. In amongst the coiled bundle of rope was a furry flat creature with wings. The creature slowly started to turn around; its eyes half-closed. It looked like the same creature he had glimpsed in the fortress. Connor didn't like the looks of it. It was bigger than a rat, bigger than a bat. It had a grey ugly mouth and spooky grey eyes. The creature scurried over to a broken stone slab and disappeared beneath it. Connor followed it. He wondered what other creatures were lurking in the floors and walls. He noticed a piece of splintered wood sticking out from under the stone slab where the ugly creature lay hidden. He kicked it with his foot. The stone slab broke in two and a stream of light rose from between the two halves. Connor knelt down and dragged the stone slabs to one side. He had uncovered a trap door complete with a rusty bolt, which crumbled at his touch.

He lifted the trap door. It grated on worn hinges. He wiped his brow and peered in. He thought he could smell the ocean. There were steps, steep ones. He saw no rails to cling to, no walls to break his fall. It had to be a portal leading to another city or village. He had uncovered a few portals when he had played the game. Sometimes they were disguised as ordinary doors, but when you went through them, you were instantly catapulted into new territory.

A scratching noise rose from outside. Light pierced the cracks in the mill doors. Someone was coming!

Connor scrambled madly to put out the oil lamp. He retrieved his bag and swung it over his shoulder. A faint trace of tar and salt-water wafted to the surface. He swallowed, fighting to keep a clear head. He had found a way out just in time.

He lowered himself through the trap door, settling on

the third step. He closed the trap door over his head. As he did so, he heard the clamour of guards smashing their way through the doors.

He was on his fourth step when he slipped and fell. He tasted soil and copper on his tongue. He felt as if someone was pelting his skull with rocks.

'No one can teleport between worlds, not even the Gifted Ones,' he heard Amelia say.

Little dots of green and yellow light flitted before Connor's eyes. Saliva oozed from the corner of his mouth. He could do nothing to stop it. He cried out under his breath and sank into the darkness.

Chapter 33

The noise sounded like a hundred steel blades being dragged across stone. If he could just get up, out of the way...

The door to the Crocksford Arms had slammed shut the instant Skelos had entered. The entrance had evaporated. He should have known from the bars at the windows and the blob of red paint smeared upon the door that the place was out of bounds. Full of danger. What appeared to be a tavern on the outside was, in fact, a muddy brown cave lit with a wall of luminous rock. Its floor was coated with sand.

He had run around for ten minutes, clawing at the rock face, frantically looking for a place to hide. There was none.

The boy had tricked him. There was no time for curses or plans of vengeance. Citizens couldn't fly, but they could jump up to thirty feet in the air. Two elegant strides in one attempt should have been enough to cement him securely to the upper surface of any structure.

He stuffed as much of his belongings as he could into a leather pouch, which he tied around his waist. The roof of the cave rose some twenty feet above him. No specialist equipment was needed to assist his jumping, from the wall to the cave roof, unsupported within a matter of seconds. So why wasn't it happening?

His first defiant leap was pathetically low and lacking in co-ordination. With each attempt, and there were many, he found himself dropping from the cave roof, spinning like a dead fly. He had already set down the Avu'lore globe, not only for safekeeping; its weight was sure to drag him down.

But what about your own weight?

He descended from his sixteenth attempt, panting loudly. He had hoped he'd feel something more than a sense of dizziness and dread. His weight was not the problem, he swiftly concluded. There were probably some enchantments cast about the place, draining him of his strength.

A deafening screech rattled through the cave, sending him into a fresh state of panic. His eyes skittered from one wall to the next. He wiped the sand-streaked perspiration from his face, rose twelve foot in the air and came crashing down, breaking his fall with his hands.

He was concentrating too hard that was the problem. He cracked his knuckles, counted to three, drew a deep breath and closed his eyes. He then leapt forward with all the brute force he could muster, tucked his legs into his chest and somersaulted, extending his body as he drew close to the roof. He spun around rather gracefully in mid-air, given his bulk, his robes twirling. He crossed his arms over his chest and flung them out at the crucial moment. He landed with his back pressed to the ceiling and his heaving chest pointing to the ground.

The Bolt-Shot whip crashed to the ground, its gems glittering in the sand. The sand rippled like silk caught in the wind and a writhing mass of heads, bodies, tails, and limbs materialised from it.

Skelos squeezed his eyes shut.

The writhing mass scattered and decelerated.

Hundreds of creatures the size of otters, sniffed at the ground, seeming to whisper to each other in low watery breaths, 'I smell Citizen.' The hair on their bodies rippled with the colours of the rainbow. Lean and long, their low bellies swept over the cave floor. They had six short legs and moved along on high-arched claws. Each had six silver tails, which thrashed and hissed wildly with every scurrying movement they made.

He opened one eye and then the other. He would have to jump. Fight his way out. But what was he going to fight with? His wits?

Several of the creatures gathered at the foot of the illuminated wall. Rising on their hind legs, they used their claws to dig out sizeable chunks of the stone, which they took between their teeth. He saw one had clambered onto a narrow ledge close by. It stared up at him with its six violet eyes. It bared its razor-sharp teeth. A quiver coursed through the creature's tail, sending out an ear-splitting hiss that bounced off the cave walls. The other Silver Tails inclined their heads, cast their eyes to the roof and then without warning, leapt against the wall in a maddened frenzy, coming together as they rose.

Skelos was appalled to discover the creatures almost matched him in speed. He soared onto the ledge, kicking at them. They tumbled down, biting at the air with teeth like iron. They hooked their claws into the ones below them to break their fall. Streams of violet blood ran from their shimmering coats.

The Six Tails turned on one another, biting, and clawing, hissing and thrashing. The sight of disarray caught

Skelos off guard. In a shot, one leapt onto his shoulder, dug its claws into his neck and pierced his skin with its teeth. He reeled in horror as it proceeded to launch itself at his head while another clambered onto his back. He screamed, struggling maniacally to tear them off. Their claws ripped into his hands. There was nothing else for it; he shielded his eyes and jumped.

The Silver Tails rushed down after him. He smashed the tails and claws that came hurtling towards him, sunk his boots into their bellies at every obtainable chance he could get. He vaulted through the air, spinning, and twisting like an acrobat, while more of the creatures emerged.

He saw the Bolt-Shot whip jutting up from the sand. He tried to call it with the power of his mind. To his infuriation, nothing happened. He hastened towards the whip. He almost had it within his grasp, when a pack of Silver Tails went trampling over it. He leaped in among the pack, booting them out of the way, determined to retrieve the only credible weapon he had. He swung his fist into the head of one of the creatures, sending it howling into the cave wall.

He wrenched the weapon from one of the creature's jaws. He attempted to activate it with his voice. 'Expand!' he cried. 'Open!'

The Bolt-Shot whip did neither. Was it that he had spent too long in Narrigh? *Or is this The Maker's Will?*

The Silver Tails were getting ready to pounce again. He resorted to the device hidden partway up his arm: the Compulog. He put the device to his lips. 'Holographic image.' The Compulog screen lit up. *At last. For a moment there, I thought I had lost my touch.*

'Which image are you requesting?' said a male voice.

'I don't know – anything!' A large enough image was sure to cause a distraction. The creatures were stupid enough to take the bait.

An image of a boy appeared on the screen. 'Grow!' he shouted into the device. 'Expand!' A miniature hologram of the boy materialised from the Compulog memory bank, a pathetic transparent hologram, the size of his little finger. 'What good is that?'

Two of the Silver Tails were trying to bite off the tips of his boots. Another had sunk its teeth into his leg. If he wasn't careful, the Silver Tails would have bitten and scratched him to pieces before he could expand the image to arm's length.

'Expand!' he said again. The holographic boy doubled in height. 'Request, fill vertical space. Request solid!'

He battled his way to a mantel of rock, launched himself from it and shot back up to the roof. 'Request, fill vertical space. Request solid, request solid!'

The Compulog grew hot. Skelos wrenched the device from his arm and sent it spinning through the air before it burned off his limb. A non-transparent image of a Citizen filled the cave. He knew the Citizen by name: Vastra. He was dressed in a long-sleeved silver tunic. Plates of armour were trussed to his legs and upper body. With his arms folded and his gaze steady, he looked striking and menacing even in the tiniest of images.

The image held fast for ten seconds. It was enough. The Silver Tails shrieked in distress at the sight of the 'giant man'. They dashed for the safety of their rotting limestone tunnel, their hissing tails flailing madly behind them. Skelos watched them stream over the bodies of the dead and dying, trailing blood that was more vibrant in colour than his own. He jumped down and retrieved the Compulog and the Avu'lore globe from behind the rock where he had hidden it.

The cave darkened quite suddenly, and Skelos looked up to see that the luminous rock had disappeared and in its place was a fresh tunnel. The mouth of the tunnel opened like the jaws of some great beast: jagged and deadly. He had opened a portal. Was it too soon to jump for joy?

'And where do you lead, I wonder?'

He shuffled to the tunnel entrance, his boots crunching on the sand. He went a little way in, rested his foot on a pinnacle of rock and sniffed the air. He smelt sand, salt-water, and something rotten. With his keen vision, he made out some malformed shapes further along the tunnel. The Compulog gave Skelos a yellow flashlight, which he shone directly onto the limestone-coated walls of the tunnel. The light then proceeded to bounce to the roof, where water and minerals had crystallised to form stalagmite drapes that compressed the tunnel's height by some fifteen feet. From there, the light travelled like a fast train across a ground littered with decaying carcasses, embedded in a thick, muddy residue. Stalagmites sprung from rock beds like church spires, obscuring the tunnel's length and trimming its width.

A hissing noise drifted eerily through the cave.

Without a second thought, Skelos bolted through the tunnel.

Chapter 34

Connor opened his eyes to a white mist. As his sight began to clear, he found himself gazing at a white ceiling. An orb of light shone down from it. It was a very faint light. The surrounding walls were dark and streaked with shade.

He lay in a large, canopied bed covered with a flannel sheet. A heavy tapestry bedspread had been cast over him, like a net. He had been stripped down to his underwear. His hair and his skin smelt of mint and honey.

He twisted his head and saw a man sitting on a chair not two paces away from him. He had a short-cropped beard and a head of rippling black and silvery-blue streaked hair. His prominent sideburns were silver.

Connor drew himself up on his elbows with effort, fighting against the weight of the bedspread and the groggy feeling in his head. He heard vague noises coming from outside his room, unidentifiable noises. Where was he? Not in his bedroom, he was certain of that.

He sat upright and stared around the room. It had a great bell-shaped window. Someone had shut the blue drapes, so he couldn't tell if it was night or day.

A crystal jug, filled to the brim with water, sat on the bedside table. A solid white wardrobe stood at the opposite end of the bed. Next to the wardrobe was an elongated piece of cushioned furniture he could not name. It was too small to be a bed and too comfortable looking to be a chair.

His gaze shifted back to the man who sat stiffly with one gloved hand perched on a glossy cane. He wore woollen trousers and a shirt unbuttoned at the neck. His eyes were different shades of blue: one a pale crystal blue, the other a dark sapphire blue. The man fixed him with his pale blue eye. The pupil expanded and contracted quite independently of the sapphire-blue eye, which appeared to be looking across the room.

Connor coughed soundlessly. 'Where am I?' he croaked.

'Baruch. Safe within the Royal Halls,' said the man. 'The Undren guards found you collapsed on the cellar steps of the old Undren mill. They brought you here.' He poured some water from the jug into a glass and offered it to Connor.

The man's voice sounded familiar, but not his face. You couldn't forget that sort of face – or those eyes. Connor gulped down the water offered him. It cleared the gritty feeling in his throat. The water was slightly sweet. It tickled the roof of his mouth on its way down. 'I thought I came through a portal.'

The man gave a wide grin, his sapphire-coloured pupil contracting. 'Better for you that you hadn't. Very few lead anywhere delightful.' He reached across the bed and took the glass from him.

Connor sank back onto the pillow. He was not sure he cared for the man's weird eyes or his over-generous smile. 'Who are you?'

'They call me The Maker.'

'The Maker?' Connor gave a long yawn and smacked his lips together. 'The maker of what?'

'This.' The man made an arc, in the air, with his head and cane.

Connor's eyes traced the arc to the orb on the ceiling, mesmerised. He could have sworn it was getting bigger. 'Let me guess, you're going to help me get home to Odisiris. I bet you can take me there right now; except I don't want to go. I'm going to look for my brother, and when I find him, we're going to our real home in London. You can't stop us.'

He yawned and sunk further into the pillow. His head felt like stone. His right hand felt heavier than his left. He tried to lift it and failed. He was as floppy as a pancake. He gazed at the jug of water and back at the man with the mismatched eyes. 'What did you put in the water?'

'A special brew to restore your Status Mark. It is the key to your abilities, your strength. You want to finish the game, don't you?'

Connor wasn't sure he cared about his abilities anymore. And this wasn't a game. It was real. His eyelids fluttered shut. 'I ran away.' It made sense now. He ran away and then forgot that's what he had done. Well, he had learned his lesson.

'Your quest is almost complete,' said the Authoritative Voice.

The strange man left the room, closing the door quietly behind him.

It wasn't long before sleep and dreams overpowered Connor once more.

Chapter 35

There are one hundred and ten portals in Narrigh. But you will not find them on any map. Those who stumble upon these concealed gateways, harbour the notion that they will be spirited to a better place than the one they left behind. For those who enter, there is no turning back...

When Skelos came to the end of the tunnel he was presented with three doors. This was something he had never seen before. *Unless I am hallucinating.*

It was Elf magic. He was certain of it. The cedar wood, dome-shaped doors were set the same distance apart. They had no keyholes or doorknobs. He had a momentary vision of pushing one open and finding nothing on the other side but a fathomless drop. One of the doors was sure to lead to the land of Theria and he couldn't abide the light-footed creatures with their flowers and glittery potions. A door with a drop seemed a more satisfactory option.

He could not deny that a few potions and magical items would have served him better than a Bolt-Shot whip and the Avu'lore. Hindsight was a gloriously, sickening thing. He could not open a magical door with the Avu'lore, nor could he do it with his mind. He had taken a handful of Barnabas's keys. They were worthless without a lock to slot them in. He could do with the Old Rogue himself. He was sure to know how to deal with dilemmas such as these.

He put his ear up to the first door. There was no sound on the other side. He knocked. No answer. *If these doors are portals, I should simply be able to walk through them.*

'Oh, what's the use.' He took out the Bolt-Shot whip. *Oh, how beautiful you are.* Diamonds and colourful gemstones were arranged in petals around the top of the barrel. Beneath the beguiling pattern, sat two thin gold bars on opposing sides. He nudged one with his finger. It rose. He pushed it up as far as it would go, precisely ninety degrees. He did the same with the other bar. With both bars raised, the Bolt-Shot whip, resembled a fat, blunt sword. *Novel.* He let the Lashes fly upon the door. They didn't leave so much as a mark. The Bolt-Shot went back into his belt. Sighing, he tried the next door along, this time pushing his weighty bulk against it. The door held fast. He went to the third and final door, and shouted, 'I command you to open.' His own cries echoed back to him.

A noise reverberated through the tunnel, which sounded like somewhere between a hum and a gurgle. He jumped, his hand went to his belt. *Is it the Silver Tails again? Are they back?* He listened for their hisses. He looked back the way he had come. There was nothing – no one.

His gaze drifted to the roof of the tunnel. Suspended above him was a smooth disc the size of a cartwheel. He almost snapped his neck in half trying to get a look at it. It was the same colour as the walls: muddy brown. It didn't seem to be attached to anything. He rubbed his chin thoughtfully. If he weren't in Narrigh, he would have sworn it was a miniature Upsilon spacecraft.

He plucked a flat stone from the ground and threw it at the disc. The disc quivered for about three seconds and then stopped.

He looked back at the doors. The door he had knocked on was open. The door itself had gone. It revealed another tunnel a straight one, very different from the one he had left behind. It was dry for a start and there appeared to be nothing sinister about it: no hidden nooks or crannies, no mist rising from the murk. The walls were even and intact. The ground was scattered with stones. Nevertheless, there was no signpost saying where the tunnel led.

The humming and gurgling noise sneaked up on him, followed by another sloshing sound. He looked down. The outer tunnel had started to fill up with water. *I could die here in this tunnel, and no one would ever know.* He hurried through the open door. *But I'd know.*

He had not been walking more than five minutes when he saw clusters of multi-sized discs moving across the roof in ultra-slow motion. They were dark brown, the same colour as the tunnel itself, but their texture was smooth and almost glossy in appearance. If he closed his eyes a crack, the clusters looked like eggs, hundreds and thousands of alien eggs waiting to hatch and invade his body. He gave a nervous giggle. *How absurd! I'm not in the Andromeda Galaxy now...or am I?*

The ground felt like warm gooey cement. His eyes bulged in horror as he watched the discs float up from the tunnel floor and drift to the walls either side of him. The tunnel was breaking up.

He broke into a run. Adrenaline pumped inside him

as he concentrated on what was ahead of him: bend after bend of winding tunnel. One of the discs smacked the side of his head. He batted it away with his hand. Large brown spots flew in front of his eyes. He felt a thump on his back and another on his shoulder, and then one on his leg. He flung his arm out in front of his face and continued to run. A sharp pain seared through his hand. *There is no way I'm going to make it out alive.*

He never envisaged having a slow, painful death. He always thought it would be unexpected, swift, and at a time when he had attained glory, not when he was on the verge of discovering it. He peered over the top of his arm. Through squinted eyes, he saw the flat stones whizzing through the air. A black dot in the distance told him the tunnel was as never ending as the last one he had come through. If the ground kept breaking up and shifting, he was never going to get anywhere.

The faster he ran, the faster the discs moved. How had he not noticed it before? He stopped quite abruptly. The discs started to float away from him, drifting slowly back to the walls and the roof. Keeping his eyes on them, Skelos took a small step. The discs froze. He took another small step. They tilted in his direction. He took another. They stirred.

All he had to do was concentrate. His eyes were roaming all over the place. He tripped over his feet, kicking his left foot with the heel of his right. A sharp stinging pain shot through his leg. He rubbed his ankle. It sprouted a lump. It was no bother, for soon the lump would be gone and the pain along with it. When he looked up, he saw the tunnel was widening. It was as if an invisible hand was stretching it open.

'How long have I been walking?' It felt like days. Realistically, it was probably no more than an hour. To his relief, the ground was beginning to dry up, but it soon became evident that the tunnel only appeared to be widening. The floor of the tunnel was narrowing. The walls grew further away from him, eventually falling away altogether.

Skelos halted. He looked down.

At least the ground was still intact. He was standing on a bridge, a ruby-coloured, and rocky from-here-to-eternity bridge. He caught his breath. Not bad. No fire and brimstone. No six-tailed beasts. No soul-sucking spirits, just rocks, sharp spear-pointed rocks about a hundred feet or so below him. He looked behind him. The tunnel he had come through had disappeared. All that remained of it were thousands, upon thousands of muddy-brown discs.

He stretched out his arms and inspected the sheer drop either side of him. The bridge was narrow. *I shall edge along it as if it were a tightrope.* With a slight hobble, he proceeded to walk along the 'tightrope'. He willed three things to happen: for the bridge to miraculously widen, for the drop to shrink by eighty-eight feet and finally for his insides to stop flapping. His arms were throbbing. His head ached from trying to concentrate on taking painstakingly small steps. The harder he concentrated, the more convinced he became that he was going to fall. Not even a Citizen could survive a drop that far. There were limitations to a Citizens ability to self-heal. He would need to be conscious at the time of impact in order for his body to mend itself.

He came to a gap in the bridge. It was no more than eight feet. Easy. He leapt over it, landing softly on the other side. He walked another thirty paces and came to another gap. This one was about ten feet. He leaped across. He landed on the other side, inches from the drop. His landing was still smooth, his confidence unbroken. He saw more breaks in the bridge ahead of him, and at the end of them, a tunnel. He bounded across each gap, each one bigger than the last. They seemed to spring out of nowhere like the Silver Tails in the Crocksford Arms. It was as if the bridge was testing him.

After successfully jumping eight gaps, he came upon one long, yawning gap. In the distance, he could see the mouth of a tunnel. He would have to take a run up to make this one. A fast run and a leap. A fast run would—

He glanced over his shoulder. He could see the muddy brown discs floating back and forth. He imagined that the moment he started to run the rest of the bridge would also start to break up. He shrugged the thoughts out of his mind and slowly walked backwards, his ample calves still burning from all the running he had done previously. He got underway, quickly picking up speed. Brown and ruby discs darted from right and left. Fistfuls of rock zoomed away from the bridge and plummeted into the gorge. His heart gave a jolt. The ground broke up beneath him and he felt himself falling fast. He lunged forward desperate to feel the ground underneath him. To his despair, he didn't feel anything. *My death came swift and unexpected after all, but without the glory.*

Chapter 36

Connor snapped awake, recalling the loss of memory, the stabbing, throbbing, burning headaches; the voice he sometimes heard inside his head, too harsh to be his own, the Authoritative Voice, belonging to the person who had invaded his mind. The one who called himself The Maker.

He had no idea how long he been asleep only that he felt different. He padded across the room and opened the wardrobe door. He caught his reflection in the long oval mirror hanging from the inside of it. He penetrated the depths of the dark brooding eyes staring back at him. He poked at the bones sticking out of his chest. He pressed his fingers gently to his neck and brought them over his face. He then stared at the palm of his right hand. The Mark was there. The italic *I* for indigo: First Status Citizen, and he no longer feared it.

The pain in his head had gone. His strength had returned, and he found his thoughts, his memories, were less jumbled in his head as they had once been.

Inside the world of Narrigh, he *was* a Citizen.

In the wardrobe, he found a long-sleeved black tunic, overlaid with plates of polished steel and a pair of padded black trousers with steel shin plates. His old clothes gone, he put the new ones on. They were a good fit. The fabric clung to him like a second skin. The steel plates concealed his gaunt frame. After he had dressed, he crossed the room to the bell-shaped window and drew back the drapes. Light poured in through the lattice panes. He threw one of the windows open and looked out.

There was a building opposite made from white stone, its high windows edged in gold leaf. He couldn't see the top of it. It soared into the sky.

He saw a white gravelled courtyard below, doused in sunlight. In the centre of the courtyard was a marble fountain, spilling water into a bowl shaped like a flower. Dotted around the fountain were stone benches. They were also people milling around the courtyard, richly dressed in velvet, silk, and wool.

A young woman in a flowing embroidered gown waved to him. He jerked away from the window, ducking behind the drapes, wishing he had left them closed. He turned to see his grubby boots sticking out from under the bed. His tattered bag was right next to them. He was relieved to see them. The soles of the boots were crumbling. There was a dent in one and a big hole in the other. They were caked in dirt and smelt rotten, but he put them on all the same.

He took up his bag. It was heavy and made jingling, clanging sounds. When he put the bag on the bed, it started to move. Connor jumped up from the bed and sped across the room. The ugly creature he had seen in the Old Getty mill poked its head out, wrinkling its nose up and sniffing the bed. It must have crawled inside his bag when he lay unconscious on the mill steps.

'Shoo.' He flapped his hand. He glanced around the room, looking for something he could throw or poke it with. 'Shoo. Go away!'

The creature spread its wings a little. He walked

around the bed, keeping his eyes on it the whole time. He opened the door. The creature was still partly inside his bag. If he could tip it out gently, grab the bag and run. He leaned forward and tugged at the bottom of the bag. Instead of leaving it, the creature started to shuffle deeper inside.

He took a ragged breath. There was nothing for him to be afraid of, not really. He was a Citizen, a warrior, not Connor the Coward. He sat on the edge of the bed and tried once more to coax the creature out. It padded towards him and licked his hand with a long sticky tongue. It tickled. He succeeded in pulling the bag away from the creature. He then set the creature on his lap. It squawked like a baby bird. 'You're not scary at all, are you?'

He eagerly tipped the bag's contents onto the bed. He saw the Shard. He slipped it inside his boot for safe keeping. And there was his Worral Stone, which he dropped into his trouser pocket. He counted three slow-burners and twenty-one gold coins. There was also an apple, a slice of cheese, half a loaf of bread wrapped in paper, strips of dried meat, a folded parchment and a full flask. The Maker must have put them, Connor concluded, or one of the servants. A place as grand as this was bound to have servants.

He unfolded the parchment and found it was a detailed map of Narrigh, showing all eight regions. A smaller piece of paper fell from within the folds of the map. It was crumpled and covered in black smudge marks. He straightened the paper out. It was a short-handwritten message:

Connor,

**I heard you were here. I asked one of the guards to get
this message to you. Come to the dungeons. Ask for
Thurden. Hurry.**

Yate

Connor heard shouting from the courtyard below. He
raced to the window. The young woman who had waved
at him had gone. A pair of armoured guards raced into
the building and out of sight, another four disappeared
into the building opposite. One bellowed, 'Get them to
the wall!'

Something terrible was going on down there.
Something he didn't want to be a part of. But he had to
go. The Sentinel needed his help, and he didn't want to
give up the search for his brother. He could always come
back later. He returned to the bed, gathered up all his
provisions and returned them to his bag. The ugly, winged
creature sat on the bed dolefully watching him. 'Okay, you
can come too, but don't blame me if you get squashed.'
He opened the flap of the bag and the creature crawled
inside.

He strapped the bag across his chest and stole out of
the door.

He padded along a carpeted corridor. Its walls were
decorated with blue and silver floral motifs. Two
enormous black crystal chandeliers, pinned to gold leaf
medallions, hung from the ceiling.

He stalked past an infinite number of closed doors

until he came to a flight of stairs leading off from the landing. At the bottom of the stairs was a set of black lacquered doors.

Connor took a deep breath. He shot down the stairs and pushed the doors open. He hadn't run away. Someone had kidnapped him. Was it The Maker? Was it The Spy? Was it the Silver Rider with the cold green eyes? He didn't know who and he didn't know why, but he was going to find out.

Chapter 37

Skelos had no idea of the amount of pain one might experience if they plummeted hundreds of feet onto rocky ground. *Perhaps there is no pain and the end comes swiftly.*

He didn't feel any pain. He didn't even feel himself land. One minute he was falling, the next he was sitting. *Where?* He vigorously rubbed his eyes to recapture his focus. He was sitting on a bed of withered leaves, peering out of a cage. A small, frail-looking boy stood on the other side. His hair was the same colour as the rust-coloured walls surrounding him.

Above him, he heard the sounds of the ocean. He looked up. He could make out the spiralling tunnel entrance above his head. There was another noise resounding in his ears: the patter of footsteps on stone.

This is quite the predicament. Citizen and boy stared at each other for a long time.

The boy wore a shirt that was far too big for him and a pair of trousers with the legs cut away at the knee. On his feet were a pair of dripping wet, brown sandals.

'What are you doing here?' said the boy. He scratched his head. His timid eyes veered off, staring at something Skelos couldn't see.

'And where is here?' There was no need to panic just yet. Skelos rose unsteadily to his feet, patting down his robes, fixing his bag across his shoulder. The cage bars were made of wood. His Bolt-Shot whip would cut right through them. His hand went to his belt. Yes, he still had it.

This was a side of Narrigh he had not experienced. He knew its history and he knew plenty about regional customs, but he had not studied Narrigh's magic. Moreover, he had no idea how the portals worked or where they led.

The boy did not reply. He stared at him blankly. *Is he too stupid to understand the question?* 'What's your name child?'

'Teffin.'

Skelos pressed his face up against the bars. 'What's your other name?'

'I haven't one. I'm just Teffin.'

The boy's gaze wandered off again. Skelos had the feeling the boy was not responsible for the cage, and it wasn't the first time a visitor had dropped onto the bed of leaves. 'Well, Teffin, would you mind letting me out.'

The boy frowned. 'I don't know that I should.'

Skelos conjured up a smile. 'I'm perfectly harmless.'

'You're wearing a sorcerer's cloak.'

'Oh,' said Skelos. He threw off the cloak and then gave the cage bars a light shake. 'You see, perfectly safe.'

'Stop that!' Teffin picked up a long stick from the floor, slid it through the bars and jabbed him hard in the shoulder. 'You stay where you are. My mistress is coming.'

Skelos took out his Bolt-Shot whip. He released the Lashes and let them do their work. They turned the front of the cage to ashes. He calmly stepped out. He tucked the Bolt-Shot inside his robes, out of sight.

Teffin's funnel-shaped jaw dropped open. Skelos's jaw did likewise when he saw a billow of red smoke rising about Teffin's ears. The smoke drifted in front of the boy's eyes.

'What is this?' He didn't like surprises and he had no appreciation for sorcery.

The red smoke thickened around Teffin engulfing his small frame.

'Stop it!' Skelos shrieked. He jumped up and down, fanning the engulfing smoke with his hands. His eyes were watering, his throat burned, and worse he couldn't see. He put his hands out in front of him and shuffled to where he thought he had seen a doorway. He felt someone poke him in the back and spun around in alarm. The smoke evaporated almost instantly and Skelos saw a woman standing in front of him. At first, he thought the woman was Teffin, until he saw the boy standing up against the wall, his eyes as big as dinner plates. Skelos recognised her as the woman he had seen watching him, from her seat by the window, in the Verity Tavern. She had long white hair and bright amber eyes. She wore a pair of puffy trousers, tucked into a pair of long boots, a loose shirt, and a short jacket. Around her neck was a metal choker.

'And who are you?' he asked.

'Worack Veros,' she said in a soft voice. 'And I believe you are Skelos Dorm.'

Skelos's heart quickened to hear his own name declared before him. He tried to see over her shoulder. There was a panelled-arched door behind her. He would destroy her if he had to. The Shardner knew him by name; outside of the Shardner his name was unknown, his indiscretions a secret. He wondered where the exit would take him. He didn't want to face another precarious bridge, just yet.

'There's little point, thinking about escaping. The Shardner and the Baruchian army are all around us. I believe the Shardner would very much like to speak with you.'

He stared at her, then at the dreary pitted walls. There were no windows. Teffin was sitting on the floor. He was studying a book filled with bizarre symbols and illustrations. 'Where am I?'

'In the Kingdom.'

He gave a small gulp. He gazed at the cage from which he had broken free. He couldn't believe he was back where he started, that his freedom had come to such a ludicrous end.

Worack bared a mouthful of milky white teeth. 'It's a one-way portal I'm afraid.'

He had options. He could bribe her or use the Avu'lore. His eyes narrowed. 'Do you serve the Shardner or yourself?'

'I serve myself through the Shardner. Now come with me.'

'Do I have a choice?'

'No, not really.'

She went through the door, leaving Teffin to his book. With wary intrigue, Skelos followed.

There were ten guards waiting outside to accompany them. Worack Veros guided him down a stone passageway with adjoining corridors veering off in numerous directions. One by one, the guards fell away, ingested by the ominous passageways until, out of the original ten guards, only two remained.

'You're fortunate,' she said. 'Few who come through the portal survive.' She pivoted on her heels, flashed him a smile, and then pivoted sharply away again.

'I hardly think myself fortunate,' he commented.

She halted outside a set of iron doors and flicked a switch on the wall. The doors grated open to reveal a lift, no more than eight feet high and six feet wide, lit with a small oil lamp. She stepped inside. Skelos and the guards bundled in after her. She pulled a lever on the inside wall. The doors closed and the lift slowly began to ascend.

The sweat rose on the nape of Skelos's neck as he caught sight of an oil-smeared Bolt-Shot whip, swinging lazily from the belt of the tallest guard. The light cut across the guard's lower jaw, the only part of his face not encased in metal, and Skelos saw that his lips were fixed in a sneer. *I could crush that sneer if I wanted to by disarming him of his weapon.* He would wait for the opportune moment, earmark his escape routes, and gage his enemies.

He had bought everything of worth with him on this wretched journey, his stone, the Avu'lore, the Compulog, the painting. If any of these items were to be discovered in his possession, then his life of confinement would be torture, his chances of escaping Narrigh minuscule.

'Where are you taking me? I've done nothing wrong.' Technically, this wasn't true, but how was she to know? The Shardner may have presumed him dead, kidnapped or simply lost in the underground maze.

'You're not here as a prisoner Sir Dorm, you are here as my guest.'

It was the first time anyone had addressed him in such a manner. He didn't know whether to be flattered or appalled. In Pareus, his colleagues addressed him as 'Doctor Skelos', his friends 'Skelos' and those who didn't know him, 'Elder Citizen.'

'You're not a Citizen, are you?'

She pulled back one side of her hair, exposing a pointed ear. 'No, I'm not a Citizen.'

A Therin Elf, he should have known. Although he had to admit, she didn't look the type to beguile him with harp music and flowery potions before subjecting him to the Shardner's wrath. *They can't kill me. They need me*, he reminded himself. Only he didn't need them.

The lift shuddered to a halt. The doors opened out onto a stone-pillared balcony, which overlooked a monumental suite. He gazed at the four Black Crystal chandeliers, hanging from the ceiling, and took a deep intake of breath. The icicle-shaped crystals, forged from glass and Velvet Opals, were seldom seen in any but the most opulent of First Status Citizens homes. The chandeliers were exorbitantly overpriced for two reasons; firstly because they were crafted by humanoids, not droids. Secondly, the Velvet Opals were rare gems that could only be extracted from one of three mines located on the planet Kaltharine, forty-light-years away from Odisiris.

'Make yourself comfortable,' said Worack. She trotted down the steps leading off from one side of the balcony.

Skelos took the other flight of steps, which delivered him to the limestone floor below where he found himself alone.

The light given off by the four Black Crystal chandeliers was not strong, and the fire cast a warm glow across the partially shadowed chamber. There were no prints on the wall, no harps, no mirrors, and no windows. He couldn't see any scratches or smudges of any kind upon the floor or the furniture. And there was no dust.

The suite was furnished with two leather couches, several armchairs and a concoction of glass and marble tables. All the furniture seemed to point at the suite's centrepiece: an enormous fireplace in the shape of a pyramid.

He deposited himself on the chair furthest away from the fireplace, afraid that if he got too close, the warmth would make him drowsy and thus vulnerable.

It was a simulated fire, exquisite in its simplicity. Its inventor had directed light onto a translucent cover so it appeared as if there was a blaze of red and yellow bursting from a stone-carved log. The fire gave a short hiss in the ensuing silence.

Skelos had hardly made himself comfortable when he heard the light patter of footsteps and turned to see a young girl running towards him, her arms outstretched.

'Uncle!' she cried.

Skelos shot out of his chair. 'Amelia!' He held the girl at arm's length before she could envelope him in an embrace. 'Where have you been?'

'I'm sorry, uncle.' Her arms dropped to her side. Her shoulders slumped. The incandescence light fell onto her tiny face and the giant silver bow in her hair. She wore a silver dress, shoes, and matching gloves. She held a silver purse in her hand. 'I wanted to find you, but The Maker summoned me.'

'The Maker summoned you. What are you talking about? Not even I can summon you, and trust me if I knew a way to do it, I would.' He stared around the room, his eyes bulging, and his stomach in knots.

'You know The Maker, uncle. You talk of him all the time.'

He clenched his jaw and his fists. 'As a turn of phrase.' He stooped, putting his face level with hers. 'Is that what they told you to say?'

'Who told me what to say?'

'Are we being watched?'

'I don't think so. Lady Veros is really kind. She gave me this dress.' She gave a twirl and a courtesy. 'Isn't it lovely?'

He gave her a withered look. 'Yes, for a five-year-old. Now drop the act. Do you have the Shard?'

'What's a Shard?'

Oh, that's right, I didn't tell her about it. 'That piece of glass I gave you when we were in my old laboratory, before those men came. The one I told you to keep for me. Where is it?'

'I don't have it, uncle. The Shardner's Special Army found me in Bluewood Forest. They asked me all sorts of questions. I was afraid they were going to cut me into pieces, so I hid it.'

'And where exactly did you hide it?'

She straightened her giant bow. 'In a bag.'

He seized her by the shoulders. Her eyes stayed fixed on his. She didn't shrink away. 'What bag?'

He could tolerate her fixation with childish dresses and her vacant expression as long as he had her loyalty. She was usually so obedient. *Perhaps, the Narrigh air is causing what's left of her brain to seize up.*

'I met this Citizen boy, called Connor, in Bluewood Forest. I put it in his bag. We travelled North together. I meant to get it back from him before he discovered it. I didn't know we were going to get split up.'

'Wait.' He took a breath. He walked around in circles, rubbing his forehead. 'Are you telling me that you were with Connor in the North?'

'Yes, uncle.'

So, Connor had the Shard, which was why he ran. He had been a fool to let the boy go off on his own. 'What I don't understand is why you left the Kingdom in the first place? And don't you dare tell me The Maker told you to.'

'I panicked. I couldn't help it. I didn't know where you were, if I'd ever see you again. When the Shardner's Special Army found me in the forest, I told them I was lost. They didn't believe me.'

'I'm not surprised. I wouldn't have believed you either. Can you not use your head? As soon as we landed in Narrigh you should have found an excuse to see me. Haven't I taught you how to produce fake tears? How to push out your bottom lip so you look sad? You should have made it a priority to get the Shard directly to me or hide it somewhere safe within the Kingdom, not drop it into some unsuspecting Citizen's bag hundreds of miles away.'

She nodded. 'Sorry, uncle. I wasn't thinking.'

'Unless you were helping the boy. Is that what you were doing? Helping him?'

'No uncle. My loyalty lies with you. I haven't betrayed you to anyone.'

'And how did you end up here? More panic, was it?' He circled Amelia, scratching his beard while considering the quickest way to return to Undren. With any luck, the boy would still be there, and Duffy and his merry band would be halfway to gypsy town.

'The Sighraith Band brought me back here after I got lost in one of their horrid tunnels. I got away from them though. I think the Kingdom is the best place for us, uncle. It's clean, warm and the Citizens here are normal. They won't jab at your hand with a knife or pretend to come from a whole other world. When I..▯'

So, the rumors were true. The Sighraith Band did exist. 'Stop your whittling. Where is the Sighraith Band now?'

'Fighting I expect. The Furnace faction is going to help them seize some land.'

I could do with a diversion. Although, I'll need to ensure no one kills me in the process. 'Were there Citizens among them? A girl and two young men?'

She shrugged, her bow bobbing about on her head. 'I'm not sure. There was an older Citizen called Yate. I didn't pay much attention to anyone else.'

'You should have!' He glared at her. 'If you're going to skip out of the Kingdom, the least you can do is find out what's going on outside its walls and report back to me, not play fancy dress in a Therin Elf's palace.'

'But this isn't a Therin Elf's palace, uncle.'

He jerked his head up, surveying the Black Crystal chandeliers. He cast his eyes to the fireplace. How could he have been so stupid? 'Which Citizen dwelling is this?' he hissed.

Amelia smiled. 'Osaphar's.'

He felt the blood rush to his head. He had not spoken to Osaphar since he was condemned to exile and the first time, he had laid eyes on him, since his arrival in Narrigh, was in Undren church. The thought of confronting his former friend made him feel faint. Sick. The humiliation would be too great. He couldn't cope with it. He wasn't ready. *He'll turn me over to the Shardner Council in a heartbeat.*

Amelia opened her purse. She took out a glass vial and handed it to him.

'What's this?'

Her smile was still fixed on her face. *Is she giving me poison? Does she mean for me to take my own life?*

'An Invisibility Potion. There's not much left. You could get some more from the Guild Vaults before Osaphar returns.'

He gave her a hug. 'You know there are times, Amelia, when I wish you really were my niece.'

'And you, my uncle.' She pointed to a set of grey doors. 'Go this way.'

He drank the tasteless potion. He observed the rapid transparency of clothes and flesh, preceding his concealment, with increasing disquiet. He was relieved to discover he didn't feel any different.

Worack returned carrying a tray set with two glasses and a slender bottle filled with a rich dark liquid. She appeared to stare directly at the spot where Skelos stood.

He was breathing loud enough to wake the dead. *What if she can't see me, but she can hear me with her big elf ears?*

'I wondered where you'd gone,' Worack told Amelia. 'And where's our guest?'

'There was no one else here,' she replied. 'Just me and my shadow.'

She ran to the grey doors, pulling them open. Skelos took the opportunity to make his exit at lightning-speed.

Shame, he could have done with a drink.

Chapter 38

Compared to the Kingdom of Baruch, Undren village was the picture of tranquility. In Undren, the streets were busy, here Connor found them manic.

The inhabitants of the Kingdom yelled and screamed in a host of different languages. Everyone was popping up in the wrong place. A gaggle of geese had succeeded in upsetting one of the market stalls. People dashed into the roads. Horse-drawn carriages mounted the pavements.

Eight streets converged into the city square. In its centre, the Shardner had erected a gold statue of the last King and Queen of Baruch. At their feet, sat twelve stone statues that represented the highest serving members of the Shardner government.

Connor was cutting across the city square, gawking at a man with a rope of onions around his neck as he chased a lurid yellow donkey, when he bumped into a woman in a boat-shaped apron. She dropped the basket of fruit she was carrying and pointed to the sky where an obnoxious black cloud was forming, drowning out the sun. 'We're under attack!'

Connor stooped to collect the scattered peaches, oranges, and apples. He carelessly tossed the fruit into the basket and followed the woman's finger with his eyes. It looked as if another windstorm was on its way.

'Be gone with you!' said the woman. 'You're getting more fruit out than in.'

'Sorry.' He looked down. Most of the fruit he had

collected had missed the basket. He had managed to smash a solitary peach on his boot. The stray fruit had rolled under the feet of dashing passers-by and under the wheels of carriages and wagons that rumbled past.

He knew he wasn't going to find the dungeons in the middle of the city square, so he headed for the outskirts where all the flies and nasty smells seemed to congregate behind a thick stone wall with a single archway.

Set within the archway was an iron door. At the top of the door was a grate. Through the grate, Connor saw the top of a guard's helmet as he sauntered past.

He was about to shout up to get the guard's attention when the door burst open and two prison guards came running out, swords in hand, gaping up at the sky. Connor sneaked through the door. Another guard immediately apprehended him.

'I need to speak with the Warden,' he said at once, struggling in the guard's iron-grip. 'It's urgent.' He didn't have a plan. He had gold. He hoped it was all he needed.

The guard's pocked face tightened in a frown.

'It's important,' said Connor. 'It's about the attack.'

The guard released him. 'Go then,' he said, ushering him towards the Warden's hut. 'Hurry!'

Connor sprinted to the Warden's iron hut. The Warden himself emerged looking miserable. His square face was set on a boulder of a neck and his fat belly was bursting out of his shirt. His teeth were set like an ivory block in his huge gaping mouth. A bunch of keys hung from the belt of his soiled trousers.

'No children!' he said, catching sight of Connor. 'No children, no children, no children!'

'I can pay you,' said Connor. 'I have gold.'

The Warden's eyes went wide and then as narrow as a nail. He looked Connor up and down. 'Why are you dressed in those clothes?'

'I'm from the theatre.' There were theatres all over Narrigh. The costumes worn for such productions looked nothing like the clothing he had on, but Connor had a feeling that the Warden didn't go to many theatres.

The Warden rolled his tongue around inside his mouth. *He doesn't believe me,* thought Connor, but he's thinking about the gold. The guard who had detained him at the door was standing by the hut, polishing the hilt of his sword. It was obvious he was eavesdropping.

'And who is it you have come to see?'

'Thurden. I was told to ask for Thurden.'

'Thurden?' said the Warden. He disappeared into his iron hut, slamming the door behind him.

Connor sensed the guard's eyes boring into him. As he turned to look, the guard went back to polishing his sword. Connor suddenly remembered the Plowmen: the half-ogres, half-humans with fangs, who possessed the power to absorb players' abilities. If there were none outside the dungeons, they would all be inside, ready to tap him with their feathery touch. You couldn't hear them coming. He would need to be vigilant.

The Warden didn't seem particularly bothered about what was going on outside his dungeons. So far, the chaos had worked to Connor's advantage. However, he didn't want his luck to run out and the Warden was taking too long. He rapped on the door, glancing across at the guard who had returned to the dungeon gate drawn by the whinnying of a horse on the other side.

When Connor got no reply, he pushed the door open and went inside.

Bowed shelves, piled with dog-eared parchment, lined the walls of the Warden's hut. At the end of the shelves, keys hung from metal hooks.

Connor found the Warden flicking through the sheaves of paper in his hand. 'Here we are,' he said, teasing out a single sheet of parchment and tossing the rest back onto a shelf. 'Thurden, Darque Goblin, brought in this morning and due for execution tomorrow at noon.'

'A Darque Goblin. Are you sure?' Connor didn't remember seeing any Darque Goblins among the Sighraith Band. Had they taken Yate hostage?

'I got it written right here,' said the Warden, waving the sheet of parchment in front of Connor too quickly for him to read. 'It's been a while since we've had a Darque Goblin cross over the barrier. Of course, he was sure to say he didn't cross over the barrier, that he didn't mean us any harm and that he only came to deliver a message, and blah de blah. You hear all that noise outside? That'll be the Baruchian soldiers readying themselves for more goblin invaders, I'll warrant. So, what do you want with him?'

'One of my friends is in trouble. I think Thurden might know where he is.'

'I see.' The Warden nodded. He put the sheet of paper on his desk. 'I'll want fifteen pieces of gold to let you go down.'

'Fifteen!' Connor spluttered.

The Warden pressed his fist to his chin. 'And not a

gold piece less.'

Connor handed the gold over to the Warden. That left him with only six gold coins. If Thurden asked for a ransom in return for Yate, then he would be in trouble.

The Warden counted the coins twice. After he had locked the money in a box on the top of his desk, he took a key from one of the shelf hooks and shouted for a guard.

One of the guards who had passed Connor, to see what was happening beyond the dungeon walls, reappeared. He had a thick white beard and pinholes for eyes.

'What's going on out there?' the Warden asked the guard.

'Don't know,' the guard replied, breathless. He had returned without his sword. Sweat poured from under his helmet onto his face. 'No one knows. Some say a storm is on its way. Others say, more Darque Goblins.'

'As long as they don't come running in here,' said the Warden, handing him the key. 'Take the boy down to the dungeons. Cell three hundred and sixty-three. Level four. Bring up five Plowmen when you're done. Just in case.'

Connor followed the guard down the rough-hewn steps leading to the dungeons.

Candles burned in sconces on the walls. Ragged shadows crept up the walls and then slunk out of sight. Connor heard the wails, grunts, and growls of humans and beasts. He kept close to the guard, hoping to use him as a shield should the Plowmen appear. He would be lost without his abilities.

The guard mistook his caution for terror. 'You've nothing to fear. They can't get out.'

The guard led him along a passageway packed with

cells on both sides. Several of the cells were nothing but iron boxes with hatches. The rest were cages with vertical steel bars. He noticed a long arm sticking out of a hatch, green and covered in boils. A bald, skinny man with hollow cheeks, poked his head through the bars of his cell. He stuck out a yellow tongue.

Connor sighted a dwarf in a blue waistcoat guzzling from a tin cup.

A Drone Elf with a broken wing and crooked antennae threw itself against the cell bars. Connor jumped and collided with the guard's back.

'Okay, calm down boy,' said the guard. 'Here.' He unlocked a cell door, two cells along from the Drone Elf.

Connor saw the Darque Goblin hunched in the corner next to a tin bucket. Its skin was pale and blotchy. Like all Darque Goblins, this one had bat-like ears, clawed hands, and feet, and a tuft of dark hair on its head. Stripped of its armour, it wore an old vest and trousers. It glanced at Connor, its violet eyes gleaming.

'You came,' said the goblin struggling to its feet.

Connor stepped hesitantly into the cell. The guard locked the door after him. 'Five minutes,' he told him.

The goblin was higher than his waist. It wrapped its arms around Connor's leg. 'You don't know how glad I am to see you.'

Connor pulled the goblin from his leg and then reeled away from it in disgust. He didn't want the thing to touch him. Its features alone were enough to give him sleepless nights. He crouched low enough to match the goblin's height. 'I got a message from Yate to meet you here. Is he okay? Where is he?'

Thurden stabbed at his chest. 'You're looking at him.'

Connor stared at the Darque Goblin's mouthful of pointy teeth in confusion and disbelief.

'I changed myself into a Darque Goblin and I can't change back until the Plowman's Touch wears off.'

Connor blinked and shook his head. 'Right,' he said. 'You're a shape-shifter. What do you need me to do?'

'I need you to get me out of here.'

'I don't know how to get myself out of here,' said Connor, a little louder than he intended. He momentarily drew the guard's gaze.

The guard who had escorted him had his back to them. He was watching the Dwarf in the cell opposite, who appeared to have a cactus plant growing out of his head. He had his foot stuck in his tin cup and was busy trying to get it out. The guard snorted with laughter.

Yate stared at the plate of armour Connor wore. 'I see you've got yourself some Citizen armour and a new pet.'

'I don't have a pet.' Connor thought he smelt burning but saw no smoke.

'So, what are you doing with a Kherrin Mawk inside your bag?'

Connor looked down to see the creature's head sticking out from his bag. So that's what it was. He pushed it back in, ignoring its squawks of distress. 'It's a stowaway.'

He heard someone shouting up ahead and watched the guard stalk off along the passage in search of the source. He had used his ability once before to remove the Dal-Carrion in the fortress. He had used the keyhole-of-light then. What if he could do the same thing to the cell bars? He studied them for a while, trying to imagine they were no longer there. He closed his eyes.

'What are you doing?' asked Yate.

'I'm going to try to use my ability.' He saw a blue halo. Vertical lines ran through it. The lines in the halo represented the bars of the cell. He took a deep breath and then let the weight of his mind bear down upon the lines and they gradually melted away. Blue light flooded his vision, bathing him. He felt warm, weightless.

He opened his eyes. The cell bars were still there. He frowned. Why wasn't it working? 'I don't think it works on solid objects.'

Yate rolled his eyes. 'Why don't you just use your armour? It's an energy weapon. It should emit enough shockwaves to blast us out of here.'

Connor stared at his chest. In *The Quest of Narrigh* game, armour could be used as a weapon, if it was enchanted. Shockwaves had nothing to do with enchantments.

Yate scurried over to the back wall and covered his ears. 'Inflate your lungs with a deep breath. Hold it for five seconds. Should be enough.'

Connor gazed at the cell bars again. He covered his ears too. He took the deepest breath he could muster and held it for one, two, three…'

His chest grew warm and started to throb. A pulsating, transparent cone emerged from his breastplate. He heard a loud crack. The blast was so powerful it ripped apart the bars in Yate's cell and in the one opposite, tearing the head off the cactus plant on top of the caged dwarf's head. The blast threw Connor into the back wall. He groaned, staggering to his feet. He could still feel the heat in his chest.

'Next time, you want to let your body go limp,' said Yate, one claw on his wrist. 'Slump forward, that way, you'll stay on your feet. Come.'

They clambered over the stone and metal debris. They made their way back along the passage. Connor could smell a grisly blend of burning flesh and straw. He could feel the smoke in his lungs, the searing heat on his skin. He heard screaming above and below him. Frantic prisoners rattled their cell bars and hammered on their cage doors.

Connor and Yate ran up the stairs, weaving through the horde of raging, stomping guards.

'The dungeons on fire!' yelled a man wearing nothing but a pair of tattered shorts. 'The North are attacking!' He careered into the chest of a Plowman coming up the stairs behind them.

As they continued their ascent Connor's eyes began to sting.

They plunged into a plume of black smoke, through a narrow doorway and up another flight of stairs. The stairs seemed to disintegrate beneath them. He struggled to see where he was going. He didn't complain when Yate, the goblin, clambered onto his back; he was featherlight.

He floundered along a series of branching passages, where cell doors hung open and deserted. He raced to the end of one passage and met a wall of raging fire. He reeled and stumbled at the sight of the lunging flames, and then he was back on his feet and away again. He careered down another passage and came to a stop on a balcony.

He saw that the balconies ran around the inner

perimeter of each level. A series of steep stairs, acting as diagonal bridges, linked each level to the one above it. Three guards, two levels down, flung themselves over the balcony engulfed in flames. Their screams were snuffed out when they hit the stony ground below.

Drone Elves were responsible for setting the fires. Connor observed them darting back and forth between levels, shooting red fireballs from their hands.

He sprinted to the foot of the diagonal staircase and started up it. Some of the steps caved in as his feet touched them, forcing him to leap across yawning rifts of stone. He reached the top of the stairs. He was only one level down from the dungeon entrance.

He didn't feel as if he was running anymore, he felt as though he were flying.

Not before long, he had reached the Warden's hut. It stood open and empty.

Guards and prisoners poured out of the dungeon door. Connor joined them, careful to avoid the Plowmen pressing amongst the throng.

He broke away from the dungeon and the crowds and ran towards the city square.

He had almost forgotten about the creature clinging to his back until Yate shouted in his ear. 'I guess you figured out by now that negotiations with the Shardner have broken down. We are at war.'

Chapter 39

The Guild Vaults in the Kingdom of Baruch are grander than all the vaults in Narrigh. The marble tiled floors are trimmed with gold motifs. A myriad of hand-blown glass lamps dangle from a vaulted ceiling, decorated with mosaic tiles.

At one end of a sloping corridor, flanked with gilded marble columns, is a gold statue of the last King: Kalgar. The bearded King sits upon his gold throne. He holds a rolled parchment in one hand and a goblet in the other. He smiles down at his Queen: Irentha, carved into the central board of the three-panel door leading to the vault rooms, where Guild membership is imperative...

Skelos liked being invisible. It was an ability no Citizen possessed. He could return to the Royal Halls, fetch Amelia and spy on Osaphar whilst there. He could sit on the Shardner's Council, and no one would be any the wiser. The Avu'lore and invisibility would be the underpinnings of his power. His name would be legend, his power absolute.

He made his way down the steep corridor, clawing his way along the marble columns. He may have been invisible, but he quickly learned that he could bump into things, and once more, things could easily bump into him, including Plowmen.

When Skelos entered the Vaults, he didn't see any Plowmen or guards. Something was very much amiss.

Cracks had appeared in the vault walls and on the roof, cracks that were certainly not there before. People were scurrying up and down the slope, laden with items they had taken from the vaults: bottles of potions, bulging sacks, armour, swords, daggers, axes, and more.

Skelos went through the three-panel door. A Baruchian guard came ambling out of the Theria Elves vault room with a cluster of tiny green and red bottles in his hands. Skelos plucked a green bottle from the guard without him noticing.

He smiled to himself and then frowned when he spotted the Guild Master. The sleeves of his obligatory red tunic peeped out from behind the panel door. There was another man speaking with him: tall, skin the colour of mahogany wood. He wore gloves and an oilskin tunic. He carried a Lightning sword in his hand.

Vastra! Skelos blundered backwards, forgetting for a moment that he was invisible. What was the Citizen doing here? *Is there a warrant out for my arrest?* If there weren't, he would have been insulted. He composed himself and marched up to Vastra. He came to a halt directly behind the Citizen.

'I need your help to obtain some items,' Vastra was demanding of the Guild Master, 'a summoning enchantment, an Invisibility Potion, one combat shield, and a□'

The Guild Master dabbed his mouth with his sleeve. Skelos noticed he wasn't wearing any shoes. 'And what is the name of your guild?'

A silly question. Citizens had their own guilds in Odisiris. They held none in Narrigh.

Vastra tapped his foot impatiently. 'I'm not in one. Just get me what I need.'

The Guild Master began to move out from behind the door. A green fire-bolt shot past his ear and he quickly retreated behind it again. Skelos joined him. He looked about for the assailant but saw no one.

The stray fire-bolt did not faze Vastra. He locked his gaze on the Guild Master.

'Am I correct in thinking that you want me to help you take items from a vault where you have no membership?' The Guild Master stared at the sword in Vastra's gloved hand.

'I am following the Shardner's orders.' He waved a piece of paper in front of the Guild Master's squinted eyes.

'I can't help you,' said the Guild Master. 'The Plowmen have been called to defend the city from the Northern attack. Meanwhile, the Vaults are left unguarded. Everyone is clearing out. All the vaults are open. Feel free to browse. Now, if you'll excuse me.'

The Guild Master slipped out from behind the door. Vastra grabbed the Guild Master's elbow before he could scamper away. 'Not so fast.'

Northern attack! Vaults unguarded? Skelos knew which served him best. He hastened to the first vault. It had a sign on the door, which read, 'Storm Faction Vault One'.

The floors of the vaults were divided into squares of wood and cobbled stone. There were still items hovering above the shelves: armour, clothing, weapons and an assortment of multi-coloured stones. Each item was surrounded by a yellow cube, a protective shield that could only be broken by Guild members with the authority of the Guild Master. *No wonder Vastra requires the Guild Master's help. He won't get it with the Guild Master dead.*

Skelos swiftly moved on to the next vault belonging to the Blade faction. Again, he found plenty of items, but no way to get at them. He tried the Bolt-Shot whip. The Lashes juddered to a stop the second they made contact with the protective shields that enveloped the prized items.

'This is useless.' Invisibility wouldn't solve his problem. Magic was required to break through the protective shields. He didn't have time to search all the vault rooms, never mind join a Guild. He thought about going after Vastra. *No doubt, he will have acquired the Guild Master's help by now. I could jump straight in, take what I need and run.*

Skelos was heading for the door when a translucent figure sprung from a shadowy corner of the vault room. The figure belonged to one of the Traceless.

'Can I offer you my assistance?' A voice purred in his ear.

Skelos froze. '*What part of me is visible?*' was his first thought. He held up his arms and looked at the floor. He saw nothing between. No robes. No feet, solid or transparent. 'You can see me.'

'No, but I know you're there and that you're not one of us. Are you ugly in appearance? Or perhaps you have an ugly character. Are you after a potion? I can get you one if you'd like.'

'I can find my own potion.' He was hopelessly optimistic. All the potions, bottles were unlabelled. You had to rely on someone else to tell you what was in them, or simply take a risk and drink.

'We help you. You help us.'

The door swung shut. Skelos tried to push it open. It held fast. There was no door handle or visible key. This was a terrible idea. *But it wasn't my idea, was it? It was my traitor niece. She had me believe that she was trying to help me, when all along, she was trying to get rid of me. But to what end?*

'I only help myself,' said Skelos. 'I'm not in the habit of making deals with non-human entities. My soul is not for sale.'

The Traceless faded from view. Skelos did not move. There was little point. The Traceless would only follow him and taunt him until it got its way.

'Did I say I wanted your soul?' said the Traceless. 'We require something of far more value than that.'

Far more value? He wondered if they knew about the Avu'lore if they could see it. *If they take it, then I have nothing.* He focused on one of the cubes. Inside it was a breastplate, etched with gilded flowers. He hoped that if he stared at it hard enough, the cube would break or the Traceless One would go away. No such miracles occurred. He would have to strike some kind of deal with the Traceless, even if it were a lie. 'Name your price.'

'The Map of the Other Worlds. It can transport you to any world at any point in time you desire.'

Map of the Other Worlds. *What nonsense!* 'Did no one tell you? It doesn't exist, not in this world or any other.'

'We have heard whispers of beings who have arrived here from Other Worlds. Last night, we heard whispers of a map that will lead us there.'

'Whispers from whom? The local gossips on the market? I don't have time to indulge in myths and fairytales. I need to leave the Kingdom, post-haste. You will have to find the map yourself.' He slammed his fist down on the cube of armour. *If all else fails.*

'It resides in a place we cannot enter.'

Skelos had always believed that the Traceless could get into anywhere in Narrigh. Evidently, he was wrong. 'And what place is that?'

'Callawly Castle.'

The mention of Callawly Castle made Skelos's skin prickle. What was it about that old ruin? 'The map resides within Callawly Castle. Where?'

'It's hidden within a painting; hidden by the one they call The Maker. An invisible dome has been cast upon the castle to prevent anyone from entering. We have never come across such a powerful enchantment. The spell can only be broken by a mortal being.'

Could they be talking about my painting? If the Traceless couldn't break through the dome, then it would have been created with science, not magic. He assumed it was a magnetic force-field, designed to repel anything that tried to cross its path. Skelos didn't need spells to break through the force-field. But that wasn't the issue.

He couldn't afford distractions. He had to put Callawly Castle, Osaphar, and Amelia out of his mind and concentrate on finding the final Shard. *And the last Shard is within my grasp, I can sense it. I'm not about to let it slip through my fingers again. How would the Traceless ever find me? They don't know what I look like. They don't even know my name. Furthermore, the Traceless think The Maker is real, which means I would truly be wasting my time.*

'I'll do it, but you have to understand, I work alone. I know the castle and the safest way to get there is underground. I'll need more Invisibility Potion, lots more and a Summoning Spell.'

'Very well. You have one hour.'

One hour. Is that all? It wasn't a lot of time, if he really intended to go. 'Yes, yes. Just give me what I need and open the wretched door.'

'If you break your word, Skelos Dorm, we will find you and we will take your soul.'

Chapter 40

The Kingdom of Baruch was on fire.

Drone Elves circled the sky, hurling fireballs. They shot through open windows and doors, sending the buildings occupants spilling into the streets. Flames licked the walls. The buildings splintered and cracked.

Connor hadn't seen one Darque Goblin the whole time he had been in the Great Northern Crater, and he had only met one of the Gamnod people. Now there seemed to be thousands of them.

Guards on horses charged at an army of Gamnod soldiers dressed in slate-grey armour. A screaming throng of Baruchians scattered to clear a path. He couldn't see where they had left to run, when all around them was chaos. Noises rang in his ears: whizzing and whooshing sounds, thudding hooves, stomping feet, clashing steel, running water.

A horde of Darque Goblins in mail, set about smashing up the marketplace, sending trestle tables and benches toppling over. The fine wares of cloth and leather were trailed through the white sand. Fruit and vegetables were mashed to a pulp.

Yate, the goblin, jumped down from Connor's back and together they ran for cover, diving under a fallen wagon. Two young boys, pushing a wheelbarrow, were in the process of filching the last of the wagon's grain.

A Drone Elf landed with a thump close to the wagon, its blue wings broken. It vanished in a flash of white light.

'My thanks,' said Yate, his goblin eyes shining. He crawled closer to Connor 'I couldn't be more indebted to you. I would have recruited you to our cause, if I'd known you were going to be such a formidable player, unlike that Citizen girl. The Worral Stone belongs to you. You're a Dream Emissary. Don't deny it. You were going to remove the cage bars with your mind.'

Connor suddenly felt a surge of importance. He had a real super-power. He bet no one else had an ability as unique as his. 'I don't think it works on real objects. I mean, I don't know how it works. When I close my eyes, I can see a keyhole-of-light and when I go through the keyhole, I can push things away with my mind.'

'Interesting.' He nodded at Connor's chest. 'And that's a fine piece of armour. Looks good on you. Where did you get it?'

Conner ran his hand over one of his puny biceps. He had rescued Yate from the dungeons. He was practically a super-hero.

'A super-hero? Get a grip,' said the Authoritative Voice.

Connor stopped feeling up his bicep. 'Erm...I found it in the Royal Halls. I think The Maker left it for me.'

Yate smiled and put his finger to his nose. 'I get it. Your secret. Your business. Do you think you can get any more?'

'No.'

Yate was regarding him with an enthusiasm that was beginning to make him feel ill at ease. He presumed that once he had rescued the Sentinel, he would be free to look for his brother and find his way home. At one point, he had deliberated asking Yate to help him. It was becoming apparent the Sentinel considered him to be somewhat of an asset to the Sighraith Band. If he wasn't careful, the man would drag him into battle and take his armour for himself. He wouldn't be much of a super-hero then.

He heard a thud and an ear-splitting crack above him. Something had fallen on top of the wagon. The vehicle groaned under its weight. He pushed himself up on his elbows. 'I have to find my brother.'

'You have a brother here in Narrigh? Is he gifted too?'

'I don't know.' He shuffled away from Yate on his elbows. He was annoyed with himself for telling Yate about the keyhole-of-light, particularly when he didn't understand it. He had to remind himself that he was only a Citizen in a game, outside of it he was an ordinary boy.

Yate started to move out from behind the wagon. Connor yanked his scrawny arm. 'Wait? Where are you going?'

'I got the Plowman's Touch. I'm going to find a Goblin Magi to heal me. It won't take long. I'm a Darque Goblin, remember? If I die I can be resurrected, but you can't so stay here. If you see trouble coming, use your armour. I'll be back, then we'll go look for your brother.' He ran out from under the wagon.

'Where have I had that before?' He clung to the wagon's large back wheel, contemplating his next move. He couldn't sit around waiting for Yate to return. He would return to the Royal Halls and ask The Maker for help.

A group of Darque Goblins were trying to bring down

a Rogghorn by lassoing it with ropes. One jumped on his back and immediately fell off. Another found itself squashed under the Rogghorn's tail.

Connor watched Yate run towards the goblins. A purple aura shot from a Drone Elf's hand, blasting him in the chest. He fell straight on his back.

'Yate!' Connor scrambled out from under the wagon, his bag swinging from his hand.

A Drone Elf went through Yate's pockets. When it was satisfied, they were empty, it took to the air and Yate, the goblin, evaporated in a ring of white smoke.

Connor saw his chance to flee. The Darque Goblins had managed to get the Rogghorn under control and were not paying him any attention.

He skirted around a warrior, who was tearing at the wings of a Drone Elf to stop it making off with his sword. He ducked under the arm of a man wielding a giant axe dripping with blood.

Enemies came charging at him: Drone Elves, Darque Goblins, Gamnod warriors, and some scruffily dressed people that he thought might be members of the Sighraith Band. He used his armour to blast a path through them, sending them scattering and dropping like lumps of wood.

Dark clouds roiled across the sky, merging with the fiery red smoke. Most of the Drone Elves had landed within the city and were fully engaged in battle.

Connor knew he wasn't far away from the Royal Halls. He could see its golden turrets in the distance, shrouded in a black fog. The problem was there were so many obstacles preventing him from getting there. The battle raged in the square. Many of the side streets and alleys that branched from it were quiet. To the east, further out of the city, stood a single stone tower. He thought if he climbed it, he might be able to navigate a safer route to the Royal Halls.

The world seemed to darken further. Connor felt the raindrops on his head. They spattered his armour. He saw a smear of black clouds. He stared at the wriggling 'raindrops' on his chest. A chill went down his spine. They weren't raindrops. They were maggots. Maggots and rushing water!

One of the buildings on the opposite side of the street exploded in a blaze of blue light, blowing out the windows. The debris showered the road. Connor ran into a doorway for cover. He found the door locked. He sunk to his knees and wrenched open his bag to check if the Kherrin Mawk was okay. One of its eyes had rolled into the back of its head and its tongue was lolling. He thought it might be kinder to let the creature go than bash it around in his bag. He set it on the ground. The Kherrin Mawk licked his boot. 'You've got wings. Why don't you fly?'

A shadow fell over him. Connor's heart lurched. His head snapped up. A tall Silver Rider blocked his path. He could see the colour of the Silver Rider's eyes through the slits in his helmet. They were green.

He leapt to his feet. He took a deep breath, preparing to use his armour and found himself crippled by a coughing fit. His armour failed to produce a shockwave.

When the last spluttering cough had died in his throat, he rushed at the Citizen like a charging bull. Osaphar caught his arms.

'Get off me! I'm not going back to Odisiris.' He shut his eyes, trying to search for the keyhole-of-light that might set him free, but there was no light, only dark. He couldn't focus. He tried to prise Osaphar's fingers from his waist. He bit, kicked and punched the Citizen, but Osaphar would not let him go.

'Let him go. You're scaring him,' said a voice more familiar to Connor than his own. His eyes flew open. He held his breath. He could hardly believe it. Standing behind Osaphar was his brother, Luke.

Chapter 41

The winged-beasts brought down races from both factions, trampling them with their claws and spearing them with their tusks and beaks. Some of the Dal-Carrion, carried off their prey, others tried to dig up the earth to bury them and found it dry and cracked. As they rapped their beaks on the ground, their terrified victims had ample time to escape.

One of the Dal-Carrion smashed into a burning roof and caught on fire. It dropped to the ground like stone, setting alight a cart stacked with barrels and the hair of a woman who was hidden amongst them. A Baruchian guard appeared with a bucket of water. He flung it over her. A Dal-Carrion then swooped down and snapped the guard up in his beak with the bucket still in his hand.

The Plowmen were on the loose, touching anything that moved, hindering the progress of all six races. Connor saw two Plowmen crushed under the weight of the winged-beasts as they thundered through the streets.

He held the Kherrin Mawk in his arms and watched the battle from the window of a tower situated close to the Bank of Pular. For the time being, he was safe. His brother had found him. However, his brother's behaviour had crushed any elation he had felt about going home. Luke was acting weird. He was wearing Citizen clothes and had two companions with him, an Eastern Asian looking-girl with long black hair, and a boy, not much older than his brother, with hair as thick as a lion's mane and a grim countenance. They had escorted him to the high tower and left him there, all alone. Luke had asked him if he was okay. That was all. And Luke didn't seem happy. He was stern, distant. Connor didn't like it. In fact, he had started to think that Luke might be an impostor; a shape-shifter like Yate.

He had no way of identifying Yate with all the Darque Goblins running around. Not all of them were wearing armour. Some had camouflaged themselves successfully. Others, in the panic and confusion, had made themselves more conspicuous. One of the goblins had turned bright green as it stood behind a white stone pillar.

How did he know Luke was really Luke? He looked like his brother (only he was skinnier), but he didn't act like his brother at all. Luke had told him to wait in the tower and Connor had obeyed. He hadn't attempted to leave. He was afraid that if he tried the door and it was locked, he would lose hope. He would be lost again.

He left the window and sat on a chair. There were two chairs in the cylindrical room, a feather bed and a table, under which sat an empty bucket.

'I'm a prisoner,' he told the Kherrin Mawk, stroking its back. He stared at the door, willing the doorknob to turn. How could his brother leave when they had only just found each other again?

He popped the creature back inside his bag and skulked over to the door. He reached for the door handle, his hand shaking. He was about to turn the doorknob when it started to turn by itself. He jerked his hand away and stumbled back.

The door opened and in walked Luke. He was dressed in a black vest and a pair of trousers cushioned at the knees. They were adorned with detachable pockets of different sizes. He wore a 'blank' watch on his wrist. He shut the door behind him.

'Going somewhere?'

'No.' Connor bowed his head in one sharp motion. He felt a tightness in his throat, a leaden feeling in his stomach. It now occurred to him that his brother's distant behaviour was nothing but controlled anger. Luke was furious with him for using his laptop without asking. The anger signs were there. Luke had dark lines under his eyes. His neck and head had sprouted inky blue veins and he had closed one of his hands to make a fist. He had put him in the tower so he could punish him when no one else was around.

Overcome with guilt and fear, Connor retreated to the chair, cradling his bag in his lap. He couldn't muster the courage to babble an apology. It would just sound weak. He hadn't just used his brother's laptop to play the game; he had stolen his passwords in order to access it. He spoke to his bag. 'How-how did you find me?'

He heard a screech on the stone floor. Luke had dragged up the other chair. He placed it in front of Connor and sat down. 'Connor look at me.'

Connor continued to stare at his bag, watching the Kherrin Mawk squirm inside it. A fat tear rolled down his cheek. This was all he needed, to have Luke seeing him cry like a baby. He tried to stutter an apology, but all he managed to do was spray his bag with saliva.

'Look at me.' Luke's voice was firm.

He raised his head and choked back a sob.

Luke wore a deep frown. He bit down on his lip and closed his eyes for a second as if fighting to form the appropriate words. 'I'm not mad at you.'

'You should be. I'm mad at me.'

He gave a long shaky sigh. 'How can I be mad at you? I haven't seen you in over a month. I thought you were dead.'

Connor sat bolt upright. A month was a long time if you were counting. 'Is mum okay? Is she with you?' He had a horrible vision of his mum staring out of the window, crying, and thinking the worst had happened.

'She's at home, waiting by the phone. She's not going to believe you're in an online role-playing game, is she? Riley had a hard enough time convincing me - and I play it.'

Connor brushed away his tears. 'What did he say?'

'He said you stayed up late playing the *Quest.* He fell asleep and when he woke up, he said you were being sucked into my laptop. The police thought he was on drugs and mum went ballistic. So, he changed his story and said he was half-asleep, and he didn't really know what he saw. All he knew was, you vanished without a trace. Things have been pretty hectic at home. The police wanted to take my laptop as evidence. I gave them my old one and played *The Quest of Narrigh* every chance I got, until one night it happened. I was here, in the Kingdom of Baruch. It was surreal. Crazy. I guess that's what happens if you play the game for too long, you end up in it. It's not the sort of thing you can talk about, know what I mean? Why's your bag moving?'

Connor lifted the flap of his bag and showed Luke the Kherrin Mawk. 'I was hoping I could keep it.' *Police or no police.* 'It doesn't make a lot of noise.'

The creature had closed its eyes. Its tongue hung from its mouth. Luke peered at it, grinning. 'It's not the cutest, is it? What if mum sees it? She'll freak.'

'She won't see it. I'll keep it in my room out of sight.' Connor lowered the bag flap. He drew his brother's right hand towards him. They shared the same Status Mark. He searched Luke's face. 'We are going back home to London, aren't we?'

Luke frowned. 'Where else would we go? We can't stay here. I've been in Baruch for over a week. Those people you saw me with are the ones who found me. I told them what had happened like a thousand times. I think I drove them nuts. They took me to the Shardner and introduced me to Osaphar. They said they were going to send out a search party to look for you, but they were taking too long about it, so I kind of organised one of my own. When I couldn't find you in Undren, I returned to Baruch. One of the guards told me, you'd been taken to the Royal Halls, but by the time I got there, you'd gone.' He stalked to the window, rubbing his temples. 'I just want us to get out of here. Osaphar reckons he can get us home. He knows we don't belong here.'

If we can trust him, thought Connor. 'What about the battle?'

Luke continued to stare out of the window. 'Looks like it's about to come to an end.'

Connor joined him at the window. He saw a great jagged crack in the smoke-filled sky. The edges of the crack were tinged purple. He was looking at the rift. Hundreds of silver birds appeared to descend from it.

'Those are Citizen spacecraft.' He pointed at the silver birds. 'They outnumber everything and everyone else.'

'Do you think there's a rift like this on Earth?'

'Let's hope not.' Luke tore his gaze away from the window. 'I'm going to speak with Osaphar and the others, find out when we can leave. Wait here.'

'Can't I come with you?'

'I can't risk you going missing again. I'll only be five minutes. You should get some rest.' He departed without closing the door after him.

Connor removed his armour and lay down on the bed, holding his bag to his chest. The Kherrin Mawk crawled out and licked his chin. 'He doesn't want to talk about it,' he told the creature. 'He wants to forget this ever happened. How can you forget?'

'By going to sleep,' said the Authoritative Voice.

He yawned. He supposed he could shut his eyes for five minutes. His eyelids fluttered shut. His head dropped to one side. His legs went as limp as seaweed. A shaft of narrow light broke through the tower window and evolved into a blaze of blue, orange, and yellow swirling colour beneath his closed lids. Shapes danced dart-quick before his eyes.

The World of Dreams beckoned him. The colours dazzled him, sucking him in. A blue light appeared. It transformed into a keyhole. Connor's eye became the 'key', flushing the blue away to reveal an unmarked dusty red road, the sides of which were shrouded in darkness. He used all his concentration to nudge it away. Like a canvas, being unveiled, it emerged first from the left and then from the right. He could not contain himself any longer, like a vessel on the verge of shattering, he could feel himself being dragged upward and onwards. His body was heavy at first, and then it became light, so light, he felt as if he were a speck of sand blowing in the wind, floating somewhere between exhilaration and despair.

Chapter 42

Hidden in the brush of the rocky hill, outside the western city wall, lies the Optic Crater. It is nothing more than a hole in the ground. The 'pupil' of the Optic Crater is a rough-edged boulder and its 'iris', gorges of skinny channels that run into its centre...

Skelos Dorm hoisted the boulder to unearth an underground passage, which delivered a strong draught. There were no stairs, only a meandering pitted slope coated in silt mud. He let the boulder drop off-centre as he climbed through the hole. He still required ventilation and light from the murky sky.

The passage, though wide, was steep and slippery. Tiny orange-green lizards dashed up and down the ramps. Skelos reached the end of the slope and hastened down a stone passageway. The ground became dry and even, and free of and dust.

He gave the cave a swift check. He was satisfied to find it inconspicuous and empty. The Invisibility Potion Amelia had given him had worn off, but he didn't need it here and he had plenty more.

So, the Traceless knew his name. He shrugged off any concerns he had about them stealing his soul. He wasn't sure he had one. With the Summoning Spell, he would bring the boy to him and take the Shard. He was a Citizen about to be reborn into an even greater one. He would have everyone under his control. There were other worlds to conquer, other Worlds where he could be both Ruling Chancellor and Emperor. He could hitch a ride on the next spacecraft to land. He would travel to Prascar, where the population was civilised and the air pleasant. From there, he would build his empire and unleash his power upon the entire galaxy.

The Traceless would be slow to realise they had been deceived. An hour wasn't enough time to travel to Callawly Castle in search of the 'Makers Map', but it was sufficient time to take what he needed for himself and escape.

The Summoning Spell required a vial of ground crystals and a few lines of ancient incantation. All very simple. The spell would allow him to summon one of his own race, only once. He was confident he could talk the young Citizen into handing the Shard over. The boy was scared and weak. However, he had to consider his options, just in case. He didn't want to hurt the boy, but if he had to resort underhanded means, he would. It was prudent that he was prepared, that there was no delay in obtaining the last Shard and putting it to work.

He quickly positioned the Avu'lore globe on a stone pedestal. Once the two Shards were in place, the Avu'lore started to glow. Skelos observed it, mesmerised. The colours wove and spun within the globe. They transformed the cave walls into a medley of vibrant streams and hues. The Maker had given him something more precious than he could have imagined. So what if he had stolen it from the one in the white robe? It was only right that he should have it, after the suffering he had endured at the hands of his so-called 'fellow Citizens'.

After the humiliation.

It irked him to know that he was leaving behind so many unanswered questions. He didn't like the idea of abandoning Amelia. She knew all his secrets. What if she succumbed to Osaphar's interrogation and blabbed? How many pretty dresses would it take for her to forget her master and seek a new one? And then there was the matter of the boy? What was he doing in Narrigh of all places? It was a mystery he would gladly like to have solved.

For the moment, his mind raced with a multitude of things that could go wrong if he waylaid his quest. What if there were beings whose minds he couldn't control? Ones that simply dropped dead before he could issue a command. There was also a battle raging above his head. Something or someone could kill him the second he popped his head above ground. Invisibility didn't make you invincible.

He supposed his timing could have been better. The prospect of going wherever he pleased excited him and the prospect of power excited him even more. *There will be no one to answer to and no consequences.* He refocused on the matter at hand, laid his hands gently on top of the Shards, and took a deep breath.

He became engrossed with watching the bright swirling colours within the Avu'lore. He felt a cold gust of wind at his back. He scratched his ear. He whipped his head around. There was no one there. He smiled and wiped his brow. The hour was not up. He would have a well-deserved nap on the flight to his new home. For now, he had to shake it off, stay focused.

He looked back at the Avu'lore. Odd? One of the Shards was missing. He frowned. Could it have fallen out or simply melted away?

He heard a loud screech coming from the upper surface. He cursed to himself. A lizard must have knocked it out. He scanned the cave floor. The ground was soft and yet he hadn't heard it drop. And if a lizard had taken it, he would have heard it, seen it. He heard another screech from outside the cave walls. 'Who are you?' he shouted. He rifled for his Binding Dust. 'If this is the Traceless, I'm working on it. I'm doing as you ask. We've got plenty of time.' *How would they know what I'm doing?*

He watched the second Shard fly from the slot in the Avu'lore globe and roll to the ground, reverting to its rod shape. The colours died and faded from the walls. Skelos dashed after the Shard. It rolled into a crack set between two rocks. He plucked it up and shoved in his pocket. Now where was the other one?

To his alarm, the Avu'lore globe began to roll across the pedestal. Skelos grabbed it in time. He hadn't tested its durability and had a nasty image of it smashing into the rock and exploding in a ball of yellow flame. He placed the globe inside his bag. He discovered the other Shard in the recess of the cave wall opposite him. He slipped it into his pocket and exhaled sharply.

Something stood on the hem of his robe. He screamed and shot upright. He was under attack. The unseen thing leapt onto his back. An unseen hand smothered his face.

'Stop this!' He screeched. The hand was hot and felt almost human. A knee went into his spine. He arched his back, trying to escape it.

'What are you doing, Skelos? I thought we had a deal.'

Skelos shook his head and tried to speak with his mind. 'You have me confused with someone else.'

'I don't think so. What is it you've got there?'

He should have known the power of the Avu'lore would be lost on the Traceless. They were soulless beings, whose minds often converged into one. *The Avu'lore won't let me control them. At least I won't be burdened with the added side effect of having them read my mind.*

He stood to attention. He was the one in control here, not them. 'You gave me one hour. When I'm finished going about my *own* personal business, I'll set about dealing with yours. I'm a Citizen of my word.'

'You think you have enough time to find all the paintings within the castle?'

'Certainly.'

'Not even with the Shardner's army on your tail? They're looking all over Baruch for you, like a pack of dogs in search of a wolf. You're a wanted Citizen, Dorm.'

'I should think so. If the Shardner are hunting me so relentlessly, perhaps you should get someone else to find your map, or better still cause a diversion to give me enough time to get away.' He peered up through the eye-shaped hole where the boulder had lain. A loud roar descended from the hole followed by a rush of air that made Skelos's hair stand on end and his robes swirl around his ankles.

'We made a deal, Skelos Dorm.' The Traceless hissed in his ear.

'Yes, and I shall honour it.' He hoisted his bag onto his

shoulder and was starting to scramble back up the slope, when a torrent of wind propelled him out of the Optic Crater into the sky.

The rift in the plane was apparent. It had become a huge vacuum, taking the world of Narrigh back to Odisiris with it. He saw humans, elves, dwarves and goblins soaring through the air, Dal-Carrion with prey in their mouths, Citizen spacecraft and Silver Riders.

He hugged his bag to him. He floated higher and higher. He saw fear etched in the faces of those closest to him. He watched them tumble away, gasping in terror. Screams and shouts thundered in his ears. He heard the rapid fire of weapons and crackling flames. He breathed in smoke.

He saw ghosts; ghosts of women, men and children hovering around him. They were dressed in long, flowing robes. They had silver hair and indigo and blue-tinged eyes. Their faces were set like stone.

He felt drawn to them. *I'm dead. Is this what death feels like?* It was beginning to make sense now. The Traceless had taken his body and his soul.

He made himself say it. 'I'm dead.'

'You're not dead,' said the ghost of a girl of no more than fourteen. She had slender limbs and a triangular-shaped face.

The rift was closing, slowly, but it was closing. The races of Narrigh started to drop. They plummeted to the ground, writhing and grasping at the empty air. Some were flung great distances, their screams reverberating through the turrets of smoke.

A number of the Citizen spacecraft had landed within

the city. Armoured Citizens came spilling out of the doors.

Skelos surveyed the blood streaming from the broken bodies of humans, dwarves, and goblins. Some vanished in a blaze of white light, while others remained. He shut his eyes. He was beginning to feel woozy. It wasn't the bodies or the blood-curdling screams that troubled his head. Something had invaded his body, something inherently terrifying. He could feel it nudging at his brain like a damp cloth. He felt it twisting like a rope inside his stomach, his chest, and his legs.

After some time, the medley of noises subsided. The air grew cooler. Skelos landed on his feet, still clutching his bag. He opened one eye, and then the other. He realised with some revulsion that his robes were hanging off him. He ran his hands over his face. It was thin, saggy and full of lines. His belt had slipped to his thighs. His hands were bony and pale. He was back in the Guild Vaults beyond the three-panel door, standing outside the Blade faction vault, looking in. The cube of armour was gone. The shelves emptied of every item. He glanced up and down the deserted corridor. A broken marble pillar lay behind him. It had created a small crater in the floor. Cracks ran from under it. The floor also had accumulated broken glass and shattered stone.

'What did you do?' he hissed at the room. His body trembled all over.

'We were going to take your soul, but then we changed our minds. The hour is not yet up, and I see you have another treasure that may be of use to us.'

'Well, you're not getting it. Do you honestly think I'd part with my soul and thus my freedom?'

'To be soulless is to be free. Imagine you will be like us. You won't have to concern yourself with food, sleep, clothes or death.'

'I like to concern myself with of all those things, thank you very much. And I preferred it when I had a lot more weight on me. I'll get you your map. I have something else I must do first. I just need more time.'

'How much time do you need?'

Skelos raised his hands. 'I don't know, a month at least, maybe two. You think this is going to be easy? Every race in Narrigh is above ground, not to mention a whole fleet of my own race. It takes careful planning, and planning takes patience. You're being unreasonable!'

'We already know that your treasure, the Avu'lore, permits you to control others. We were there when you were thinking about it. Tell us, is it only your mind we can read or others?'

'Only mine,' said Skelos. *Think of flowers, blue flowers, nothing but blue flowers.* 'And it is easily veiled. You won't learn anything from reading my thoughts. Only I have the power to control the Avu'lore. No one else. And I can't control it without a soul. Therefore, it is quite useless to you. You've asked a great task of me, and I'll need the time to deliver. We're wasting precious time already. Give me two months. If you don't hear from me in two months, you can have my soul or what's left of it.'

A mesh-covered face flickered into view for about an instant and then it was gone.

'We'll hold you to your word, Blue Flowers. One of our kind lies dormant within you. If you fail in this quest, you will become one of us.'

Chapter 43

Connor's eyes flew open. He had a sense of something being dragged out from underneath him. He was falling. Flying. Cold air whistled past his head. He felt the hairs rise on the back of his neck, felt his heartbeat quicken.

'Hurry!' said the Authoritative Voice.

Connor scrambled up, spinning around, searching for the Voice. Sweat leaked from his pores, tickling his skin. Had he travelled in his sleep-dreams? If so, why here?

He was standing on a desert-cratered floor, studded with rifts, pits, and bowls coated in a rusty orange powder. Light bled in through tiny holes above his head. His bag was on the ground beside him. He picked it up. It contained a few gold coins, the crumpled map of Narrigh and an apple. There was no sign of the Kherrin Mawk. He swung the bag over his shoulder and took a sharp breath. He scanned the great expanse of dust-filled depressions and the scars caused by the yawning fissures surging the length and breadth of the underground plane.

He jerked his head up, sniffing the air. He followed his nose a little way to his left where a matrix of ridges gave off a colourless steam.

He felt the heat. Some of it seemed to come from inside him, the rest emanated from the rock itself in low inconsistent waves. The smell that rose through his nostrils was not one of flame, but of the rusty grains beneath his feet, chalk, built-up residue, and deadly fumes.

He coursed along the rusty carpet, spurred on by a loathsome feeling of dread.

Someone had been spying on him and he did not attempt to hide from the one he pursued. In fact, he wanted them to see him.

The roar of fires deep within the crater pulsated in his ears. His skin prickled from the heat rising from the searing rock. Red lizards with bold yellow eyes exploded in his vision as he sped across the terrain like a Citizen possessed.

And he was gaining.

The Citizen he pursued was far older than he was, and though he moved like a whirlwind, he could not have hoped to outrun one so young.

Finally, the older Citizen dropped his pace, and then came to a stop beside a deep-pit-of-a-crater, raging with fire and brimstone. Panting heavily, the Citizen trailed a sweaty palm across his surly mouth. His neck and face were smeared with the orange dust. Sweat dripped from his straggly hair, oozed from his tangled beard.

He looked like a man who had lost a lot of weight too quickly, standing there in his voluminous purple and gold robes. Loose skin hung around his jaw and his neck was as scrawny and as wrinkled as a turtle. There was something about the way he moved. Hunched. Awkward. Sly.

'What an utter and pleasant surprise,' said the Citizen, forcing a smile to his chapped lips.

Connor sensed it wasn't surprise that made the Citizen's eyes widen, it was fear.

He stopped several paces away, watching him mindfully.

He needed to be on his guard. 'Did you summon me?'

The older Citizen gave a weighty sigh. The skin under his bloodshot eyes looked swollen from lack of sleep. His boots were practically hanging off his feet. And as he straightened up, his back creaked like an unoiled hinge. 'Why that's no way to greet a fellow Citizen now, is it? Skelos, House of Dorm.' He waved a soiled right hand. It was marked with the letter 'B'. He tottered on the balls of his feet, bridging the distance between them. 'I don't believe we've met.'

'You know we've met. Don't come any closer.' Connor studied the Citizen before him. Yes, it was him. Although there was nothing distinctive in his features: beady eyes, pencil-thin lips and a nose that took up half his face.

The Citizen's eyes swept back and forth across the glowing terrain. Seemingly satisfied, they were alone, he returned his gaze to Connor. He gestured to Connor's bag. 'My niece tells me you have my Shard.'

Connor's fingers tightened on the bag's strap. The Shard was still sitting in his boot, but how was Skelos to know that? 'It's not your Shard. You stole it. I saw you.'

'Unlikely, but I'll run with it. I didn't steal it. It's an old family heirloom gone astray. I've been looking for it everywhere. I'm grateful you found it. If you'd like to hand it over and then I'll be on my way.'

'You brought me to Narrigh, didn't you?'

Skelos put his hand to his mouth to stifle a laugh, which sounded like a pig's snort. He pointed to his feet. 'What here? You think I brought you to this infernal pit. You must have suffered some brain damage during transportation. I hear it can happen on transit through the rift, if you're conscious that is. I was exiled here months ago from the City of Pareus. And you can't have been here as long as I have, otherwise, I would know about it. Narrigh is running a little short on technological advances, so I wonder how I would accomplish such a feint or why I would spirit you to another world where a Citizen's Status stands for nothing. Tell me, what would I have to gain?'

Connor clenched his fists. He felt a surge of anger and frustration. It angered him that Skelos had laughed at his accusation, and he was frustrated because he couldn't answer the question: what would the Citizen have to gain? If Skelos stayed in Narrigh, he would never have his freedom. The only thing that bound them together was the Shard, an item that Skelos's niece had clearly planted on him after his arrival in Narrigh.

Skelos came to a stop. 'As I thought, you haven't the slightest idea what you're talking about. Your brother couldn't tell me how you got here either.'

'You're lying. You're behind all this.'

'If you must know, I'm on the run and you're the only one who can save me by giving back what you stole.'

'You stole the Shard from someone in a white robe. You were spying on him. I saw you.'

'When did you see me *spying*?'

'In a dream.'

An abundance of frown lines congregated around the Citizen's eyes and mouth. 'So, you're one of them? One of the Gifted. That's why you're here, slaving for the Shardner.'

'I'm not slaving for anyone and I'm not going to give

you the Shard. I know what it does. You're going to use it to control people.'

Skelos's left brow fervently twitched. His respectful demeanour turned sour. 'What are you a Sentinel now? A protector of the realm? Or just a young Citizen playing at being a hero. Be warned, you're wasting your time. What I plan to do with the Shard is none of your business. Now if you don't mind, I'd like to conclude this tedious conversation. The Shard, if you will.'

Without his armour, Connor was defenceless. He was thinking about making a run for it when he saw a jewel-encrusted knife fly from under Skelos's robes. It hung in the air and then it snapped into life. He heard a crack like thunder. There was a flash of white light, and then a silver mass shot out of the knife's hilt. It transformed into seven squirming tentacles, all hungry and radiating heat.

Skelos's jowls shuddered in fury. 'Looks like you're not the only one who's gifted.'

Connor's stomach gave a lurch. He backed into the wall of a fire-pit. His eyes trained on the Bolt-Shot whip's fiery tentacles, he reached inside his boot and pulled out the Shard. He held it aloft.

'Call it off or I'll drop it,' he warned. He dangled the Shard over the pit. His hand was shaking so much he was sure he would drop it whether he intended to or not.

Skelos advanced on him. 'Throw me the Shard, young Citizen. Let's get this over with.'

Connor felt the heat rise in his neck from the furnace below. His heart was flapping in his chest. If he gave Skelos the Shard, he would use it to make him take his own life, just like the man in the dream.

A smile graced Skelos's lips. He continued to advance. His poisonous eyes never left Connor's own. He stretched out his hand and seized the Bolt-Shot whip. The deadly tentacles vanished in the same way they had appeared: with a crack and a flash of white light. 'Throw it to me!'

Connor stared back at him, daring himself to breathe, daring himself to move.

Skelos lunged, bridging the gap between them. Connor smelt Skelos's hot rank breath in his face. He could see the greed and corruption swimming in the Citizen's eyes. He had had enough of being a coward. He had nothing more to lose.

He lashed out, knocking the Bolt-Shot whip from Skelos's hand with his fist. He swung his leg in an upward arc, catching Skelos's limp wrist on the sole of his boot.

Skelos fell to the ground clutching his wrist and squawking.

Connor spun away from him, his face flushed from both heat and panic. The Shard had fallen from his hand and landed with a thump on the edge of the pit. He grabbed it and shoved it down the neck of his tunic.

A blow, which felt like a barrel of lead, caught Connor in the hollow of his spine. It knocked the wind from his lungs. He pitched forward, tumbling over the fire-pit's rim.

He met an unwelcome sight: bursting, hissing flames about a hundred feet below him. The view was dizzying and the heat searing. He clawed at the scorching rock with his hands, gritting his teeth through the pain.

Skelos peered at him, a leer on his face. 'Quite the

predicament,' he said, tapping on his lips with his fingers.

The surface was too hot for Connor to travel along. He kicked at the pit wall, his feet working furiously to find a ledge on which he might launch himself from. He was good at that, launching with the correct amount of leverage. It was a pity there wasn't any.

'What? Can you not jump, young Citizen? I would gladly give you my hand,' he rubbed his forearm, 'though my arm is a little sore you know.'

The hot rock crumbled under Connor's fingers. He clawed like a cat on a slated roof, scrambling wildly to find a niche more solid than the last. 'Get me out,' he begged.

Skelos grinned mercilessly. 'If you say please, I will gladly oblige.'

'Ple-please,' said Connor, his voice cracking with the strain. The heat tore at his throat. He thought he smelt his flesh burning.

'Please, what?'

'Please...sir.'

'That's hardly the right address for someone of my Status, but I suppose it will have to do. Now, let's see what we can do for you.' He pushed up his sleeves and gave his knuckles a brisk crack. He leaned into the crater, and gripping Connor's right shoulder nimbly tugged at the neck of Connor's tunic. 'Hold still now, young Citizen.'

Connor should have known that Skelos would go for the Shard. No doubt when he had it in his grasp, he would waste no time in pushing him to his death, if he hadn't already fallen by then. He didn't know how much longer he could hold on.

And so, he redoubled his efforts, frantically working

his feet across the crumbling rock until he found a foothold on a sliver of a crevice. It held strong. The fingers of his left hand scuttled to the right, finding their way to a slight overhang. He grasped it, groaning.

There was no time to rest. Skelos's hand was still stuck down his tunic, foraging for the Shard. Connor brought his other hand up from the crater, gathered a fistful of the fabric shadowing his face and twisted it into a knot. He then yanked on the knot with all his strength.

Startled, Skelos squashed the handful of lizards that had gathered at his feet and collected under the skirts of his robe. His eyes were close to popping out of his head. 'What are doing?' He plucked fervently at his robe, his face convulsing in panic. He had not taken the initiative to plant his feet, and they had started to leave the ground.

Connor puffed and pulled.

Skelos's chest thudded into the edge of the crater. His upper body hung over it. He stared into the fiery abyss. And he might well have stayed there, had a lizard not chosen to scamper up his leg at that very moment. Skelos lurched forward in alarm and slid headlong over Connor's shoulder, bashing his spine on his descent.

He grabbed hold of Connor's waist to prevent himself from falling. 'Don't you dare let go,' he screamed, his feet doing a merry dance beneath him.

Connor expected them to go together. He pressed himself into the sizzling rock face, dug his fingers further into the ledge, clenching every muscle in his body.

Skelos found his own sparse rock cleft to support one leg. He clung to Connor's weathered belt. The heat from the metal buckle scorched his fingers and he squealed like a pig. Then he fell, letting out a blood-curdling scream that was cut off by the fire spewing beneath him.

Connor shut his eyes, waiting for his turn. The pain was unbearable. He had the strange sensation of firm hands gripping his wrists, working their way up his arms, clawing at his burned clothes. He groaned in agony as the firm hands peeled his weeping fingers from the rock.

'You're okay. We've got you.'

He opened his eyes and looked into Yate's bronze face, knotted with determination. Wolth appeared alongside him, grunting and snarling. Connor's feet nudged the lip of the crater and he slithered to the ground like a wet fish loosened from a net.

He heard voices coming from the other side of the pit. He couldn't tell if Yate and Wolth had heard them. His tongue protruded from his inflated lips, desperate to warn them of the impending danger.

Chapter 44

'We have to get him above ground,' said Wolth, spitting sweat and saliva. He threw water over Connor's weeping blisters.

Connor cried out, unable to help himself. The warm water did little to deaden the pain that consumed him by the second. His forearms were burnt. His trousers were torn and curled like paper from the knees down. His eyes had become horribly swollen; he could not fully open them. He stared helplessly up at Yate, who was holding him down. He tried to communicate with the Sentinel through his raw lips.

Yate brushed his sleeve across his face. 'Don't try to speak. You're safe now and back where you belong.'

Connor responded with a moan. 'What?'

'Let's take him over there,' said Yate, nodding his head in the direction of a rock, shaped like a shark's fin, some feet away, 'out of this heat.'

'You can't move him,' Wolth said, squinting at Yate through dust-covered lashes. 'Not like – look at him.'

Yate retrieved Connor's charred bag and slung it over his neck. He hoisted Connor over his shoulders, ignoring his howls of pain. He covered the distance to the rock in four short strides. He gently laid him down. He then squatted beside him, his elbows resting on his thighs.

Wolth went down on one knee. He took a long breath and laid a hand on Connor's chest. 'A slow painful death for one so young. It hardly seems fair. Is there nothing we can do to ease his suffering?'

'He's not dying,' snapped Yate. 'We're of the same blood – Citizen.' He wrapped his arm around Connor's neck, his fist clenched. 'So, save your pity. He is not as weak as you think. He'll be back on his feet within the hour. His powers are unimaginable and he's in good with the Shardner. You've no idea what he can do for us.'

Wolth took his hand from Connor's chest. 'Then we could do with ten more like him. What's in the bag?'

Yate tugged open Connor's bag. 'Gold coins and ashes. He had some good armour on him earlier. Keep a look out for it.'

'How much gold?' said Wolth. He rubbed his hands together and licked a boil on his lip as if it had a good taste.

'There are those who would give all of Odisiris to have your gift for themselves,' the Authoritative Voice reminded Connor.

Connor gave a series of throaty growls. They weren't helping him. They were helping themselves.

Wolth responded to his growls by throwing the last of his water in Connor's face. 'Least I don't need to waste my healing potion. We'll have to get far away from the Kingdom and then drum up more recruits. We took a lot of casualties.'

Yate's head snapped up, his muscles tense, the blood popping in his veins. 'Quiet. We've been followed.' He poked his head out from behind their hiding place, inconspicuous as it was.

'By how many?' said Wolth.

'Ten maybe. All armoured.'

'There are eight to be precise. Excluding me,' a voice proclaimed.

Yate jerked his head in the direction of the voice, his muscles tightened in expectation.

Wolth was on the feet, coughing and swaying. He reached for the dagger tucked inside his belt.

A man stood a mere five paces away: tall, pale, and not in the least perplexed. He had closely cropped salt-and-pepper hair. He was wrapped in a silver-grey cloak stained with mud and grass. There were dark stains on his tunic and dents in the breastplate he wore over it. The seam of one of his trouser legs was unravelling. Tucked under his arm was a battered helmet. The man's nose was shaped very much like the rock he was leaning on. Connor recognised him by the colour of his eyes. It was Osaphar.

'You can try to arrest us, but we won't go easy,' said Wolth. He pulled himself upright and pushed out his chin, his eyes wide with fright.

Connor admired his courage, for what it was worth.

'The battle is over and you lost,' said Osaphar, in a voice like steel. 'Now, release the boy.'

The swelling on Connor's eyelids had gone down. The blisters on his skin had ceased weeping. He watched Yate morph into a big cat.

Connor rolled out of the way as the cat bared its ferocious jaws at Osaphar.

A lizard scampered onto Osaphar's shoulder. He stroked its tail, and then lazily brushed it from his cloak. 'It's forbidden to enter these caves.' He looked off into the distance and then back at the big cat.

'I didn't see any sign saying that,' said Wolth, his hand

fumbling for the hilt of his dagger. His white shirt was soaked through. Fat beads of sweat burst out all over his face.

'I'm a sign,' said Osaphar in a crisp tone. 'Seize them.' In a flash, eight guards, donned in black and silver armour appeared beside Osaphar.

In a deft stroke, one of the guards' snatched the dagger from Wolth just as he pulled it from his belt. The Gamnod Hunter crumpled to the ground, choking in dust.

Yate, the big cat, pounced at the group of guards. The guards scattered as fast as they had appeared, and the big cat went crashing into a Plowman, crouched behind the spot where they had gathered. The Plowman wrapped its great arms around Yate. The big cat writhed in the Plowman's powerful embrace. It snarled and snapped its jaws. It raked its claws across the Plowman's face and then it went still, drained of energy.

'Secure him,' said Osaphar.

A guard produced a coiled silver rope from a bag strapped to his back. He wrapped the rope over the big cat's jaws, binding them shut. He then wound the rope around its neck, leaving enough length on the rope to bring the cat to heel.

'Have you seen its claws?' said another guard. 'I'm not taking any chances.' He pulled out his coiled rope and used it to bind the big cat's paws together.

'Let us be!' cried Wolth. 'We're worthless to you.' A Plowman strolled up and tapped him lightly on the shoulder. Wolth didn't notice.

'That's a matter of opinion,' said Osaphar. 'Not mine

you understand, the Shardner's.'

A guard, not an inch shorter than Osaphar, lifted Connor in his arms, cradling him as if he were a baby.

A guard hauled Wolth to his feet by his arm. Another, thumped him in the back with his steel baton.

'Where are you taking us?' said Wolth.

Osaphar spoke into a device strapped to his wrist. It was like the one Connor had seen on his brother's wrist. 'We've found him. Bring us up.'

A white light surrounded them like a curtain. It fizzled and cracked. Then the floor of the cave was gone, replaced by a shiny black one.

They had arrived on a raised platform with steps leading from it. The structure was set with four evenly spaced steel pillars. A pulsing blue light lit the black-tiled floor.

'What magic is this?' said Wolth, his jaw steadily dropping. 'Where are we?'

'On board a Citizen vessel,' said Osaphar. He stepped off the raised platform and removed his gloves. He turned to the guards. 'Bring the boy. Hold the others here.'

Connor felt as if his heart was beating on the other side of his chest. Luke came running out. The guard slipped Connor into his brother's arms.

Luke staggered, taking Connor's weight. He set him down and gave him a crushing hug.

'We found him in the caves,' said Osaphar. 'The Sighraith Band were after him. Isn't that right, Connor?'

Connor stared back at Osaphar. Only he knew the whole truth.

There are those who would give all of Odisiris to have

your gift for themselves.

He pushed his hand into his pocket. His fingers found his Worral Stone. He had seen the change in Yate, once he had learned about his Gift. How would Osaphar react if he knew? What if the Citizen already knew, and he was going to take him to Odisiris. Separate him from Luke. He wasn't sure if he should mention his Gift or the Shard.

Luke frowned at him, waiting for an answer. Osaphar's eyes were as cold as ever. His Adam's apple bobbed up and down.

Connor stumbled up, shrugging off his brother's attempts to help him to his feet. 'Wolth and Yate saved me from the firepit.'

'For a reason,' said Osaphar. 'They used a Summoning Spell to extract you from the tower. They were going to recruit you to their rebellion.'

So, his sleep-dreams had not carried him underground, Yate had. He curbed his disappointment. 'They just want some land.'

'Do you know why Yate was exiled here?' said Osaphar.

Connor shook his head.

'He doesn't need to know, does he?' said Luke, resting his hand on Connor's shoulder and glowering at Osaphar. 'He's been through enough.'

'He murdered someone,' said Osaphar, his eyes on Connor, 'in cold blood.'

Connor swallowed. 'I didn't think Odisiris had any crime.'

'Oh, there's crime,' said Osaphar. 'The government doesn't publicise it. The culprits are swiftly caught and brought to justice.'

'Yeah, sure they are,' said Luke, nodding at the big cat.

'What's going to happen to them?' Connor stared at the forlorn-looking big cat with its eyes half-open, and The Hunter with his head bowed in defeat.

'They can help rebuild the dungeons,' said Osaphar. 'The Plowmen will be their shadow, the sunlight a dream.'

Connor wrestled the Shard out of his tunic and gave it to Osaphar. 'I found this in my bag.' It was better that he hand it over. It was no good to him. No good to anyone now.

Osaphar took it from him. He rolled it between his finger and thumb. His forehead creased. 'I'll have the Shardner Council look at. Let us proceed to the cockpit. I don't want to delay your departure any further.'

Luke and Connor followed Osaphar into another grand arena. Soft spotlights lit up the space.

Connor's senses were not dead. He heard a faint noise coming from beyond the walls, but he could not make them out. And the air was surgically clean. Odourless. The space was darker and more sinister and filled with an array of cubic and circular metal-cast structures.

A cylindrical structure spurted up from the floor. A huge glass chamber jutted out from the wall. It housed three holographic control panels, some twenty feet high. The central panel projected a holographic image of a circuit board with blue and white transmission lines. At the base of the screen was a wide shelf and a row of metal stools.

Connor saw a man, with a head of dark hair, dressed in black, standing inside the glass chamber, mopping up the sweat pouring from his brow. The man held his hand up to an access control panel set in the glass door. The door made a popping noise and slid open.

Osaphar went into the chamber first, followed by Connor, then Luke and a guard, holding Connor's charred bag. The door slid shut after them.

Connor heard a familiar chirp and was surprised when the Kherrin Mawk emerged from between two metal stools. It stared up at Connor, flapping its useless wings. Connor scooped the creature up in his arms. 'Did you miss me?'

'You know that thing bit me twice,' said the dark-haired man, licking the sweat off his top lip. He met Osaphar's steely gaze with an uneasy twitter. 'No harm done though. I'm Thorn, by the way.' He held out his hand to Connor.

Connor positioned the Kherrin Mawk in the crook of his arm so he could shake Thorn's hand. 'Connor.'

'Your brother's stubborn, isn't he?' said Thorn.

Connor looked over at Luke leaning on the wall. He didn't know if Thorn was paying his brother a compliment or an insult. Either way, he wasn't going to answer with Luke there in the same room. He shrugged, stroking the creature in his arms. He had something else on his mind. If the government in Odisiris had exiled Yate for committing a crime, then they must have exiled Skelos Dorm for the same reason. He had to say something. He couldn't just leave it. The Shardner would know Skelos was missing. It wasn't as if he had killed the Citizen. It was an accident.

He blurted it out before he lost his nerve. 'I saw another Citizen when I was out there. Skelos Dorm. He wanted the Shard. He fell into one of the firepits when he tried to grab it off me.'

Osaphar staggered briefly, dropping his helmet and his gloves.

The guard tossed Connor's charred bag on the floor and gathered up Osaphar's belongings. He placed them on one of the stools. 'What would you have me do?' he asked Osaphar.

Luke peeled himself from the wall, looking anxiously from Thorn to Osaphar. 'Do you know him?' His eyes finally rested on Connor.

Connor couldn't believe it. His brother was giving him the Look of Awe.

'He was expelled from Narrigh,' said Osaphar hoarsely, 'for carrying out unlawful experiments on Citizens.' He turned to the guard. 'Return to the place where you found Connor and search all the pits. Take five more with you. Leave behind all Odisirian weapons and devices. You will stay in Narrigh until you find him. Do you understand?'

The guard gave a short bow and left the room.

'You think he's still alive?' said Luke.

'There's a slight possibility,' said Osaphar. 'But let me worry about it. Thorn, prepare for transportation will you.' He collected his gloves and helmet from the stool and walked to the door. He lingered there, his focus on Connor. 'You can't take the creature with you.'

'Why not?' said Connor. He was already planning to smuggle the Kherrin Mawk through, in his bag, once

Osaphar had left.

'When you go back out there,' said the Citizen pointing to the grid. 'You will be stripped of your Citizen Status and every reminder that you were ever here, and that includes the Kherrin Mawk.'

Connor gazed at his brother, willing him to say it wasn't true.

Luke stayed silent.

'I don't want my memory erased,' said Connor. He hugged the Kherrin Mawk tightly to him. He had finally learned what it meant to be a Citizen. He hadn't fully mastered his Gift. Now it was all going to be taken from him. He wanted to go home a Citizen – a hero that had fought in battles and had a cool pet, not some kid who everyone thought ran away because his mum had told him off.

'We're not going to erase your memory unless you want us to,' said Thorn. He smiled with his lips tucked inside his mouth.

'You probably erased it when I got here,' said Connor. He went to pick up his bag. The strap snapped. He tied a loose knot in it and hung it from his arm.

'It was a joke,' said Thorn. 'You don't need to get tetchy.' He cocked his head at Luke and raised one eyebrow. 'I see you've a similar temperament.'

'I hardly think they're in the mood for jokes,' said Osaphar, shooting Thorn a look. 'I suggest you get back to the task at hand. Return them to Earth.' He opened the chamber door. His face was grim. 'I wish you well.' He exited the chamber.

Connor and Luke stared after him.

'Right,' said Thorn, he led Connor by one arm and Luke by the other to the centre of the chamber, right in the midst of the grid. 'If you want to stand side by side.'

Connor felt as if Thorn was assembling them for a family photo.

Luke slipped his arm around Connor's shoulder. His hand was trembling. 'It's okay, buddy.'

It didn't feel okay. 'I thought we were going through the rift.'

'You didn't arrive in Narrigh through a rift,' said Thorn. 'To be honest, we've no idea how you got here, but we do know a way to send you back. Luke's given me the approximate time you disappeared from your home in London, which means I can return you to the exact location you were in, moments before you landed in Narrigh.'

He used one finger to move around the holographic gridlines. He dragged a section of one of the control panels towards him. He dropped it into a space within the grid. 'I'm going to sync the coordinates, so you'll both return at the same point in time. You may want to shut your eyes for this.' He tapped the transparent keys hovering in front of him. The section of the panel zoomed away, returning to its former position.

Grids rocketed from the control panel. One by one, they surrounded Connor and Luke. The grids flashed off and on. Connor heard a weird pulsating sound in his ears. He watched in wonder as the Citizen clothes he wore, his bag and the Kherrin Mawk were diced to minute pixel squares. Thorn and the glass chamber disappeared.

The lights were blinding. This was it. Connor squeezed

Luke's hand. They were going home.

Chapter 45

Connor's arrival home was less dignified than his departure. When he opened his eyes, he found his brother sprawled across his lap, crushing his thighs. Riley was standing over them yelling his lungs out.

Luke scrambled to his feet, leaving Connor to gain control of the spinning swivel chair. He grabbed the edge of Luke's desk and slammed his feet on the floor.

Luke's laptop sat open on his desk. Connor slammed it shut and took a breath. He felt hot and clammy all over. He was wearing his tracksuit bottoms and a vest – the same clothes he had been wearing when he had been playing the game.

'Will you shut up!' said Luke, seizing Riley by the shoulders. 'You're going to wak'

Too late.

Their mum burst through the door. Her upper lip was hitched in a snarl. Her mascara was smeared across her eyes and there were lipstick smudges on her chin.

'What's with all the noise?' she screamed, yanking down her nightshirt. 'I'm trying to sleep! I thought you were out Luke. And Riley, I thought you went home.'

Connor wanted to run and hug her, but not in front of Riley and *never* in front of his brother. So, he said the only thing there was left to say. 'Sorry mum.'

'Yeah, sorry mum,' said Luke, releasing Riley, and giving him a hard slap on the shoulder. We were just messing about. I'll walk Riley home in a minute.'

Riley had stopped yelling and started wheezing. He raised his finger, pointing at the laptop on Luke's desk. Luke smacked Riley's finger with the back of his hand. 'Okay, that's enough joke's over.'

Connor stared at the laptop. The screen-saver had appeared. It was a photo of him, and Luke taken on a beach over a year ago. He examined his hands. His palms were red. His Status Mark was gone. So, Osaphar was right. He had lost his bag, his Citizen clothes, and the Kherrin Mawk. He was no longer a Citizen.

His mum glanced suspiciously around the room, at its pale blue walls, made-up bed, and double wardrobe. She stared at the large bookshelf laden with Luke's collection of books, comics, and DVDs, at his football boots hanging from a hook on the door, and at his beloved football rammed under his bed.

Satisfied with her inspection she said, 'I'm going back to bed. And if I hear any more noise coming from this room, I'll give you hell. Understand?' She glared at them.

Connor swallowed. 'Yes, mum.'

'Yes, Ms Brailey,' said Riley. 'Sorry.'

Their mum gave a satisfied grunt and stomped out of the room.

Riley collapsed on Luke's bed. 'Whoa! I can't believe that just happened. Where'd you go?'

'Narrigh,' said Connor.

'No way,' said Riley. He sat up, clutching the sides of his head. 'I saw this purple light, and then bam', he slammed his left fist into the palm of his right, 'you were gone and then I started freaking out, and then bam you were back again with Luke. What are you like aliens or something? I mean you could have told me, I've only known you for, like, five years.'

'We're not aliens,' said Connor. 'It's the game. We got sucked into the game. And I was gone for weeks, and then Luke got sucked in and came to find me.'

'How come?' said Riley. 'You've only been gone seconds.' He frowned. 'And I saw Luke go out.'

'We got sent back in time,' said Connor. 'If we'd have got here a few seconds earlier, you wouldn't have remembered a thing.'

'Time travel? No way,' said Riley, he looked from Connor to Luke enthralled. 'I wanna go.'

'It's not like a ride at the funfair,' said Luke, wheeling Connor away from his desk, and grabbing the laptop. 'It was dangerous. Real. Not the kind of thing that happens every day, not the kind of thing that happens ever, so don't go bleating about it to the next person you see. And while you're at it, you had both better say goodbye to my bedroom because it'll be the last time you set foot in it. Riley, get your stuff together, I'm taking you home.'

'That's a bit harsh,' said Riley. 'You haven't even told me what happened yet. Can't I sleep here?'

'No,' said Luke. He slipped his laptop into a filing cabinet and locked it. Connor watched him slip the key into his pocket.

'It's a long story. I'll tell you about it tomorrow.' Connor had the good sense not to argue with Luke. He deserved what he had coming to him. He was lucky Luke hadn't given him a clout round the ear.

'Okay, see ya,' said Riley. He gave Connor a stiff wave goodbye as Luke ushered him out.

'Connor?' Luke paused by the door, a stern look on his face.

'Oh, right,' said Connor, he rose to leave and said a silent goodbye to the room. He followed Luke out. Riley was at the bottom of the stairs, fishing out his trainers from the stacked shoe rack.

'Luke, can I ask you something?'

'Is it about Narrigh?'

'No.'

'What then?'

'Did you think I ran away again?'

Luke grinned at him. 'Course not. You hadn't packed a bag and I know you wouldn't have broken your promise. At one point, mum thought you went looking for dad again and that we'd find you in the place you went missing the last time.'

'I couldn't remember his name?'

'Whose name?'

'Dad's – do you?'

'It was Eron. Why?'

Connor shrugged. 'No reason.' How could he tell Luke about the man he has seen in his Past-Telling, lying dead on the slab of granite? It was now no more real than the Status Mark he had once had embedded in his hand and the Indigo blood that had pumped through his veins. Forgotten.

'I'm not done with you,' said Luke. 'Wait in your room until I get back. It looks like we're going to need to set some new ground rules.'

Connor gave a shaky sigh. Maybe he would get that clout round the ear after all.

He dug his hands into his pockets. His fingers closed around a stone. He took it out. His Worral Stone. He stared at it. So, Osaphar was wrong. Something had come through: his Gift.

'The game hasn't ended,' he whispered. 'It's only just begun.'

Something told him that his destiny lay in the hands of The Maker and one day he would become a Citizen again.

Chapter 46

Before the sun has risen, he believes he owns the day, that the day is his to command, and that he will overcome every obstacle laid before him. For he does not know that he lies in the palm of his Maker, and with each twist and turn of his Maker's hand, he is moulded, and as he sleeps, time rises up to steal another day.

Skelos tore at the rope with his fingers until the frayed ends slipped to the ground. The doors gave a gentle creak. One of them was near coming off its hinges. He struck a piece of flint on his Worral Stone. It flared, producing a tiny flame, which he used to light his slow-burner. He then jostled the doors open and went inside, drawing them shut after him.

He walked along the mill's perimeter twice. The first time, he glanced at the ceiling, the second time at the floor. *At least I am safe here.*

He had returned to Undren. The Shardner had long since vacated the village. The villagers themselves had settled back into their old routine, the fear of a northern invasion firmly behind them. Every last mine had been packed with craybine and there was no more talk of mysterious strangers appearing like puffs of smoke on the horizon. Even when talk arose of thick black clouds seen racing, like a band of horses, across the Northern skyline, the people of Undren did not dwell on it. The summer harvest was plentiful, and the Northern sky was not 'their sky'.

Skelos had no such contentment. The Traceless had saved him from the fiery pit. They thought he owned them a debt for saving his life, so they had taken the Avu'lore as payment. They had then come to him shortly after to complain the Avu'lore had failed them. Skelos had almost collapsed with relief. The idea of them controlling his every move was enough to make him want to end it all. He had six weeks to find a way to rid himself of the Traceless being dwelling inside him – if not more. He was not going to fret over it. The Traceless were easily persuaded and he was skilled at using his tongue as a bargaining tool.

He spotted a small object sitting under a broken ladder, glowing like polished silver. He snatched it up without thinking and held it up to the light of the slow-burner. A rock that shines in the dark. Rainbows Rock. It was the size of a small potato, harder and not half as smooth. He set the rock down beside him and positioned the slow-burner in a cog he found propped against the wall. He went down on his knees, dragged the canvas from his rucksack and laid it on the ground, poppy side up. This had been his daily ritual since leaving Baruch. Travelling at night to a new location, attempting to find a map within the only painting he possessed. He was a wanted Citizen who was down to his last gold coin. He had paid for shelter, paid for silence. He had even brought a Divulging Potion on the black market, in hopes it would reveal the secret map. It hadn't worked. Nothing had worked thus far.

The Traceless had informed him that the Shardner

had removed the impenetrable dome from around Callawly Castle. Skelos had returned there only to find the Shardner had stripped the place bare. He didn't know what prompted him to believe the map existed. Had his desperation to escape Narrigh skewed his judgment? Was the Traceless One inside him, sending out subliminal messages? Or was it a mere collection of the facts as he understood them? The Traceless said the painting belonged to The Maker, which meant it would have to have come from Odisiris. How many paintings from Odisiris could find themselves on the wall of Callawly Castle? It would explain the Shardner's brief presence there.

He studied the canvas every day, poppy side up. He had scratched at a section of the painting with a small knife in order to test a simple theory: that the map was sitting beneath the sea of poppies. His theory proved wrong, and he had left a thumb-sized hole in the canvas to prove it.

After a while, he turned the canvas over and spent another fifteen minutes staring at the yellowing blank side. He thought his inborn intuition, if nothing else, would have revealed a secret map to him by now.

He heard a sudden rustling noise outside and was on his feet in an instant, at the door in a flash, yanking it open and sucking in his breath. He heaved a sigh of relief. There was no one out there. It must have been the wind or a Ticket shrew burrowing into its home. He pulled the doors shut and returned to the canvas to find a small section of it glowing. He had accidentally trodden on the rock, crushing a small fragment of it into the canvas. The fragment had left a trail of glittering dust in the uppermost right corner.

Skelos lifted the canvas. He gave it a shake, expecting the dust to fall away. It remained stuck to it as if secured by invisible glue. 'It was under my nose all this time.'

He set the canvas back on the floor, locked the last fragment of rock into a groove in the sole of his boot, and then trampled it into the canvas, grinding the remnants underfoot until they were reduced to nothing more than a fine powder. He lifted the canvas and gave it one last decisive shake.

He squatted down to examine what he had found, dragging the cog with the slow-burner close. There were lines on the canvas in more detail than he had ever imagined. The dust had hardened leaving a silvery residue made up of crooked lines and bumps. At the top of the canvas in large italic letters were the words, 'Map of the Other Worlds.'

'Other Worlds.' Skelos ran his finger over the letters. The map consisted of horizontal lines, labelled from Level One to Level Three. Along each line was a spate of headed dots.

Above one of the dots were the words, Old Getty, on another, Levistan Woods. He also saw Shile Point, Olva Mountains and a whole host of other landmarks in other cities and other places, he had never even heard of. All were marked above the dots on the map.

He frowned. He did not understand a map made up of lines and dots. There were no such maps in Odisiris. His frown deepened. *If this is a map to the 'Other Worlds', then how do you reach your destination? There are no other worlds on here.*

He flipped the canvas over; flipped it back again. Some of the dots were unmarked. One of them, on Level Three, had a cross through it and a series of digits: *87, 23,* and *16.*

He trailed his finger along the horizontal line labelled Level One. The Old Getty Mill, Levistan Woods, and the Olva Mountains, were all above ground, on Level One, which meant the other two levels, had to be below ground.

He stood up, map in hand. He strode around the mill again. Treading carefully this time, he left no crack unchecked, no clog unturned. He noticed two broken stones. They looked quite out of place in the mill. He surveyed the floor around it. It had been disturbed and not too long ago. Skelos crouched and shifted the stones. He discovered a trapdoor without a handle. He slid his fingers into the surrounding gaps to raise the door. There were scraggy steps running into the ground, steep and fathomless. A faint trace of tar and salt-water wafted to the surface.

He cupped his hand to his mouth. Was this the Will of The Maker? An underground passage? If the road to the Other Worlds were as simple as walking down a flight of steps, surely, he would have discovered it long ago. He picked up the slow-burner and gathered up the small bag containing his belongings.

He journeyed cautiously down the steps, hewn from rock. His heart quickened, thinking of the cross marked on the map and what awaited him there. The road would be long, arduous, and filled with danger, but it was a road he was accustomed to and he took it without fear.

Chapter 47

The Maker sat behind his desk studying the Herming Moth Wing handed to him by his friend and confidant, Osaphar Kulane. It didn't look any different from the one he was handed this morning or the one he was handed the morning before that, come to think of it. The Wings were the least of his troubles.

Osaphar stood in front of him with his hands clasped behind his back. He had fine lines around his eyes and pale forehead that were not the telling of his age. His own worries were making him haggard. The Maker pursed his lips, struggling to recall the last time he had seen him smile.

'There has been no word of Skelos Dorm,' said Osaphar. 'No sign. He wasn't on any of our ships. We also put out all the fires in the pits. At the rate our tissue regenerates, if he were dead, we would have found his charred body in one of them. He has simply vanished. It is a grave mystery.'

The Maker rolled his sapphire-coloured eye. Osaphar frequently used the word 'vanished' to explain the mysterious disappearance of both creatures and persons alike. It sounded more theatrical, he supposed than 'gone into hiding' or 'gone underground' or 'bit the dust'. Anyone would think that someone had tapped them with a magic wand, making them disappear in a puff of smoke.

'And what of the Sighraith Band? I suppose they've vanished too.'

'The Traceless helped most of them escape. Some remain in the ruins of Baruch. My men are rounding them up as we speak.'

Vanished.

How many more had slipped into Narrigh unnoticed? Unannounced? Unchallenged? Others who did not want to be part of his worlds; others who were not welcome.

'I thought you should also know that one of your maps has gone missing. It found its way to the Undren Auction House where it was purchased for one bronze coin by an alleged sorcerer.'

The Maker let the Herming Moth Wing clutter noisily to the floor. His friend winced. He reached for a bottle of fifty-year-old Zaskian and poured some into a glass. He was less concerned about the map. He had others and no one knew how to read the maps but him. He had engineered them that way.

'No excuses. Skelos must be found and quickly.'

Osaphar had warned him about Skelos's ruthlessness, but he had paid no attention until it was too late. The Citizen had found a way to make himself quite undetectable, which was a concern. He could only hope the Technopath was still in Narrigh and not a world in which he could put his techno-wielding talents to better use.

'I'm astounded that you let him get away from you on so many occasions: Bluewood Forest, Callawly Castle, you and your elf woman's home. I thought your feelings for your former friend had waned since his expulsion from Odisiris. Was I wrong? Do you think loyalty is the mark of a good Citizen?'

Osaphar shuffled closer to his desk, the dusty soles of his boots crunching on the floor. His face darkened. 'At one time, he was my best friend and then we grew apart. I could never condone what he did. There is no friendship. Worack didn't know how much of a threat he posed when he arrived at our dwelling, or else she would have gone to greater lengths to detain him. I warned you about him. You know he could have killed the boy.'

'But he didn't. Strange that he and his brother should come to Narrigh.'

'I thought you had something to do with it?'

'Come now, you know me better than that. I don't get pleasure from tormenting children. What happened to Connor and Luke was entirely outside my control.'

Osaphar stamped his foot, his nostrils flaring. 'Outside your control? They were playing *The Quest of Narrigh*, a game that you created. That's not a coincidence.'

'I didn't force them to play it, did I?' He shook his head. 'It was an unfortunate accident. I will have to see to it that it doesn't happen again. I'll be leaving shortly for home. Do you have any other business you wish to discuss?'

Osaphar's eyes flashed with anger. 'You're returning to Earth, now? What about the Herming Moth Wings? Since Skelos vanished, there is no one here qualified to complete his work.'

The Maker rolled his crystal blue eye. 'What have I always said to you, Osaphar? If you can't find what you want in this world, then look in another.'

He lifted his glass to toast his good friend. Unfortunately, Osaphar didn't have a glass to reciprocate.

'Maker's Will. Don't give up your search for Skelos. I want him found, preferably alive. He must never return to Odisiris.'

Osaphar gave an abrupt nod and left the room, his face grim.

The Maker drained his glass of Zaskian. He then ran his tongue over his lips and poured himself another.

Building worlds was a very delicate business. Creating species, shaping cultures, building new lands out of old ones. Trying to control and manipulate everyone and everything down to the last itsy-bitsy detail. *It is rather like being an artist. You painstakingly apply your brush strokes to the canvas. You stand back to admire your work, only to find smudges. Why are there always smudges?*

He was staring at one now: the part-humanoid sitting on a leather stool by the window. She stared at him with her usual blank expression and fiddled unconsciously with the pale-yellow ribbon in her hair.

'Will I see Connor again, sir?'

'I wouldn't count on it.' He stared into the doleful hazel eyes of the part human, part robot girl. Disappointingly, she was more human than droid.

'Is my uncle coming to collect me, sir?'

It was a good question, one that would be answered with a curt 'no', when the time was right.

'In due course,' he replied.' He set down his glass and opened the logbook belonging to the former Stores Administrator, Gyan Sputworth. Osaphar had discovered it next to one of the fire-pits. It made for an interesting read. The most recent page showed a child-like sketch of the Avu'lore, minus two Shards. If the Administrator hadn't labelled it, 'invention', the Shardner would have assumed that Gyan had grown bored with his duties and had taken up doodling.

Osaphar had given him the Shard that Connor had passed on to him. The Avu'lore globe and the other two Shards had not been recovered. He would have to get them back. You couldn't unleash the Avu'lore's full power without all three Shards in place. With three, you could open rifts between worlds. With just two, you could still achieve a lethal amount of damage: control another's mind for a short duration. Steer their every move.

Skelos must have seen him using the Avu'lore when he was in the Red Caves. It looked as if he would have to be more careful with his possessions from now on.

Most of the guards stationed within the immediate vicinity of the Stores had suffered partial memory loss. The last thing they *claimed* to recall, before they were discovered sprawled out unconscious on the floor of the Stores most secure chamber, was Gyan screeching at them about an emergency. The guards were now occupying a space in the Court of Justice prison, one of the few buildings that was undamaged in the fire. Not that he thought a good flogging, poor light, and a meagre diet would refresh their memories, but security had been breached and appropriate punishments had to be carried out. He could not hold the Stores Administrators accountable. Belstien, the other Store Administrator on duty, had been declared brain-dead. Gyan was dead (despite supposed sightings of him in Undren village). The one guard worth questioning, Vastra something-or-other, was nowhere to be found.

He flipped up the lid on his cane and gazed at the fragment of Rainbows Rock sitting on the velvet cushion fitted inside it. Why were there always smudges?

Sci-Fi Fantasy series, THE OTHER WORLDS

Dorm

The Quest of Narrigh

The Plague of Pyridian

The Chancellor of Odisiris

To learn more about **The Other Worlds** visit
tridanentertainment.com

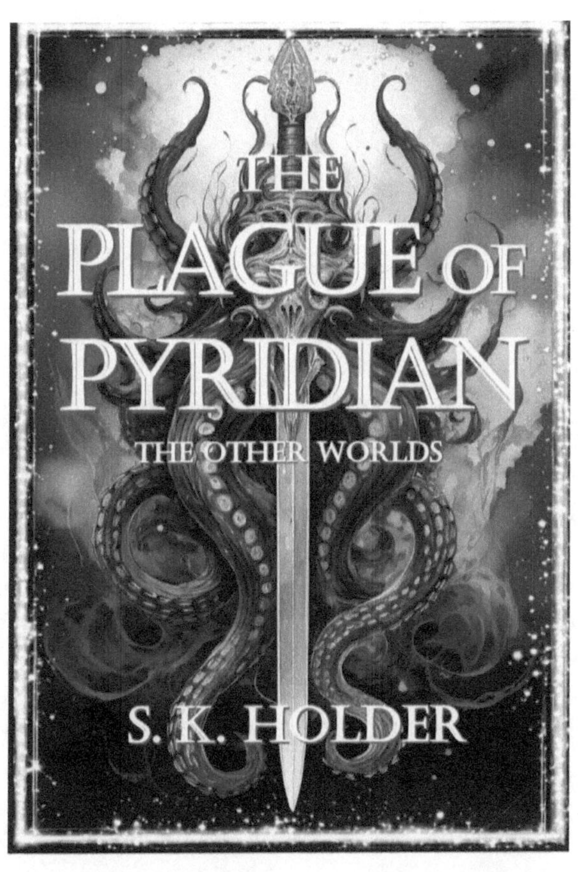

EXTRACT FROM BOOK TWO

Chapter 1

Lin launched herself down the rock face. Leaping the last two feet, she unsheathed her dagger, lunged at the alien and ran the coarse blade down its back. She immobilised another before it descended on her by pinning a flap of its skin into the dirt and then hacking off its head. It gave a shriek of indignation and a grey mucous bubbled from its mouth.

That's what you get for killing aliens: no respite and little reward.

She whirled in the direction of the screams. They came from a young woman dressed in civilian clothing. Caught in the grip of the alien's tentacle, she looked a bloody, fleshy mess.

Lin clambered back up the precipice and over to where she lay writhing, drew her Ryber weapon from its holster and thrust it into the creature's tentacle. The alien screeched and its tentacle went slack. She gripped the civilian by the waist and attempted to haul her back to her feet. The woman screamed and slammed her arm into Lin's legs. She howled in pain as Lin's spiked armour pierced her skin.

'Get up. Get up you fool!' Lin yelled at her. 'Can't you see I'm trying to help you?' It became clear that the woman could not. Her eyes were closed; one had a purple bruise. Her clothes were spattered with blood. She had a bloody lip, half of her lustrous hair looked as if it had been ripped out at the root and she had a deep gash in her leg.

Her hand jerked towards the lifeless limb. 'I can't feel my leg.'

Lin slapped the civilian's arm away and shook her by the shoulders. 'You need to stand. Try!' Did the woman not grasp the urgency of the situation? And what was she doing out here anyway, without combat gear and without courage? She suspected she was another half-wit who thought they would try their luck at hunting aliens.

'My leg,' she screamed. 'Help me. My leg!'

Lin released her hold on the civilian and told her the truth. 'Your leg is the least of your worries.'

The woman flopped on her side and made a feeble attempt to crawl away. She cut a pathetic figure, squirming and clawing at the dry rock bed with her bruised fingers and her eyes shut.

Another alien closed in and Lin drew her Ryber weapon again. She hit the protractor key on the alloy steel device, extending it by seven foot. She took a firm grip on the Ryber and raised her right knee to her chest. She ran with mighty force, using her raised leg to drive herself through the air. She vaulted over the alien and rammed her blade into the top of its head before it had seen her.

The creature crashed to the ground, emitting a rattling sound before disintegrating in a cloud of ash. The Ryber contracted in Lin's hand. She then slapped it to the magnetic strip on her belt.

The civilian had witnessed Lin's kill. She started to scream again. She squirmed dangerously close to the edge of the rock face on which they were situated. Sighing, Lin resigned herself to mounting a rescue before she tumbled off the ledge or into an alien's open mouth.

Grunting with effort, she dragged the civilian away from the precarious edge by her feet. She then knocked her out with the handle of her blade. She parted the civilian's hair on one side in search of the tattoos that were the Peltarcks hallmark. She was not surprised to find no sign of them. She did not bother to check the palm of the woman's right hand. If she were a Citizen, her Mark had failed her as her wounds had not healed.

She heard the whir of a fleet carrier above her and saw it in the distance banking south. The fork-shaped carrier flew low on approach.

Massaging the knots in her shoulders, she watched it land close to the mottled blue corpse of the eighth alien she had killed that day. She thought she heard two more carriers drawing in from the west. They sounded close. She shifted her gaze west where a band of white light dripped over the horizon and a single star sat over the steep ridge tracks of Baya Mountain. Lin could have sworn she saw the mountain quake. Baya Mountain does not quake she told herself. It had been a long day and her eyes were tired. She closed them for a moment and caught her breath. When she opened them, the quaking had stopped and so had the sound of the carriers.

Lintheia Aroda had done a great deal of killing in her eighteen years. Too much, she thought. In her infancy, she had killed alien hatchlings. As she grew older, she moved on to the bigger ones. She had once killed an alien with her bare hands.

She had joined the Citizen Taskforce at thirteen years of age. The Taskforce had many guises and many names.

On Narrigh, it was the Shardner's Special Army, on Kaltharine it was the Military Academy, and on Pyridian it was the Octane Resistance. They all had one thing in common: they were all led by a Citizen, and their chief aim was to resolve war and conflict by any means necessary. Or so one would think. For while Odisiris had peace, it was a well-known, yet unspoken fact that all the other worlds occupied by Citizens were plagued by wars and unrest. Lin did not have the heart to read into it. She was a warrior born and raised. She spent most of her time on the battlefield. And while she had the utmost respect for the superhuman race of Citizens, her loyalties lay with her own race: the Peltarcks.

A laser gun went off, blowing the head off one of the alien's she had taken out earlier. Given the chance, she would have finished the beast off herself.

'You're slacking,' said a voice over her shoulder.

She waited for the cloud of rock dust to settle around her, and then turned to address her commanding officer, Garis Kyson. His eyes were the colour of algae, and his white hair made him look older than his thirty-eight years. 'I don't think so sir. It was half dead when I found it.'

She held the First Status Citizen in high regard. As her commanding officer he reminded her when to step up and when to step down. Nonetheless, he spent more time above the battlefield than on it, and as a consequence had no idea how many aliens, she had killed that morning or the day before.

His eyes lingered for a moment on the unconscious figure lying on the rocks. He jammed the laser gun into his leg holster and met her gaze. 'You missed cadet training yesterday.'

Lin scowled. 'I had other business to attend to.' She disliked teaching anyone and had not given the cadet training any thought. Most of the new recruits were Citizen youths. Eager to take up the family mantel, they joined the fleet with little notion of what awaited outside their city walls until it was too late.

Garis ran his thumb under his chin, watching her thoughtfully. 'Other business?'

'Killing things.' Lin threw her Ryber weapon into the open jaw of the alien looming up behind Garis, the one he thought he had killed. The alien gave a long screech and drew itself up before crashing to the ground. Garis hopped forward with wide eyes, and then spun round to survey the alien's corpse.

'What was it you said about slacking?' she asked.

His cheeks coloured and he fixed her with a glare. 'I was saving it for you.'

'I'm sure you were.' Eager to retrieve her blade, she strode over to the alien's carcass and prised open its mouth. 'You haven't been the same since Narrigh. Did something happen?'

'You've been talking to my father.' Her father had conveyed his concern about her well-being in front of the entire family. The recollection of it made her cringe. He had wanted to counsel her regarding her feelings for Thorn. Her father had said she had not stopped speaking of him since she returned home. He didn't know she had used Thorn's name in place of another. In the past she had spoken of Thorn with such venom it was no wonder her father thought that he was the cause of her brooding moods. 'Take no notice of him. I'm fine. And as to your question. Yes, something did happen. It always does. That's why I went.'

'You seem less focused.'

'I'm always focused.' Holding her breath against the stench, she stuck her hand into the creature's mouth and felt for the handle of her dagger. She tugged it from the alien's porous tongue with effort. She plucked up a rock slate from the ground and used it to wipe the gore from the blade. Then sheathing her weapon, she made her way over to the groaning civilian, who was slowly regaining consciousness. She knelt over her.

In a short time Garis had joined her. His arms folded, he circled Lin, keeping a look out for more alien scavengers. 'I thought she was dead.'

'I had to knock her out. She was hysterical.'

He spared the civilian a swift glance. 'Where's she from?'

'Not this world. Her screams were too raw. Peltarcks know that screaming won't help them.' She examined the woman's right hand out of protocol more than anything. 'No sign of a mark and her wounds aren't healing.'

There were no pockets in the civilian's shirt or trousers for Lin to rifle through. The woman had a blue ribbon around her neck. Lin lifted it free. Suspended from it was an identity card made from an unfamiliar material. The civilian at her feet matched the one in the photo: a woman in her late twenties dressed in an unappealing grey and white striped blouse with dark brown hair and a mole-speckled face.

Garis read the identity card from over her shoulder. 'Beth Crosswell. Senior Level Designer. Tridan Entertainment.'

'I've never heard of Tridan Entertainment. You?'

'No. We'll take her into custody. And when she wakes, she can tell us.'

At that moment, Beth Crosswell's eyes popped open. She took one look at Lin crouching over her and screamed.

www.ingramcontent.com/pod-product-compliance
Lightning Source LLC
Chambersburg PA
CBHW030530190726
48283CB00006B/1840